Was this the proof I needed that Sam was murdered?

I wheeled my cart along the corridor in the basement, which was even dimmer than the hall on my floor, thanks to our negligent super, and headed for the laundry room. *Good*, I *thought, I won't have to wait for a machine. There's nobody here.* But I was wrong.

I heard moans coming from the floor in the corner. Rose Adelman lay half-buried in a pile of laundry. I dropped my cart and rushed over to her. "Rose, my God!" I bent down to her. "What happened? How did you fall?"

She looked horrible. Her face and arms were purple with bruises, and one of her legs was at a strange angle. Her breath was coming in gasps.

"I don't want to leave you, but I have to go upstairs to call EMS." This was downright scary. I glanced around for her cane. It was under her laundry cart, broken in two. This was strange. That cane was rock solid and had served Rose well for years. Not only that, but she was always careful about walking, including wearing non-slip shoes.

As I turned to go upstairs, she reached up and touched my leg.

"What? Tell me, Rose."

"Didn't—fall—pushed," she whispered.

When Marabella Vinegar's favorite neighbor, Sam Lipschitz, dies, everyone, including the NYPD, thinks it was
natural causes. After all, Sam was pushing eighty, with a
heart condition. But Marabella knows Sam's heart problem was mild and under control with medication—and
she's already acquainted with Sam's greedy relatives—so
she doesn't think there was anything natural about it. Neither does her sleuthing sidekick, her mother-the-ghost-
detective, who has recently dropped back into Marabella's life, happy to interfere again. Not only that, but Rose,
another elderly neighbor, tells Marabella she overheard
Sam arguing with someone in his apartment about money, and was threatening to change his will. Rose caught a
shadowy glimpse of the person fleeing Sam's apartment
and is worried the person saw her. The next day, Marabella finds Rose, severely injured, on the floor of the
building's laundry room, saying she was pushed. Marabella can't convince her old nemesis, NYPD Detective,
now Lieutenant, Rivera, that people are being murdered.
So she vows to track the killer down with her mother's
help, by investigating the heirs to Sam's considerable estate. Can she and her mother find the killer and get
enough evidence to convince Rivera? Or is Marabella
doomed to become the next victim?

KUDOS for *Grave Expectations*

In *Grave Expectations* by Sandra Gardner, Marabella Vinegar is back, investigating the murder of her neighbor and friend, Sam. Her mother-the-ghost-detective is also back, determined to help her daughter, and of course, interfere in her life again. Marabella would love to leave the matter to the police, but they don't seem to think Sam was murdered, or care if he was. Marabella also has to find a way to tell her boyfriend John why he can't come to her apartment anymore, unless she wants him to meet her mother. And she has no idea how to explain that. Cute, clever, and full of wonderfully eccentric characters, this is a cozy mystery that fans of all ages should love. ~ *Taylor Jones, The Review Team of Taylor Jones & Regan Murphy*

Grave Expectations by Sandra Gardner is the second book in her Mother and Me mystery series. In this story, our intrepid heroine, Marabella Vinegar, is devastated at the death of her favorite neighbor, Sam. It seems to be natural causes, or so Marabella thinks—until another neighbor, Rose, tells her of the argument she overheard between Sam and a relative. When Rose dies too, Marabella is sure that Sam was murdered. But the police don't believe her and won't investigate, so Marabella decides to do it on her own—with the help of her mother the ghost, of course. Gardner's character development is superb and her plot full of surprises, making *Grave Expectations* a worthy addition to the series. I thoroughly enjoyed it. ~ *Regan Murphy, The Review Team of Taylor Jones & Regan Murphy*

ACKNOWLEDGMENTS

I would like to thank my good friends and critiquers: Susan P. Baker, Judith Lechner, and Robin Kramer. And thank you to my New England Crime Bake critiquers: Hank Phillippi Ryan, Kate Flora, and Paula Munier for their valuable advice. I would also like to thank Sunny Frazier for suggesting that I send the series to Black Opal Books.

Grave Expectations

A Mother-and-Me Mystery

Sandra Gardner

A Black Opal Books Publication

DEDICATION

I'd like to dedicate this book to my husband, Lewis Gardner, with enormous gratitude for his encouragement, patience, and excellent editing advice.

Chapter 1

She was back again, landing on the needlepoint rug on my living room floor with a familiar clunk.

I gasped. Then I bent down to help my mother up. "You *could* give a person a little warning," I said. Then I flashed on why she'd come back the last time. "Am I in trouble again?"

My mother, who was supposed to be resting wherever it was that seventy-year-old women who'd died rested, shook her head. "No, it's Sam. Go check on Sam."

"Why couldn't you—" I started to ask why on earth she couldn't go herself, through the walls or floors, or something.

"A lady doesn't go into a man's apartment alone, Marabella," said my-mother-the-mind-reader, a talent she seemed to have perfected since—

She drew herself up, still in the satin-and-lace dress she'd been buried in, which now looked a bit worse for wear.

"Don't they let you have new clothes up there?" I said.

"Please, I'm lucky I still have this old thing. You should see what some of them are wearing." She shuddered. "No taste."

I wasn't going to try to process that one. From the time I was a little kid, I'd wondered about ghosts. Sometimes, I thought I heard my dead grandmother whispering to me, but I never saw her. As for my mother, when I asked her how it worked, how she got here, she threw up her hands.

"It's complicated," she said, as if that was that.

Knowing she'd recently developed certain special instincts, along with other abilities, I hurried out the door into the dimly lit hall of my apartment building and rang Sam's doorbell. No answer. Then I knocked, very loud, since he was hard of hearing. Nothing.

"Sam! It's Marabella. Are you okay?" Dead silence. Now I was really worried. He hardly ever went out, and never at night. "Going out at night is not for old people," Sam would say. And I'd say back, "You'll never be old, Sam," which made him smile.

Sam, who was pushing eighty, was a favorite of mine. And my mother's, too, in life. And afterward. I'd introduced them before my mother became seriously ill with congestive heart failure, and they'd enjoyed each other's company.

Since moving into the rent-stabilized building on Manhattan's Upper West Side…was it almost twenty years ago?…I'd learned to appreciate older people, like Sam. Like other old folks I'd come to know, Sam had more than his share of compassion and was genuinely interested in others. Spending time with him warmed my heart.

Come to think of it, I hadn't seen or heard Sam since yesterday. Which was unusual, since he lived in the next apartment and I always heard him after I got home from work, emptying his trash in the trash room across the hall.

I ran back to my apartment. My mother was standing in the middle of the living room where I'd left her. "I'm calling nine-one-one. He's not answering." I picked up my cell phone.

She nodded. "Hurry! There may still be time."

Time for what? I wanted to ask, but I already had the dispatcher on the line. "It's my elderly neighbor. I'm worried about him. He doesn't answer his door, and I haven't seen him today."

"Name and address?" the nasal voice said. Then, "Lady, maybe he's out. Or taking a nap."

"No, I banged on the door very loud, for a long time. And he never goes out this late in the day. Please, hurry, I think there's something wrong."

Finally, the voice agreed to send the EMS. I hung up and started pacing the floor.

"Mmmrowwrrr!"

I whirled around. Zilla, a ball of furry orange fury, was growling at my mother, who'd usurped his place on my maroon Victorian sofa.

"Zilla, down, boy!" I said.

My mother sank back against the lacy sofa cushions. "Go away, cat, I don't like you," she sniffed.

This produced another growl. "That's not helpful, Ma," I said.

I bent down and scratched behind his ears. That was all the human contact he'd put up with most of the time. I gave up trying to pick him up to cuddle months ago. Not only was he much too big, but I didn't look forward to more scratches on my arms.

"Zilla? What kind of a name is that for a cat?" My mother glared at Zilla, who hissed at her.

"I'll explain later, Ma," I said. Hearing noises and voices in the hall, I told them both to behave and ran out the door. Two EMS workers and two cops were standing in front of Sam's apartment, towering over Tony, the super. "I just hope he's okay, that everything's okay," I babbled, while Tony opened the door. I trailed in after them, saying a silent prayer that this sweet old man was all right.

I looked in. "Oh, no!" Sam was slumped in a chair at the desk in the corner of his living room. His mouth was wide open, his glasses dangled from one hand, and his eyes were fixed in a frightened stare. I felt tears welling up.

After taking his pulse, the taller EMS worker shook his head. The shorter one gave me a handkerchief, and I wiped my eyes. "Why?" I choked out, sinking into Sam's overstuffed armchair. "He was fine when I saw him the other day."

"Looks like a heart attack, miss," the tall one said. "He probably couldn't get help in time, dying alone like that."

The idea that Sam spent his last moments alone made me even sadder. "But he had family. And he had me, and—" I stopped myself before I mentioned my mother. Who was dead.

"And who?" the shorter EMS worker asked.

"Um, friends. He had other friends," I said, blowing my nose into the handkerchief.

The heavier of the cops came out of Sam's bathroom. "Nothing much here except aspirin, bandages, antacids." He headed into the kitchen. "There's a half bottle of nitro on the kitchen counter," he said. Then he asked me about Sam's medical history.

I told him what I knew, that Sam had a mild case of angina, which was under control with medication. And that seemed to be it, other than failing eyesight and hearing.

"Doesn't look like any sign of foul play," the heavier cop said. "Miss, he needs to go to a funeral home. Can you get in touch with the family and find out where?"

I nodded. The taller EMS guy gave me his card and asked me to let him know the name and location of the funeral home. I pushed myself out of the chair on wobbly legs and thrust the sodden handkerchief at its owner, who winced and told me to keep it. I thanked them for their kindness and made my way back to my apartment.

When I got inside, I sagged against the door. Sam had been so kind, so good to me. I remembered how frantic he'd been when my life had been in danger from the killer I'd been tracking down. I'd thought of Sam as a surrogate father.

My father died when I was only twelve. My mother's parents, Marvin and Bella, whom I was named for, were long dead, as were my father's parents. I was an only child, so no older brothers to protect me from evildoers on the playground and elsewhere. Not even a doting uncle around. We were the type of family that stayed away from each other as much as possible, to avoid the hostilities that were sure to break out.

My mother shook her head, saying, "He's gone."

Unfortunately, the sound woke Zilla up from his new perch on my royal blue velvet-covered armchair. After a stretch, he let out a couple of loud "Mmrowws," before going into the kitchen.

"Is that what they call 'caterwauling'?" My mother put her hands over her ears.

"Never mind that. First, please tell me why you're here."

She took her hands from her ears and sighed. "I came back to try to save Sam's life. I guess my sense of timing was a little off."

I knew she came back when there was trouble. And that there were certain things she knew and was able to do, and others that she couldn't. Which ones and why, she wouldn't, or couldn't, tell me.

"It's all the way it should be, sweetheart," she'd answer, not answering anything.

Okay, whatever. I'd deal with my-mother-the-apparition later. Right now, I had to think. "I have to let Sam's family know what happened. I know he has…" I couldn't bring myself to say had. "…much-younger half-brothers and a sister and their families, and another niece."

"Do you know where they live? How to reach them?" she said, diving right in. My mother was a devoted mystery lover who'd harbored a desire to be Jessica Fletcher. Or Miss Marple. Well, better late than never. If there was even any mystery here.

"Of course there is, sweetheart."

I shook my head. "Damn. I should have looked for his address book."

"Don't swear. But no problem, sweetheart. Back in a few minutes." And she took off.

"Are you sure it's not too much for you? You just got here."

But she was already gone, into whatever ether she operated in. She had acquired the ability to appear and disappear, wafting through walls and doors.

I should mention that for some reason, which I had yet to find out, my mother's present incarnation had only been visible and audible to me. That must have been torture for her since there were few things she loved more than voicing her opinions to everyone within earshot.

It seemed that my mother's emanation was also available to Zilla. Maybe animals had a sixth sense about spirits, who knew? My boyfriend John, a veterinarian, might know, but asking him could cause major problems in our relationship. I didn't have the courage to broach the subject of my mother's materialization with him, yet. I was afraid he'd think I was certifiable.

Anyway, having an invisible mother-ghost around had already proven to be an asset in scoping out bad guys and situations. It also created situations where the people around me thought I was nuts: talking to myself and gesturing. And made John's and my sleeping arrangements more complicated.

I went into the kitchen to feed Zilla, who was emitting kinder, gentler sounds, since he knew food was coming. Before I could open the can of Fancy Feast Chicken in Gravy on the counter, I heard my mother land with a groan in the living room. "Just a minute," I said, not wanting to face the temper tantrum if the food didn't make it into the bowl right away.

Zilla was my concession to the sensibilities of my boyfriend, John Adriance, DVM. Even though I was finally becoming less terrified of the Marx Brothers, John's three huge St. Bernards, I still approached most large animals with fear and trembling. So I figured a cat would be a kind of starter pet, in a small, soft, and kittenish, way, right? Wrong. By the time he was six months old, the tiny, cuddly orange sprite, who I'd named Puck, had grown into Catzilla. He was humongous, and I'm talking muscle, not fat. That and his curmudgeonly personality accounted for his name, Zilla, for short.

"Why is he so big? Does he bite?" my mother asked.

"Don't know. As for biting, only if I don't feed him on time," I said.

While Zilla was wolfing down his pricey dinner, I got a marker and a legal pad from my desk in the bedroom, trotted back to the living room and sat down next to my mother on the sofa. She fished her bifocals from her bosom.

No point asking her how she managed to transport them. Did she stash the glasses somewhere up…wherever she came from?

"It's no problem. Everything's taken care of," said my-mother-the-mind-reader." She pointed to the ceiling.

Let sleeping bifocals lie. Her bosom was still substantial, much more so than the rest of her now, which looked almost transparent. I hoped she didn't still feel the terrible pain she'd undergone during the last stages of congestive heart failure. "Are you all right?" I asked.

She smiled. "Yes, sweetheart. I'm just a little tired, that's all. It was a long trip."

Right.

"Now let's get to work." She handed me Sam's old leather address book.

I inputted the names and phone numbers into my Droid. I read the names to her while she wrote them down.

"Jeremy Lipson, brother, Riverdale, Bronx, wife, Tamar."

"Lipson?" my mother asked.

"Sam told me Jeremy's wife insisted on him changing his name to Lipson, before they got married."

"Tch, tch," my mother clucked.

"David Lipschitz, brother, Glen Cove, Long Island, wife, Cheryl; Abby Goldfarb, sister, Tarrytown, husband, Larry; Jennifer Lipschitz, niece, Park Slope, Brooklyn." Then I read off the street addresses.

"Email addresses, too," my mother said. "You never know."

Fine. I never could figure out her reasoning when she was alive, so why now?

I seemed to recall that Jeremy and Abby had children and David didn't. But I didn't know the children's names or anything about them. Jennifer was an only child. I flipped through Sam's address book, to see if there were other people and phone numbers I might need. "Oh, his doctor, Dr. Allan Bornstein, and his pharmacy, the one down the block." I inputted those and gave my mother the particulars. I already had Sam's lawyer's numbers, office and home.

"The niece, Jennifer, what about her parents?" she said, chewing on the marker.

"Jennifer's parents were killed in a plane crash a year ago." I remembered how hard Sam had taken the news.

My mother shook her head. "Sad."

"Jennifer is, was, Sam's favorite, maybe because her mother, Sam's other sister, the baby of the family, was, too." I got up and paced the floor, working myself up to making the dreaded phone calls: first, because I was afraid I'd break down and second, because I didn't know Sam's family well and wasn't eager to expand our acquaintance.

I'd already had the displeasure of meeting some of them on occasion at Sam's. And when Sam, terribly distraught, had begged me to go with him to Jennifer's parents' funeral and the *shiva* at Jennifer's apartment, I went. Only my fondness and concern for Sam made me do it. The sisters-in-law seemed to be shallow social climbers. Abby, Sam's sister, was nice enough but over-the-top materialistic, and her husband drank too much. The brothers appeared totally cowed by their wives. Only Jennifer seemed to be a real human being, who'd genuinely cared about her parents and her Uncle Sam.

In fact, Sam hadn't trusted his siblings enough to make them executors of his will, except for his deceased youngest sister. After she'd died, he'd asked me to step in, making me the executor. I couldn't say no. As for Jennifer, he thought she was a little young and busy with her own affairs. He didn't want to burden her with the responsibility.

At the service and the *shiva*, poor Jennifer had been in a state of shock and had to be medicated. Sam was in even worse shape, given his age and the fact that he'd been so close to Jennifer's mother. Fortunately, the sisters-in-law, Tamar and Cheryl, stepped up to the plate. Abby and the brothers were either in no condition to do anything, or pretending.

I stopped pacing, sat down next to my mother and my cell, and groaned.

"What's wrong?" she asked.

"I hate having to deal with that crew. They're pretty miserable people, except for Jennifer."

"Well, at least they're somebody else's family. Not nice, like ours," my mother said smugly.

I stared at her. "What planet have you been living on?"

"That's no way to talk to your mother."

"Sorry, sorry," I mumbled. "But what about all our relatives who never spoke to each other except through interpreters, even the ones married to each other? Or the ones we never mentioned?"

"Silly misunderstandings."

"And then there were…" I recalled some of the really bad situations, the ones nobody thought I knew about. Amazing what listening at doors and peeping through keyholes can do. That was how I'd managed to blackmail my obnoxious cousin, Sybil, about stealing her mother's cigarettes, among other things, when we were eleven. It kept me in comic books for months. That was the beginning of my fascination with detecting, okay, snooping, which I'd recently fine-tuned trying to solve two murders and almost becoming the third victim.

My mother just folded her arms across her chest.

The rest of her had gotten a lot thinner. I was afraid she'd really disappear one of these days. "Why are you so thin?" I asked her.

She laughed. "I used to ask you that all the time

when you were little. You were never a good eater."

"I'm asking about *you.* What does it mean? Are you going to disappear one of these days?"

"Don't worry, sweetheart," was the answer.

Grrr. I checked the time, not too late to call, picked up my phone, and scrolled to the first names on my list: Jeremy and Tamar. I got their voice mail. I left my name, phone number, and email, saying I was Sam's neighbor and would they please contact me as soon as they could. Then I thought, *they'll be afraid it was an emergency.* Well, it was, dammit. Next were David and Cheryl. After two rings, a woman answered. "Is this Cheryl Lipschitz?"

"Yes. Just who is this, please?" a wary voice said.

"This is your brother-in-law, Sam's, neighbor, Marabella Vinegar."

A snicker. Then another snicker. "S—s—sorry. Something—" Snicker. "—went down the wrong way."

I waited for her to stop choking on my last name, the result of a mistranslation of my Vinnaucyers' ancestors from Poland, at Ellis Island. Besides the name department, I'd inherited a few other family blights: too-generous hips and hair that tended to frizz at the least opportunity. My generous bosom, I guess, was one...two?...of the only family assets. Even so, my mother's chest still beat mine by at least a cup size.

Some nerve, you with the last name Lipschitz. "Ms. Lip...schit...z..." I said, drawing out the name to its fullest. "I need to tell you that Sam has just passed away."

"Ohhhh, nooo! Don't tell me!" Sniff.

"From what appears to have been a heart attack."

"Ohh! David will be absolutely heartbroken." Sniff.

"The EMS workers need to know what funeral arrangements have been made."

"Oh." The "ohs" were getting shorter by the minute. "Let me check in David's desk. Hold on." When she came back on the line, she said, "Stein's Funeral Parlor, Sixty-Ninth Street near Madison. I'll let the director know. David and the others made special arrangements for…" Sniff. Then a quick switch to business mode: "Should I assume that you'll contact the others about Sam?"

"Yes."

"Thank you sooo much for your help."

We hung up on her last sniff.

"One and a half down, two to go," I said. As I picked up the phone again, it rang.

"Hello, this is Tamar Lipson. I believe you left me a message."

"Yes. I'm Sam's neighbor."

"We've met," she said dismissively. "What is this about?"

I gritted my teeth and repeated my message. Any more conversations with these people, I'd wear my teeth down to nubs.

There was silence on the other end of the phone. Then: "Sam died? How did you know? Why weren't we called?"

Grrr. "It just happened. I called the EMS because I hadn't seen or heard him around today. They found him, um, in his living room." I cleared my throat. "David's wife is contacting the funeral home."

Silence again. After a brusque goodbye, she hung up. I didn't know which was more revolting, phoniness or rudeness. After gritting my teeth again, I reminded myself that I was doing this nasty chore out of fondness for Sam.

"God, these people," I said to my mother.

She and Zilla were both stretched out full length—my mother on the sofa, Zilla on the chair. I called the

EMS worker and gave him the funeral information and David's phone number.

Before I could make any more calls, the doorbell rang. It was Rose Adelman, another elderly neighbor, leaning on her cane, wearing one of her trademark flowery dresses, tears running down her chubby face.

"I just heard about Sam," she said. Then she whispered, "I'm so afraid."

Chapter 2

"Take it easy, Rose." I ushered her into the living room, directing her to Zilla's chair.

Zilla jumped down and flew out of the room, his tail a twitching orange blur.

"Oh, poor kitty. I'm so sorry I disturbed the nice kitty," Rose said, sinking her flowered bulk into the chair, dropping her cane, and planting her sensible-shoe-clad feet firmly on the floor.

"Nice, humph," from the mother-ghost.

I had to admit, nice was not one of Zilla's finer attributes. "Tell me what's worrying you, Rose. First, how about a cup of tea?" That made me think of Sam, who always offered me a glass of Swee Touch Nee tea when I dropped in. I brushed back tears.

"Tea makes me think of Sam. So, of course, I'm not all right." She wiped her eyes with a large flowered handkerchief. Rose, a longtime widow, had moved into the building a few months ago. She and Sam became constant companions, spending afternoons in one another's apartment, playing cards, and drinking tea. "But..." She shivered.

"What is it?" I said, sitting down at my mother's feet.

"Late this afternoon, I saw something when I was taking out the trash. Somebody. And I heard something, somebody, too," she whispered.

"You don't have to whisper, Rose. There's nobody here who will repeat anything to anyone." I glanced at my mother.

Rose, ignoring my disclaimer, kept whispering. "I heard loud yelling, including Sam."

I couldn't imagine soft-spoken Sam yelling at anyone or anything. "What were they yelling about?"

Rose shifted her considerable weight, which made the chair groan. "The person said, 'Why are you so against this, you stubborn old man?'" She paused. "Then the person said, 'Can't you just give me my share of your estate now? After all, you can't take it with you.' Imagine that. What kind of a person—"

"A disgusting person," my mother-ghost said.

"A terrible person. Could you tell if it was a man or a woman?" This was probably a total waste of time, since Rose's hearing, like that of some other elderly people I knew, was really bad. If the voices weren't so loud, chances were she wouldn't have heard anything at all.

She shook her head. "No, I couldn't tell. The person had a low voice, but…"

"Did you hear anything else?"

"Yes. Sam said, 'You want your share of my money? You'll have to wait till I die.' Then he said that person was so greedy, it made him sick. And that he was going to change his will."

"This is making me sick," said the voice from the sofa.

I digested this for a moment. "Oh, my God. Then somebody, one of his family, might have decided not to wait."

Rose nodded. Then she whispered, "Marabella, I'm

scared to death. I think whoever it was saw me, too."

Trying to comfort her, I said, "I don't think so, Rose. Remember, the light in the hallway is not very bright. We can thank Tony for that."

"I guess so," she said slowly. "But…"

"Did you get a look at the person? Did it look like a man or a woman? Young or old?"

She shook her head. I realized I sounded like I was interrogating her, and I said, in softer tones, "It must have been too dark. Don't worry about it."

"I sure wish I'd really seen them rather than them seeing me." She let out a long sigh, heaving herself out of the chair.

"Can I get you anything? You don't need to rush off," I said, fetching her cane.

She patted my shoulder and headed for the door. "Thanks anyway. But I'm tired out from crying, so I think I'll go lie down for a while."

Impulsively, I bent down—she was a few inches shorter than me, and I was just over five feet—and kissed the top of her gray head. She gave me a hug and left.

I thought about what Rose had heard. Somebody didn't want to wait until Sam died of natural causes to collect his or her share of the estate. And maybe decided to hurry the process along.

"Hmmph." My mother folded her arms across her chest.

"Hmmph what? What's this all about?" I tried to take Rose's place on the comfortable chair, but Zilla beat me to it. Since Zilla wasn't into sharing, I got back on the end of the sofa.

"She knew about Sam's will."

"Ma, she heard him arguing with a person, probably a relative, about it, that's how she knew. And that's much more important."

"I don't think that's the whole story. She'd know, believe me. They always do," she said darkly.

"They?"

"Those…that kind of woman. I remember when one of them tried a move on your father. So I know, believe me."

"You don't even know her," I said. "You're just jealous, that's all."

She actually blushed. *Can they really blush?* "Don't you have more phone calls to make before it gets too late?" she said.

Ha! I thought. When the going gets rough, my mother changes the subject. She was always good at that when things got uncomfortable. Like the time I caught her reading my diary when I was fifteen. Without making an excuse, she'd started downstairs, announcing that I'd better get dressed or I'd be late for the restaurant we were going to. The fact that the restaurant wouldn't be open for another three hours didn't faze her, of course.

I shook my head, knowing better than to say anything. Then I thought again about what Rose said she'd seen and heard. Did Rose really hear what she thought she heard? She was practically deaf, so maybe she misinterpreted the conversation. I inwardly cursed Tony the super's lackadaisical attitude even when it came to replacing light bulbs. If I had a ladder, I would have done it myself.

On the other hand, Tony's laziness might have been a blessing in disguise, at least this once. Otherwise, whoever was in the hall might have gotten a really good look at Rose. I shivered.

Well, I couldn't deal with all that now. I had to make calls. I picked up the list of names and phone numbers and scrolled to Abby Goldfarb's number.

A man answered.

"Is this Larry Goldfarb?" I asked. After getting a confirmation, I introduced myself and asked for his wife. "Not here, not here. Went to spa for th' week," he said, slurring his words. "You know, one of those fat farms. I said be hellava lot cheaper if she jus' stop stuffin' her face." He chortled.

Well, this couldn't wait till Abby finished fasting and juicing, so I gave him the news.

"Oh. Thass terrible. Poor Sam. Sush a nice fellow," he mumbled.

"Yes. Would you please get in touch with Abby as soon as you can?" I gave him my contact information.

"Cer—tain—ly. Thank you so mush for lettin' us know."

After we clicked off, I thought, he might be drunk, but he did seem to remember his telephone manners.

"Being polite doesn't mean he didn't do it," said my mother-the-mind-reader. "It just means he was brought up right. The way you were."

"But what could possibly be his motive? He's only a brother-in-law, a relative by marriage. I'm sure he wouldn't be in Sam's will."

"But his wife would be. So, what do you think, sweetheart?" She lay back against the sofa cushions.

"I don't have a clue. But I have to let Jennifer know. Poor thing, she really cares, cared about Sam." I reached for the phone, scrolled to her number and she answered. "Jennifer, it's Marabella, your Uncle Sam's neighbor."

There was a sharp intake of breath. "Oh, no. Don't tell me there's something wrong with Uncle Sam. Please tell me he's okay." I heard a tremor in her voice.

I took a deep breath. "Jennifer, I'm so sorry."

She began to cry. Then, hope in her voice: "Is he sick? In the hospital? Tell me where."

This was really hard. *Why me?* I thought. I felt like

the Angel of Death. "Jennifer, I'm afraid he's gone."

She was crying harder now. "How? What happened?"

"The EMS workers think it was a heart attack. So it must have been peaceful. I don't think he suffered."

Still crying, she said, "I know he had a heart condition. That must have been it. I kept telling him to take better care of himself. Where—where did they take him?" She blew her nose.

I gave her the information and said I'd already called the others, and she thanked me.

"Please let me know when the service will take place, so I can pay my respects," I said. Jewish law dictated that the funeral should take place as soon as possible, preferably within twenty-four hours. She said a tearful goodbye and we hung up.

"Poor kid. It really hit her hard. They were so close. She used to visit pretty often, even more after her parents died." I said to my mother.

"How old is this Jennifer, anyway?"

I thought for a few minutes. "Let's see, her mother was the youngest of Sam's half-brothers and sisters, about sixty when she was killed in the plane crash. She married late and Jennifer was her only child, so Jennifer must be around twenty-five. She's a bright, attractive, successful young woman, works for a health care company. Why?" What was she thinking?

"I just wondered. She sounds like a lovely, considerate young lady. Caring about an older relation like that. Not many young people would be so thoughtful. I know whereof I speak. Remember Uncle Leonard's son, Jeffrey? When Leonard got sick, Jeffrey was nowhere to be found."

"Well, Jennifer had just lost her parents. And Sam was very close to her mother. So Jennifer probably clung to Sam for comfort, something that would be a good thing for both of them. And not every young person is as cold-hearted as Jeffrey," I said.

She nodded. "You've got a point."

I picked up my cell again. "I've got to call Sam's lawyer."

Harold Cohen, who'd known Sam for years, was not only upset to hear that Sam was dead, he was shocked. "I saw him a couple of weeks ago and he seemed just fine. I guess you never know." He sighed.

Since I was Sam's executor, Harold walked me through the procedure. The will had to be probated, which meant proving to a probate court that the will was genuine. Harold would file the will in the court and petition for my temporary letters of administration. Once I received these, I would be able to act on behalf of the estate, selling the stocks and bonds. Harold said he'd notify Sam's broker about obtaining the stocks and bond certificates.

"This will all take some time," Harold told me.

"That's fine. Thanks so much for explaining it to me," I said.

He promised to keep me informed about the progress of the estate, told me to let him know if I had questions or problems, and we said goodbye.

I turned to my mother. "What a nice man. Very patient. And he was shocked about Sam, said he'd seemed fine when he saw him last. Well, I thought so, too."

"Hmmm. Maybe Rose was onto something after all," she said.

"Let's talk about all this later. I'm starving. I must have something in the fridge."

Actually, the only edible food occupying a shelf was leftover takeout Chinese from last night. A cook I was not and I blamed my mother's genes. Her meals had always been barely digestible. Even with seltzer to wash them down. I still got the dry heaves when I flashed back to her lethal attempts at chopped liver, when I was a child.

I couldn't remember what her digestive system did these days. "Are you hungry? Do you still…"

"I could eat, but I don't—" she said.

"Enjoy it as much as before," I said.

Chapter 3

The next day, the day of Sam's funeral, was windy and rainy. A typical March day. Well, it fit my mood. When the packed I think crosstown might be one word cross town bus finally came, I squeezed myself as small as I could, to give myself room to inhale.

I tried to find a cab to take me the rest of the way, forgetting that available cabs in New York were nonexistent in rain, sleet, and snow. So I took the subway and walked the two blocks to the funeral home, my head down against the now-stinging spray. All the while, trying to stay in the middle of the sidewalk, to avoid getting splattered by the unavailable cabs passing by. Unfortunately, so did the other pedestrians, who shoved me to the sidewalk's edge. By the time I got there, my trench coat was a wet, muddy mess. I peeled it off inside the door in the lobby.

Stein's Funeral Parlor was the fanciest Jewish funeral home on the fancy Upper East Side of Manhattan. I knew Sam hadn't been particularly observant, preferring to practice his beliefs quietly, in his own way. I'm sure he would have wanted his passing to be marked in the same way: quietly. But his relatives had a different idea: a big show, a lavishly decorated, satin-lined casket. And an

imported rabbi from the area's most prestigious synagogue, to eulogize a man he'd never met.

The few people who'd really known Sam, elderly
men and women, were weeping into handkerchiefs at the
back of the room. I was betting they felt too uncomfortable at the over-the-top display to mingle up front. Speaking of Sam's friends, I looked around and didn't see Rose
Adelman. That was strange, I thought. Maybe she was
too worn-out with grief to make it.

I hung up my damp coat, expressed polite condolences to the family, and gave Jennifer a hug. The siblings, who were on the short side, all had the prominent
Lipschitz nose. Except Abby, who'd obviously had hers
miniaturized.

My mother always had a lot to say about girls who'd
had their noses "fixed."

"And what's so wrong with a good-sized nose, I ask
you, that you have to go and get it chopped off? It's
something to be ashamed of?" She also had strong opinions about people who'd changed their last names, except
for those who'd had them changed for them, like ours, by
immigration officials.

I took a seat in back with Sam's friends. Their good
suits smelled of mothballs. I sat down next to Bennie.
Bennie was a genial, white-haired man who recently had
to depend on a walker, which hurt his pride. He'd known
Sam for years. During warm weather, they'd set up a
folding table and chairs outside the building for hot
games of checkers, played while sipping *schnapps*. As
the glasses kept getting refilled, the games got fiercer and
louder, interspersed with laughter and mock accusations
of, "You bum, you're cheating." And the retort: "Oh,
you're becoming an *alter kaker*." I stifled my giggles
when I was within earshot of their banter. It was obvious

that their friendship provided them a lot of happiness in their old age.

Poor Bennie was devastated. His black-suited shoulders shook, and he leaned against his walker. I patted his shoulder. "I loved him too, Bennie," I whispered into the ear that still had some minimal function.

Bennie reached into his jacket pocket for a handkerchief, blew his nose loudly and slowly sat up. "What happened to Sam? All of a sudden, he's gone. I can't believe it. He was in pretty good shape for an old man, better than me. And I'm here and he's gone. Why?" Tears ran down his cheeks.

"Bennie, they think it was a heart attack. You know he had heart trouble, don't you?" I kept whispering, hoping he'd take the hint and lower his voice. This was probably hopeless, since he was totally deaf in the other ear.

"*Bubkes.* He never had what you call real heart problems. It was just a little angina, and he was very good about taking his medication regular, I know."

"Well, maybe his condition got worse. You never know with those things."

He snorted. "All of a sudden, it gets worse? Baloney. Matter of fact, I went to see him just last week. He didn't have trouble with the checkers or—" He chuckled."—with the booze. And when I asked how he was, he said he was feeling good. And so?" He looked at me.

And so, he got me thinking. Bennie was no dope, wasn't senile, and really knew Sam. So did Harold Cohen. And so did Rose. And where was she, anyway? I bit a cuticle, hoping she was all right. But if she was all right, she would have been there, wouldn't she?

I tried not to inhale through my nose on the bus home. My fellow passengers smelled like wet dog. Unfortunately, my nose had the fine-tuned sensitivity of a dog, wet or dry. I could sniff the remains of dead mouse for months after the creature had gone on to that big mousetrap in the sky. But I could also detect the scent of an oven-baked pizza blocks away from the pizza parlor. Same with baking brownies. Whether this was a blessing or a curse usually depended on the state of my hips.

All the way home, I thought about what Bennie and Rose had said. Then life, in the form of clean clothes, took over when I got there. Tomorrow was a workday and I had nothing clean enough to wear.

After checking on my mother and Zilla—both were fast asleep on their separate pieces of furniture—I quietly dragged my laundry cart from the closet and stuffed it with clothes, detergent, water softener, dryer papers, and hangers. I checked to make sure I had enough quarters and took the creaky old elevator down to the basement.

Why did they put laundry rooms in the basement of apartment buildings? I wondered. In my best friend Toni-ann Di Lorenzo's building a few blocks away, it was on the mezzanine floor. Much nicer and lighter and much less scary, and the building included a doorman. Then again, her building, like her salary, was a notch up from mine, since she'd been working for Otis Pinckney, attorney and new city councilman, not to mention sleazebag. Otis was a self-promoter who pretended to care about his clients. But he'd usually only take a case if it promised to make him a lot of money or get him a lot of votes.

I wheeled my cart along the corridor in the basement, which was even dimmer than the hall on my floor, thanks to our negligent super, and headed for the laundry room. *Good,* I *thought, I won't have to wait for a machine. There's nobody here.* But I was wrong.

I heard moans coming from the floor in the corner. Rose Adelman lay half-buried in a pile of laundry. I dropped my cart and rushed over to her. "Rose, my God!" I bent down to her. "What happened? How did you fall?"

She looked horrible. Her face and arms were purple with bruises, and one of her legs was at a strange angle. Her breath was coming in gasps.

"I don't want to leave you, but I have to go upstairs to call EMS." This was downright scary. I glanced around for her cane. It was under her laundry cart, broken in two. This was strange. That cane was rock solid and had served Rose well for years. Not only that, but she was always careful about walking, including wearing non-slip shoes.

As I turned to go upstairs, she reached up and touched my leg.

"What? Tell me, Rose."

"Didn't—fall—pushed," she whispered.

Chapter 4

After I called 911, I told my mother what happened and went back down to Rose. I waited by her side for the ambulance, stroking her hair and holding her hand, gently, not wanting to aggravate her bruised arm. Soon, she either slipped into sleep or, I was afraid, unconsciousness. I silently sent out good thoughts: *Please, Rose, don't die. I can't bear it if another one of my kind, good-hearted neighbors dies on me.*

When the ambulance came, I told her, "Don't worry, Rose, I'm staying with you." I didn't know if she could hear me. The EMS workers agreed to let me ride to the hospital with her, and I climbed into the back of the ambulance. One of them asked me what happened while another one took her vital signs and radioed them into Riverview Hospital. I gave them the little information I had.

"Is she just passed out? Or is it something worse?" I asked.

They said her condition would be assessed by an ER doctor. I chewed a cuticle and worried. When we got into the ER, I repeated the same scanty details that I'd given before to a nurse. I sat down on one of those hard plastic chairs that hurt your behind after five minutes, while they wheeled her into a cubicle and pulled the curtain.

To make my already stressed-to-the-max self even more so, the ER, like emergency rooms everywhere, was filled with people in distress, sitting on the chairs against a gray wall: mostly anxious mothers trying to control their screaming babies and whining children. A little girl with a blonde ponytail and big blue eyes, who looked about three or four, gave me an adorable smile and I smiled back. Bad move. Next thing I knew, she trotted over and greeted me by spilling orange soda on my sneakers. Her mother apologized over and over for little Bethany's mishap, while little Bethany screamed for another orange soda.

"It's okay. She didn't mean it." I lifted my sticky sneakers to walk to the ladies' room. After cleaning off as much goo as I could with wet paper towels, I went back to the waiting room, thanking the gods that little Bethany and her mother had moved on. I sat down and tried to think of what I knew about Rose's family, which wasn't much. She had a sister who lived in Brooklyn, Flatbush, I thought. What was her name? *Think, Marabella. You don't have anything else to do right now except worry.*

I chewed a cuticle then decided to meditate, hoping it would clear my mind and bring her name forward. A few silent "Oms," and a couple of deep breaths later, I felt more relaxed. And there she was: Miriam, Miriam Kravitz. Aha! I tried for her address, but I must have maxed out my powers of concentration for the moment. No wonder, with everything that had been going on: My mother coming back again from…wherever. *Sam, oh, Sam.* I couldn't face the fact that I'd never see that kindly face or drink a glass of tea with him again. And now, Rose.

I stood up, went over to the nurses' station, and told

a stocky nurse in a kitten print pantsuit about Miriam Kravitz in Brooklyn. Hopefully, there weren't too many Miriam Kravitzes in the phone book and since she was a couple of years older than her sister, she probably still used a landline.

I'd tried to get my mother to use a cell before she got really sick, but it didn't happen. Even though it was one of those Jitterbugs, designed for seniors, she'd balked, saying, "What do I need that thing for, when I've got a perfectly good telephone in my kitchen?" When I tried to tell her it was a good thing for when she wasn't home, she said, "And why would I call someone when I'm not at home to talk to them?"

I went back to my uncomfortable seat to wait and worry and gnaw. Finally, a tall, thin man wearing a white coat with a stethoscope around his neck popped his head out from the curtain around Rose's cubicle. I jumped up and ran over to him. "How is she?"

He peered at me over his glasses. "Are you a family member?" he said.

"No, I'm her neighbor. I found her on the floor in the basement of our building. Please, tell me, how is she?"

He shook his head.

Oh, no, I thought, *please, no.*

"I can't discuss her condition with anyone but a family member."

"But is she…"

"She's alive."

Thank you, God. I felt tears in my eyes.

"More than that I can't tell you," he said kindly. The stocky nurse came over and whispered in his ear. Turning back to me, he said, "I understand that Mrs. Adelman has a sister."

I gave him the information. Then I dug into my pocketbook for a pen and paper, scribbled my name and phone number, and handed it to him. "Could you please give this to Mrs. Kravitz and ask her to let me know how her sister is? "

He took the paper, nodded and went back into Rose's cubicle. I headed for the exit and home, thinking that after I checked on my roommates, it was time to call the cops. Even though my previous encounters with them had been less than pleasant, for the most part.

Chapter 5

After a sleepless night, feeling miserable about Sam and worried about Rose, I woke up spitting out a mouthful of fur. Zilla was in his usual first-thing-in-the-morning position, sitting on my face, emitting loud "Mmmrrrooowws." Translation: breakfast, now. I opened one eye, looked at the clock, and shut off the alarm.

"I'm lucky I don't get hairballs," I said, dragging myself into the kitchen, Zilla at my heels. I emptied half a can of Fancy Feast Flaked Tuna and Mackerel into his bowl, filled the water bowl, and made for the bathroom, which we shared. *Well, at least he makes sure I'm not late for work anymore*, I thought, stepping into the shower. After brushing my teeth, I cleaned the litter box and went back to the bedroom to get dressed. I unearthed a light gray blouse, a royal blue skirt, and a gray blazer and fished around the bottom of the closet for a pair of gray flats.

After trying to do something with my unruly chestnut hair and giving up, I went into the kitchen, boiled hot water for tea, and shoved a piece of whole wheat bread in the toaster. Sipping and chewing, I looked in on my mother, who was snoring away on the sofa, in one of the flannel nightgowns I'd bought her the last time she was here. My clothes were too tight in the bust and too big in the behind for her. I grabbed my trench coat and pocketbook, took the elevator down, and headed out the door.

The sun was bright and warm as I stopped to say hello to Lucy and tossed a couple of dollars in the Yankees cap at her feet. Lucy was a homeless woman who'd been stationed on this corner for as long as I could remember. She never seemed to look any older and always managed to appear neat and clean.

She pointed heavenward and gave me a toothless smile. "He gave us another lovely day. Old Lucy thanks you for your kindness."

Since it was indeed a lovely almost-spring day, I set off to walk the twelve blocks to Chelsea College, where I'd had the misfortune to be employed in the public relations department for almost twenty years. As usual, on my way, I had to duck the skateboarders and deposits of stinking dog poop that people let their dogs leave on the sidewalk. Being a pedestrian in New York could be hazardous to your health, not to mention the bottom of your shoes.

Chelsea College, built in the 1980s as an affordable neighborhood college, had the distinction of being among the lowest ranking community colleges in New York City. Except for its science department. The college had put lots of money into the science faculty, which gave it an outstanding reputation. It also gave me my boyfriend, John Adriance, the handsome—in a shaggy, country doctor sort of way—smart, funny, and very sexy head of the veterinary technician program.

John and I had lots in common—romantic restaurants, Victorian inns, classical music, old movies, crossword puzzles. And oh, yeah, sex. Great sex. Wonderful sex. Our steamy relationship had been going full steam ahead.

Until the advent of Dr. Lisa—call me Li Li—Chang. John had founded the veterinary technician program at Chelsea College. Unfortunately for me, he'd done such a great job the program was growing like Jack's beanstalk, so he'd needed another pair of hands. He hired an assistant director. Enter Li Li Chang.

Li Li was bright, hard-working, petite, and gorgeous, with long, jet-black hair, beautiful teeth, a perfect oval-shaped face, and a throaty laugh. Not to mention being an incorrigible flirt. The type that had every man in sight not only drooling at her graceful figure, but eating out of her finely shaped hands. She accomplished this by preying on weak masculine egos, saying things like: "Oh, you men are so wise, so much smarter than a little girl like me." Wise, my behind. The only thing real about this statement was that she was little, ninety pounds soaking wet, if that, and barely five feet tall. And the tiniest bones I'd ever seen. She looked fragile as hell, but was far from it. I found out that she was a martial arts expert, a fact that she kept secret from all those big, strong, wise men.

And she was spending more and more time with John at work. Even though my better sense told me it was perfectly natural, since they were working together, I worried. What if it turned into something else? How would I know? I didn't want to be made a fool of, having had enough of bad relationships in my life, thank you.

So one afternoon, when I found them bent over some charts on a table in Li Li's office, a subtle scent…was it jasmine?…wafting around their heads, I had to stop myself from reaching out and banging their heads together. Then Li Li turned around and gave me what I thought was a superior smile. As in, "Ha! I can have him anytime I want him." Her smile for women was vastly different than the one she used on men. Especially good-looking ones.

When I confronted John about the whole thing, over tea (me) and coffee (him) in the college cafeteria, he laughed. Which made me even madder.

"Don't be silly, Marabella. She's new and she needs my help sorting things out, that's all. Pretty soon, she'll be able to work on her own. After all, she's very bright," he said.

Grrrr. And a very good manipulator, who knows just how to handle you, you who don't have a clue about such women, and are thoroughly taken in by the little witch.

But then he flashed me his dimpled smile, which, as usual, made me melt. With John, I'd thought I'd finally found "Mr. Right," after years of "Mr. Wrongs," and after a number of relationships where my screw-up mechanism had reared its ugly head: do something so they'd reject you. This time, I seemed to be doing things right. Until Li Li, that was. I couldn't help the jealousy. Well, maybe I could, but not very easily.

When John and I first started our relationship, I was still insecure about mostly everything. Not exactly the queen of self-confidence. But I'd been doing a lot better, these days. Until Li Li. *Stop that, Marabella, get your mind onto work*, I told myself, walking up the concrete steps to the college's front door. I waved a greeting to the ever-present group of protesting students. This time, it was about the food in the cafeteria, and I hoped they'd be successful. I would've joined them in a heartbeat, especially after the last time I tried eating one of the so-called specials. It didn't even measure up to my mother's dreadful cooking.

Going to my tiny office, I reminded myself how lucky I was now, boss-wise. My old angrier-than-thou boss, Donna Tomiello, was fired after the administration finally caught on that she spent a major part of her day on the phone with her hairdresser, nail stylist, and leg waxer, when she wasn't catering to her nasty little dog. And the amount of time she actually spent working consisted of her giving orders to me and Lionel, the child science prodigy working in our department who'd since gone on to MIT. Wasn't one of Sam's great-nephews at MIT? I brushed back tears. *You can't do anything about Sam now, Marabella. Or Rose. Wait till after work, when you'll have a chance to think.*

In addition to being tiny, my office was painted institutional beige, with a prime view of the red brick wall of one of the other campus buildings. I'd tried to brighten it up with a couple of easy-to-care-for philodendrons and a few photos. My favorite was a headshot of Harpo, one of John's St. Bernards. John had sent it to cheer me up while I was wrongfully incarcerated for two murders related to my former therapy group. Whenever I looked at that huge, drooling face, I had to smile.

Susan Davies, my boss, had left a note on my desk about the college catalogue. Susan was an attractive, stylish African-American woman in her mid-forties with an Ivy League MBA. She'd been a columnist for a business magazine before she took the job as public relations director, for a more secure position, she'd said. I thought she could have done better, but I was happy that someone with a brain and a work ethic was in charge. I didn't think I'd be good at her job—meetings, dealing with the board, faculty egos. I was better off being left alone to write and edit.

But there was a faculty member, Professor Myra Newsome, who *did* want that job, and insinuated at every chance she got that Susan was an affirmative action hire. The fact that Newsome was rumored to have gotten her own job by sleeping with a rich alumnus…the real kind of affirmative action? Screwing for your supper?…did a lot to quash her ugly accusations around the campus. But that didn't stop her ugly mouth.

I popped my head around the door of Susan's office. "Marabella, good, come in," she said, giving me a warm smile, which I still wasn't used to. Donna had never talked when she could bark or yell, and certainly never bothered to smile at her minions, namely Lionel and me.

Susan and Carmen were already sitting around the long table Susan used for laying out publications. We'd go over the outline for the college catalogue and divide up the work.

Carmen Rodriguez was the newest member of the public relations department. A divorced mother of two young kids, she lived with her widowed mother who took care of the kids while Carmen worked. Carmen was short and slightly overweight, with long dark hair, a dazzling smile, and a potty mouth. She had a personality that made people instantly comfortable, except for those who got offended by her less-than-PC language.

Lucky, for me, Carmen was not only a science maven, which I was so not, but also a bona fide techie, thank the gods, who could whisper to all things electronic. Her favorite line was: "Who ya gonna call when your computer plays dead, your internet acts weird, and your printer goes nuts?"

And Susan and I would yell, "Carmen!" I couldn't imagine Donna and me ever being collegial.

We got the parts of the catalogue sorted out, with Carmen on the science section; me on writing, editing, and proofreading (my specialties) the rest of the copy; and Susan, who had a great visual sense (another thing I didn't), on design.

When I got back to my office, the phone rang. "Marabella, I've been missing you," John said.

I tried to erase Li Li from my brain for the moment. "Me, too," I said. "What are we going to do about that?"

"For starters, how about dinner 'aanndd' Saturday night?"

"And? You mean like 'coffee and'?" I giggled.

"Not exactly. More like mmmm."

I could hear the loving leer in his voice.

"I think I've got it. Where are we going?"

"How about La Suisse Romanze? And then, my place or yours?" he said.

Oh, no, I thought. *Here we go again.* No more my place, currently occupied with my roommate, the-mother-ghost-watchdog. Speaking of dogs, John's place meant a date with *his* housemates, the Marx Brothers, whom I was still skittish around. Zilla was about my limit, size-wise.

"How about yours, for a change?" I said, adding, "I'm really looking forward to seeing Harpo again." I hoped that sounded sincere. Harpo had claimed me as his personal dog toy on our first date, John's and mine, that was. Now, whenever we ended up at John's place, I'd have a panting Harpo between John and me on the sofa, with Groucho and Chico at my feet on the floor, lying in wait for Harpo to leave.

We agreed to meet at the restaurant at seven and said goodbye. For the next couple of hours, I tried to keep my focus on the catalogue, ignoring the phone, letting voice mail pick up.

But thoughts of Sam and Rose kept intruding. Sad thoughts, then angry thoughts about a possible killer—who was more than likely a member of Sam's own family.

Chapter 6

My mother and Zilla insisted on having dinner as soon as I got home. My mother was wearing one of the tops and sweat pants I'd bought her. She was heating up a meatloaf she'd concocted by smothering the meat with ketchup and breadcrumbs, together with side dishes of liquefied powdered instant potatoes, and canned green beans. Not only was her meatloaf tasteless, but the ketchup managed to dull any real meat aroma.

I emptied half a can of Fancy Feast Roasted Turkey for Zilla. If I didn't lay out different food every night, he wouldn't eat. This left me with three choices: try to disguise it, throw it away, and start from scratch or eat it myself. Sometimes even a leftover Fancy Feast dinner looked a lot better than my mother's terrible cooking. Then again, I wasn't a bad-tempered cat with a delicate palate.

While I tried to get some of the meatloaf down, my mother asked how Rose was.

"I hope her sister will let us know soon," I said.

"Well, now we need to…" she said, between sips of seltzer, still her favorite drink.

"Call the cops," I said. "Unfortunately."

She belched then nodded. "At least this time, they can't try to put the blame on you."

"Ha!" I said. "Just wait and see."

But it wasn't as if I had a choice, with one neighbor dead and another one assaulted. Unless the cops did an investigation, I'd have to figure it out myself. Not only was I broken-hearted about my two friends, especially Sam, but I was becoming seriously angry at whoever did this.

"Oh, no, you don't," said my-mother-the-mind-reader, a characteristic she'd had in life and had perfected afterward. "Don't you remember what happened the last time? How you almost got killed, three times? And if it wasn't for me, you'd be a dead duck."

I did not need reminding. My mother had come back the first time when she somehow knew that my longtime therapist, Dr. Ditstein, was about to be killed. And that I'd been about to become a suspect by Detective Eddie Rivera of New York's finest. After there was another murder connected to Dr. Ditstein, I was upgraded to prime suspect status and sent to jail. Meanwhile, the real killer kept trying to kill me.

Not that I'd recommend being targeted by a killer, but one of the good things that came out of it was that I'd become a stronger person, much more confident. Maybe it was because I was no longer dependent on a shrink.

Or my mother, with whom I'd had a love-hate relationship ever since my teen years. That relationship, in fact, was the main reason for my years of psychotherapy.

I'd even gotten off Xanax recently, taking care to reduce my pills so gradually, I hardly noticed. But I still had my crosswords to help me wind down from the day and aerobics, when I could drag myself there. I also had my new hobby of knitting, which included joining a knitting group. As for Zilla, I had my doubts as to whether he qualified as a stress-reducer.

After chugging down a cup of tea to help my digestive juices, I picked up my cell, looked up the police non-emergency number, and inputted it.

"Officer Baker speaking," a male voice said.

I gave my name, address, and phone number and said, "One of my neighbors died in a suspicious manner and a woman who heard something was attacked, and now she's in the hospital."

"I'll connect you with the Detective Bureau," he said.

A minute later, I heard, "Lieutenant Rivera speaking."

Oh, no! My *bête noir* from the last time, the cop who'd had me in his crosshairs from the get-go. Who must have gotten promoted since our last unpleasant encounter. Which gave him more authority to harass me. But why was he here in my backyard, so to speak?

"Hello? Is anyone there?"

There was no help for it. "Lieutenant Rivera, it's Marabella Vinegar."

He sounded as if he were choking. "You! I thought I heard the last of you!"

"Are you all right?" I asked. "What are you doing here, on the West Side? Last time, you were on the other side of town."

He cleared his throat then bellowed, "Why did I get so lucky to be moved closer to you? And what *do you want*?"

I repeated what I'd told the officer.

"Is there something in the water over there? Are you at it again, butting into things that are not your business?"

I thought he wasn't playing fair. But that wasn't important right now. "Look, I really need to talk to you about the whole thing. As soon as possible."

He sighed. "All right. I was having a lousy day anyway, so you might as well finish it off. I'll see you at the station in an hour."

"Thank you, Lieutenant. And by the way, congratulations on your promotion," I said, playing nice, even though he didn't deserve it.

A grunt and the click of a phone was my thanks.

Chapter 7

After waiting on a hard metal bench in the grimy main room of the police station for at least twenty minutes, I was directed into Lieutenant Rivera's office. He yawned as I sat down in a chair across from him, at his desk. The man didn't look as if he'd gotten any more sleep than the last time I'd seen him. Or developed any better fashion sense, even with a better job. He was wearing a navy blue blazer with a yellow shirt and brown pants. Either he got dressed in the dark or just didn't care.

"Still off caffeine?" I said, trying for pleasantness.

He threw me a black look, taking a gulp from a can of caffeine-free soda on his desk and making a face. "I suppose you're innocent of this one, too? That is, if it really *is* a homicide."

"I think Sam was murdered, even though the EMS people thought it was a heart attack," I said.

He sighed and took out a notebook and pen. "What makes you think so?"

"I've known Sam for years, he's my next-door neighbor. He's—he was—not a youngster, but I don't think he had a life-threatening illness."

"How old was he?"

"Probably pretty close to eighty," I said.

Rivera shrugged. "It happens. A person that age usually has some kind of health problem. What kind of shape was he in?"

"Well, I know he took nitroglycerin pills, but it was just for mild angina."

He held up his hand to stop me. "And just how do you know it didn't develop into something more serious, with somebody almost eighty?"

Unfortunately, Rivera was having his usual effect on me, that was, making me furious. I tried to keep my temper by taking a few deep breaths, which caused him to give me a strange look.

"Are you turning weird again?" he said. "Thank God I'm due for a mental health day."

I gritted my teeth. "Lieutenant, may I please tell you the rest of the story?"

He sighed again and picked up his pen. "Okay, from the top."

"I hadn't seen or heard Sam for a day, and I usually see or hear him going to the trash room, which is across from my apartment and his. I rang the bell and knocked loud on the door, because he's—he was—hard of hearing. I called EMS and the super let the EMS and the cops into Sam's apartment." I felt my eyes getting watery.

Rivera dug into a drawer and pulled out a box of tissues and shoved them over to me. "Go on," he said, his tone a little less hostile.

I wiped my eyes and blew my nose. "Thanks. It's hard for me to talk about it."

He nodded. "Take your time."

I took a few deep more breaths, even though I knew it would provoke more strange looks. "We found him at his desk, in his living room. It was horrible."

"You haven't told me why you think it was murder," he said, yawning again.

"Because another neighbor, Rose Adelman, told me she heard loud voices, arguing, coming from Sam's apartment."

He grunted. "Another Nosy Parker."

Grrrr. "She's an elderly woman, a friend of Sam's, who was taking her trash to the trash room, which, as I said, is across from Sam's and my apartments. She heard someone ask Sam if he or she could have their share of the estate now, and Sam said they'd have to wait till he died. Then she heard Sam yelling at whoever it was that the person was so greedy, he was going to change his will. And Sam was not a yeller. Besides, there's a lot of money involved. I know, because Sam made me executor of his will."

"This all doesn't prove anything, except that she heard people arguing."

"Then why was she attacked?" I challenged him.

He raised his eyebrows and made some notes. Now he seemed interested, or awake, or both. "Go on."

"The next day, after the funeral, I went down to the basement in the elevator, with my laundry, in my laundry cart—"

He started tapping his foot. "Get to the point."

Itching to kick that foot, I said, "I'm getting there. I found Rose on the floor, badly beaten, with bruises all over her, and her leg was at a funny angle, maybe broken, and she was moaning in pain. She told me she didn't fall, she was pushed. I called EMS." Now I had his attention.

"Where did they take her?"

I told him, adding, "Now do you believe me?"

After more scribbling in his notebook, he stood up. "We'll check it out."

I guessed that was the signal for me to leave and I

got up, too. "Will you please let me know how she is? The hospital wouldn't give me any information because I'm not a relative. I told them about her sister in Brooklyn, Miriam Kravitz, and I was hoping she'd call me. I haven't heard anything yet and I'm really worried about Rose."

"We'll take care of it, and I'll relay your message to her sister, when we contact her. But you are to stay out of this. Do you hear me?" He glowered at me.

I nodded. "Believe me, I'm not eager to meet up with any more killers."

"That's good. That's very good. Now I've got things to do and I'm sure you do, too." With that, he directed me toward the exit.

Subtle, he was not.

Chapter 8

The next day, before I left the office for lunch with Toniann, I picked up my phone and scrolled to Rivera's station house. When the officer got him on the line, Rivera's tone was softer than usual. Oh, God, I thought, not Rose, too.

But he was saying, "I'm sorry, Ms. Vinegar. Mrs. Adelman passed away about an hour ago. The injuries must have been too much for her, what with all the internal bleeding."

"No!" This was too much. Poor, innocent, kindly Rose. I couldn't speak for a few minutes. Rose had been Sam's special friend. My friend, too, no matter what a certain jealous ghost-mother thought.

Ugly thoughts whirled through my brain: the fear and pain Sam and Rose had experienced because of a vicious, evil human being. Finally, I got out the words, "Lieutenant, are you going to investigate? And find out who did this terrible thing?"

"We're checking into it, as to whether or not it was an accident or foul play."

Trying to keep my temper, I said, "But you *know* it wasn't an accident. She told me she didn't fall, she was *pushed.*"

"And I told *you* we're checking it out, Ms. Vinegar." The old hostile Rivera was back.

I could feel my teeth gnashing. "Fine. If you won't try to find out who did this, to Rose, and to Sam—"

"We don't have any reason to think that Mr…

"Lipschitz."

"Lipschitz died of anything but natural causes."

"But what about—"

"Ms. Vinegar, we'll let you know about Mrs. Adelman. Meanwhile, don't call us, we'll all you." He laughed and hung up.

This is all a joke to you? I banged down the phone. *No, it's not that,* I realized. *He thinks whatever I think is a joke. Okay, Mr. Lieutenant Rivera, see if I care. And just you wait and see what I can do.*

When I related the whole story to Toniann, her wide blue eyes got wider. "Geez Louise, two old people in your own building, dead. That's terrible. Maybe there's a serial killer loose in your building," she said between mouthfuls of at least 1000 calories of a deliciously aromatic hot pastrami sandwich. Plus potato salad. And macaroni salad.

"Many thanks for that opinion," I said. It went over her curly brown head, as usual.

Toniann Di Lorenzo had been my best friend since we'd met working in the PR department at Chelsea College. She resigned because our boss before Donna, Joe Sawicki, used to hit on her regularly. Now she did publicity for Otis Pinckney, fat slob, city councilman, ambulance chaser, and conniving wheeler-dealer. But not a chauvinist pig sexual harasser, she always reminded me.

Toniann could eat like a longshoreman and never gain a pound. "Don't hate me, it's genetic," she'd said when we first met, after I'd thrown her hateful looks. She also could wear the off-white silk suit she had on today without getting a spot on her. Whereas I was not only wearing dark colors, but had a double napkin in my lap. As if that would do any good. When I looked down, I saw two pools of salad dressing decorating my blouse.

Trying not to drool over the pastrami, I said, "I really cared about these two people. I considered them my friends."

She nodded. "Especially Sam, I know. I'm really sorry." Toniann was extremely loyal and had a big heart.

"And there's about a three-million-dollar motive for a greedy someone to do away with Sam. I know because I'm executor of his will. About seven-hundred-fifty-thousand dollars divided four ways, to family members."

She whistled. "Where did he get all that money?"

"Savings bonds, mutual funds. He had plenty of them, held onto them for years. Plus he made some investments in oil, Exxon-Mobil."

"Smart man," she said.

"Not smart enough around his family, unfortunately."

"Do you really think some sonuvabitch in his family bumped him off?"

"Um, yes, I really do."

Toniann could be crude, which wasn't improved by her longtime association with Otis Pinckney.

She called the waitperson over and ordered dessert—fudge cake with whipped cream—which I was already salivating over. But my hips told me to take a cold shower. I sighed and ordered another tea and got more Splenda. Then my mind drifted back to Sam and Rose. Rivera didn't seem to be overly concerned, that was for sure.

"Marabella?"

"Sorry, I got distracted."

Toniann was totally focused on her wedding plans. She and Peter had been waiting till he graduated from law school, which he did this fall, first in his class, and was now about to take the bar exam.

Licking the whipped cream off her fork, she said, "Of course, he'll pass with flying colors. My family is so proud, they could burst. The first lawyer in the family, imagine that. And from the wrong side of the Bronx, yet. My father doesn't even think there's a *right* side of the Bronx."

Her parents were the third-generation in their townhouse in Carroll Gardens, a middle-class, family neighborhood, in Brooklyn, that never seemed to change over the years.

I munched on my Skinny Minnie Lunch Special: cottage cheese salad, complete with limp tomato slices, and a couple of wilted lettuce leaves that collapsed on my tongue. I choked a little on the acrid taste of too much vinegar in the dressing.

Except for a flat chest, Toniann had lucked out in the genes department, tall and slim, with long legs that wouldn't quit and an excellent metabolism.

I, on the other hand, gained weight when my lips touched anything that tasted good. Which was probably why, considering my mother's cooking, I'd never been a fat child.

She barreled on. "My parents decided on the flowers and the menu and I picked out the rest of the stuff. The band, the invites, the photographer. And checking off the guest list, of course."

The ceremony was going to be at the traditional Roman Catholic church Toniann had grown up in. Her father had hired two limousines to transport the wedding party to the reception at a caterer in Howard Beach, near JFK airport in Queens. "Are you really going to make me wear yellow? It makes me look sick." I sipped my Splenda tea.

"Don't be silly. It's a butter yellow, practically not even yellow, and you'll look fabulous," she said, drinking her coffee and taking bites of fudge cake and whipped cream.

How yellow could be practically not yellow—and make me look fabulous was beyond my imagination, but I let it go. It was her big day and I was her maid of honor. "Okay, when do we go for the fittings?"

"Friday afternoon. Oh, by the way, I'm glad the sexy animal doctor will be able to be there." She made lascivious animal sounds.

"His name is John," I reminded her, "and he'll be there, barring an animal emergency." Or a Li Li emergency, I thought. To add to her other charms, she had a habit of calling him at the most inconvenient times, such as when we were having lunch together, begging the big, strong, wise man to help her with a problem. Grrrr.

"Tell him to bring his pager. What a riot if it goes off, not during the ceremony, of course, and it turns out to be a horse. Or a sheep. Sheep emergency!" She started to laugh and it turned into a snort.

"I don't think horses or sheep know how to use a pager," I said. Which went right past her.

When we paid the bill, left a tip, and got up to leave, she said, "Seriously, Marabella, I'm worried about you. Two people in your building were already knocked off, you said. You're not gonna stick your nose in this, are you? Remember how you almost got killed when…" She gave me a stern look.

I gave her a hug. "I know. I'll be careful."

"I sure hope so. Don't want to have to get another maid of honor at this late date." She swatted my arm. "Just kidding, of course."

We said goodbye and left for our respective offices. I was happy to have the fifteen-minute walk, hoping to forget about murder and mayhem for a little while. Happy to be warmed by the sun, with only a slight breeze disturbing the air. Guess the lion's part of March was quiet for a change.

Chapter 9

When I got home after work, my mother and Zilla had their eyes glued to *Animal Planet* on TV, on their separate perches.

"Ma, I thought you always hated that program." I hung up my jacket and kicked off my shoes.

Both pairs of eyes swiveled to me then back to the stalking tiger hunting down a small, helpless creature. My mother, wearing a red tee and gray sweatpants, shrugged. "Lousy programs on the other channels," she said.

Zilla, tail twitching, looked ready to join the tiger on the hunt.

I chortled. "Don't tell me you're trying to make nice with Zilla."

"If you can't beat them…"she said with a sigh.

I should pick up some new sexy underwear after work some time. God forbid John should see the same black lace bras and panties and teddies all the time. Then again, he never seemed to notice anything till he took it off me.

My mother probably thought I still wore lollipops, those colored cotton briefs for little girls. Certainly not black lace underwear. I stifled a laugh, remembering the look of horror on her face when she first saw teddies in the window of Victoria's Secret. She'd turned to me and said, "Only a prostitute would wear something like that."

Welcome to the twenty-first century, Ma.

As soon as the program was over, I told my mother about Rose Adelman.

She shook her head, worry lines on her forehead. "Terrible, just terrible. This is a scary business," she pronounced.

"I know." I leaned back on the sofa, feeling very tired.

"But it's not *your* business. It's police business," she said.

"Right." I decided this wasn't the time to mention my resolution after my frustrating conversation with Lieutenant Rivera.

"What did the detective say?"

Sometimes, I swear she had a direct channel into my brain. "Nothing much. He said he'd 'check it out,' and let me know." I rolled my eyes. "And he's a lieutenant now. But just as unpleasant."

"Patience has never been one of your virtues."

I fed the tiger-in-training and sat down with my mother for a meal of her leftovers. It was like the old joke: Was there ever an original meal?

"No sense putting good food to waste," she said, wagging her finger at me.

Right. Why throw garbage away when you could eat it? But I was hungry, so I shoveled in some of the boiled chicken, gravy made from canned cream of mushroom soup, and canned corn niblets. Washed down with seltzer. A blessing if there ever was one.

After I put the leftovers of the leftovers in the fridge, I opened the letter from Sam's lawyer that came in today's mail. It was a handwritten note, which read: *Dear Marabella. Though I am greatly saddened by the passing*

*of my longtime friend, Sam, I am grateful that he entrust-
ed this responsibility to you. I know he thought highly of
you, and I'm sure you will carry out these duties with the
utmost care and diligence. I'll keep in touch with you
about the estate. Yours, Harold Cohen.*

I felt myself tearing up. *Sam, wherever you are, I
promise to faithfully take care of this last thing for you.*

Harold had noted that there was a little money desig-
nated for my work as the executor, which I was thankful
for. My job paid *bubkes*. My previous boss, Donna, never
granted me a raise. Susan had tried, but all she'd managed to get for Carmen and me was another $50 a month
each. Chelsea College was perennially short of cash,
since they spent so much on the science department. I
was probably lucky I still had a job.

After I showed the lawyer's letter to my mother, the
phone rang. It was Rose's sister, Miriam Kravitz I gave
her my condolences and told her how much I'd enjoyed
her sister's company. It was true. She was a warm, bright
woman with a good sense of humor. And she'd been
Sam's companion, which earned her a gold star in my
book.

"Thank you, Marabella," Mrs. Kravitz said. I could
hear her blowing her nose. "And I appreciate your telling
the hospital to call me."

"I'm so sorry, Mrs. Kravitz. I know it was a shock. I
guess her injuries were too much for her."

"Miriam, please," she said. "I feel like we know each
other. My sister—" She blew her nose again."—told me
so much about you."

I must have been one of the few younger people in
the building who'd been friendly. "I was very glad to
know her."

She was quiet for a moment. "Marabella, let me tell
you something. I went to visit my sister this morning. She

was awake and alert. They had given her a transfusion and her nurse said she was stable and holding her own."

A chill went through me. "She was doing better this morning?" I could see my mother mouthing a question about time. "What time was that?" I asked Miriam.

"About eight, eight-fifteen. You know, Rose was a strong woman. Other than the arthritis in her hip, she was doing okay."

I thought for a moment. My mother was pointing to a pad, where she'd written: *anything unusual? See anyone?*

"Did you see anything unusual? Anyone who shouldn't be there?"

I heard her gasp. "Do you think someone—"

"Miriam, I don't know. But it's a possibility."

She was silent for a few minutes. "Marabella, could you please do two things for me?"

"Whatever I can do to help."

"Can you come to my place one day this week for the *shiva*?"

"Of course."

"And can you find out what happened to my sister? I know you're the one who found her. But there's something funny about it. She was always so careful about her balance. She didn't take chances."

I needed to approach this with caution. "I know," I said, debating whether to relate Rose's words to Miriam. And my mother. I'd left out that part when I told my mother what happened, afraid that she'd think I was in danger. Which I probably was.

"You *know* something. I can tell by your voice. And Rose told me you were like an amateur detective, good at solving crimes," Miriam said.

I knew when I was beaten. "I didn't want to worry you," I said. Not only that, I didn't want *her* to be in danger. And I didn't want me to, either. I'd promised myself

I'd had enough, thank you, the last time I chased down a killer.

She gave a harsh laugh. "What's to worry me now? My only sister is dead."

I took a deep breath. "When I found Rose, I asked her how she fell. She said she was pushed."

Miriam gasped. So did my mother.

"It's possible that someone already tried to kill her in the laundry room. And maybe that person came to the hospital to finish the job." I sneaked a look at my mother. She turned even paler than she'd been before and sank back against the sofa pillows.

Miriam was silent for a few minutes. Then her voice hardened. "I *knew* something wasn't right. I just knew it. Well, we're just going to have to make sure the police go after the bastard."

We? Me and a woman who was probably around seventy-five? I would have laughed, but I didn't want to hurt her feelings. "Miriam, I've already spoken to a police lieutenant, and he didn't take me very seriously. I'm sorry. I don't think there's anything else we can do."

"Oh, yes, there is. My son is an assistant district attorney. He'll see that this lieutenant…what's his name?"

"Lieutenant Eddie Rivera," I said.

That was all I needed, for Rivera to find out that I went over his head. I didn't even want to think about his reaction. I could say that Miriam dragged his name out of me, that I told her it wasn't a good idea to do this, that I really was going to leave everything up to him. Ha. One thing Rivera wasn't was dumb. In fact, sometimes I thought he could sniff out what was on my mind .Like my mother.

"My son will see to it that this Rivera takes it *very* seriously. I'm going to call Ronnie now, I have to call him about his aunt anyway, and the *shiva*. I'll call you when he tells me he's fixed it with the cops." She gave me directions to her apartment building in Flatbush.

"But…" I started to say, realized it was useless, and said goodbye. This was one determined septuagenarian. What was it about these women of my mother's generation, anyway? I had to admire that fighting spirit, even when it was being directed at me.

"What's the plan?" my mother said, sitting up and ready for action.

Chapter 10

I told my mother about Miriam's ace-in-the-hole, her idea of using her son, the ADA, to get Rivera to investigate Rose's death.

"Good, but that's not enough. Just a minute…"She fished out her bifocals from her bosom. Next came one of my pads of paper and a marker. She liked to work out her thoughts (plots?) on paper, making lists of who's who and what their motive for murder might be. I wondered if the chemicals she ingested chewing on the marker gave her brain an extra boost, in addition to chemical poisoning.

I joined her on the sofa. "Well?"

"Wait, wait, let me think," she mumbled through a mouthful of marker.

I heard the patter of big cat feet, and Zilla landed on the chair. I patted a spot next to me on the sofa and beckoned. He was having none of it and stayed where he was.

With a smile of satisfaction at her plotting, my mother said, "Okay. First, do you know if they cleaned out Sam's apartment yet?"

"I don't think so. We would have heard something. Cleaners aren't usually quiet, right?"

She nodded. "So, I'm going to first have a look around."

"What do you think you'll find?"

She threw up her hands. "Who knows? But it couldn't hurt."

With that, she took off, her essence slowly evaporating. I didn't know if I'd ever get used to her doing that. I worried too much about her disappearing altogether, or hurting herself, or getting stuck somewhere in the ether.

"Mmmmorrwww!" All of Zilla's fur was standing up. He was a furious orange-spiked ball, his eyes wild and his tail twitching nonstop.

I tried calming him down, but he was too deranged. He ran back and forth, dashing from room to room, finally burrowing under my bed, shaking. I bent down, speaking softly, hoping to coax the poor thing out, and got my arm scratched for my trouble. He obviously needed to chill by himself for a while. I closed the door of the bedroom, so he wouldn't be further traumatized when my mother landed, and went back to the living room.

A few groans later, she was back, with something in her hands, and collapsed on the sofa. "Take a look at this."

It was a small pad of paper, with faint ballpoint indentations on the top page. After rubbing with a pencil, I could just make out the words: *I, Samuel Lipschitz, being of sound mind and body, hereby change the instructions in my previous last will and testament to…*

The date at the top was the day Sam was found dead. "Rose was right," I whispered.

My mother nodded. "Unfortunately for Sam. And for her."

I started to think out loud. "The killer must have stopped what he or she was doing when they heard Rose in the hall, near Sam's door. So they grabbed the page from Sam, but…"

"Didn't have time to check all the pages underneath," she said.

"Now we've got more ammunition to bring to Lieutenant Rivera," I said, hoping this piece of information and Miriam's son-the-ADA would do the trick. Not to mention Miriam herself. I had no doubt that she could knock Rivera out, verbally speaking, in a New York minute. Now that was something I'd really look forward to seeing.

"Me, too! Power to the seniors!" my mother said.

Chapter 11

The next few days flew by at work, with Susan, Carmen, and me putting in long hours to finish the college catalogue. By Wednesday, we were wiped out, but it was done.

Susan leaned back in her chair at the table in her office. "Looking good. We're done except for the proofs." She had on one of her no-nonsense work outfits: black pantsuit with a royal blue shirt that she said could hold up through anything.

"Thank God," Carmen said, chomping on a piece of nicotine gum. She'd also been plucking at fluff on her red woolen sweater for the past couple of hours. Her kids and her mother had begged her to stop smoking. This time, she was really trying. I hoped she'd finish with the plucking before she ended up topless.

Sometimes, when we could catch our breaths, we'd take a coffee and tea break—tea for me, coffee for Susan and Carmen—and discuss our love lives, or lack of them. Mine used to be the most pathetic, since before John, I hadn't had a real relationship in years. Dates, yes, but nothing meaningful.

Susan had an on-again, off-again, long-term relationship with her boyfriend, Theo, a great-looking African-

American guy who was a senior medical researcher at Rockefeller University. The on-again was because they really clicked—attraction, interests. The off-again was because he was a senior medical researcher, meaning he'd get so caught up in his projects that he'd forget minor events like dinner dates, Susan's birthday, Valentine's Day, New Year's Eve.

Carmen was still dealing with the detritus of her ex-marriage. Occasionally, she'd mutter things like, "That f-ing bimbo," not exactly under her breath. She said that she'd been so hurt by her ex, she even resented the kids' every-other-weekend visitations with their father and his new trophy wife. I reminded her that this gave her a chance to go out and have fun.

"Fun, excitement," she groused. "What's that? I haven't had a date in who-the-f—"

Susan shot her a warning glance.

"—God knows how long," Carmen finished.

Speaking of excitement, for some reason, probably nostalgia about her old, crime-ridden neighborhood, Carmen thought my horrible, scary experience tracking down the killer of my late therapist and a group therapy member was thrilling, including my being wrongly imprisoned and almost killed. The whole thing had been splashed all over the tabloids, thanks to yet another member of the group.

When Carmen and I first met at work, she gave me a high-five, saying, "Way to go, Bella!" I guess some people couldn't help giving me nicknames. Lionel, who'd worked part-time in our department, used to call me "Marybelle," when he wasn't annoyed with me. I should get in touch with him some time, I thought. He was a nice kid and had been so out of place in college as a fifteen-year-old science prodigy.

Getting ready to leave for the day, I dug out my cell

phone and called my mother, just to check on her. She picked up after she heard my voice on the landline's answering machine, our signal. "Is everything okay?" I asked.

"Yes and no," she said.

Oh, God. "What?"

"The good news is that your cat and I seem to be getting along better, which I thought you'd be happy to—"

"What's the bad?" I interrupted.

"I heard noises in Sam's apartment a couple of hours ago. Maybe the killer came back and..."

"And?"

"And realized that he, or she, left the pad of paper in the apartment."

I took a deep breath. *Okay, Marabella, concentrate on exactly what there was to worry about.* "Hold on, Ma. First, did you see anything or anybody? And second, what exactly did you hear?"

"I didn't see a thing. But I heard some kind of rustling sounds, like paper. And what sounded like drawers opening."

This was not a good thing. They had to be thinking someone else had been there and found the pad.

"Marabella? Are you still there?" My mother's voice was getting anxious.

"Yes, yes. I've been thinking. The killer had to know that nobody could get into that apartment without a key, right?"

"But then how did he—"

"Used a credit card, probably. Easy." I thought about something else. "Anyway, there was no name on the pad of paper. So what could anyone learn that could be a threat, right?"

"Right."

Something else occurred to me. "Except, the killer might think the nosy old lady they murdered might have told somebody else about the argument and the will."

I heard a deep breath on the other end of the line.

"That's just paranoid thinking, right?" I said, trying to calm her and myself down.

"Right."

But whoever said killers weren't paranoid?

Chapter 12

Monday morning, I avoided getting a mouthful of fur by waking up early and feeding Zilla before he had a chance to land on my face in bed.

"Gotcha!" I said, slogging to the kitchen for Fancy Feast Salmon in Gravy. While he scarfed it down, my mother, bundled in the terry cloth robe I'd bought her, served me one of her specialties, burnt French toast. I managed to nibble at it by swilling down plenty of OJ and tea.

Giving my mother a kiss on the forehead and trying to give Zilla a pat before he could turn tail, I dressed for work in a dark green blazer, green striped blouse, and black skirt. I grabbed my trench coat and pocketbook, went out the door, and faced into the strong wind. The March lion was roaring away, so fierce I could hardly get my breath.

Lucy was at her usual corner, bundled up against the cold blasts, blowing on her fingers. Neither rain, nor sleet, nor wind could drive her away. But she looked worried. I found out why when she beckoned me over to her side. She looked up and down the street and whispered in my ear. "Marabella, I saw something strange yesterday."

"What?" I said. Lucy was not usually a worrier. She tended to take things as they came, relying on God's good grace to fix the world's problems.

She looked up and down again. "Somebody came into your building, like they were sneaking in, yesterday afternoon around three o'clock. I acted like I didn't notice, but I did."

That was about the time my mother had heard noises in Sam's apartment "What happened after that?" I asked.

Lucy had been occupying the same corner for years and knew who belonged in the building and who didn't. And she had an eagle eye for details. In fact, she once helped the cops identify a thief who'd been robbing apartments in the building.

She whispered, "He or she, I couldn't tell which, went upstairs in your building. They were up there for maybe a half an hour. When they came out again, they sneaked out, just the way they came in."

It was my turn to whisper in Lucy's ear. "Did you get a good look at them?"

She nodded and said in my ear, "Medium build, not too tall, not fat, or skinny. But I couldn't see the face or the hair. They were all covered up with one of those sweatshirt jackets, a gray one, that kind with the hood."

A hoodie. That could be anybody, since they were popular. But it was usually young people who wore them, right? Well, an older person could wear one, too. Borrowed from a son, a daughter, a grandson, or granddaughter. Or they could just buy their own. "Lucy, Thank you for this information. But please be careful, okay?" I said.

She smiled her toothless smile. "Ah, don't you worry. The good Lord will look out for old Lucy, I know." Then she frowned. "There was something familiar about that person, but I can't think what it was. I'll let you know when I remember." She shook her head, as if to clear it.

"Lucy, even though the Lord looks out for you, you need to look out for yourself, too, okay?" I dropped a couple of dollars in the Yankees cap.

On the subway, I worried about Lucy and the intruder. When I got to work, snorts and fits of laughter coming from the ladies' room got my attention. They stopped when I poked my head in the door. "What's so funny? Can I hear, too?"

"Take a look," Carmen said, pointing to the mirror on the wall, where she and a bunch of other women were gleefully admiring their handiwork.

Somebody had written in bright-red lipstick:

There once was a girl named Lisa.
A real little piece-a teas-a.
Little did she know.
What can happen to a ho.
Better look out, watch your step, little Lisa.

"Guys, guys. This is not a good thing." I picked up some paper towels and made for the mirror.

"Stop!" Carmen grabbed the towels out of my hand. "Why would you wanna do that?"

"Um…because it's not nice."

Loud sneers. Margaret Wilson, from accounting, hands on fleshy hips, twisted her lips in a snarl. "Neither is she! Do you know what that little bitch did? Arnie and I were practically engaged, when she—she—stole him away from me, the dirty, f-ing whore!"

"Look. She's not my favorite person, either. But this could be considered workplace harassment," I said.

Bronx cheers, aka raspberries.

"*Somebody* could get in trouble," I said.

Silence. Carmen planted her feet apart. Then: "How would anybody know who did it? Tell me that, huh?"

"By the handwriting? The shade of lipstick?" I said.

Carmen drawled, "Riiigght. Well, kids, I guess we better make tracks outta here, if we don't want *trouble*."

When they began filing out, she whispered to me, "Listen, this is just between us, right?"

"Us?"

"Hey, everybody knows you hate her guts, too. They could even think *you* did it," Carmen said, with a sly grin.

Was this a not-so-subtle threat? I glanced at her, but I couldn't tell. Her face was smooth as glass. We'd always gotten along, had even become office friends. At any rate, there was no room in my brain to deal with one more problem. "Okay, it's between us," I said.

Then I flashed on what could happen if John found out about this—of course, he would—and thought that I did it. Just when things seemed to be going along swimmingly, well, except for Li Li and the fact of my apartment now being off-limits to romance. Not to mention a murderer on the loose in my apartment building. My home. I sighed. A person was supposed to feel safe in her home.

Chapter 13

The next morning when I got to my front door on my way to work, I heard a commotion outside and remembered last night's forecast of snow. *Yes, it can snow in New York City in March. And no, the city doesn't handle it well.*

I peeked outside. No plow. Police, an ambulance, and a crowd were gathered in front of my building. I hurried out the door into the piles of already-dirty snow.

"Stay back, lady," a beefy cop said, escorting me onto the slippery sidewalk.

"What happened? I live here. I've got a right to know."

Tony, the building's super, came over to me. "It's that homeless woman, Lucy. She's dead."

"Oh, my God! What happened? Was it an accident?" I asked him, hoping against hope.

"Not unless you call being stabbed in the chest an accident."

Oh, God .Poor Lucy. It was all my fault. I never should have encouraged her to tell me about the person she saw sneaking into the building. And if I didn't get involved in all this in the first place, chasing after a murderer, she wouldn't be dead.

I stopped myself from asking Tony if he'd seen or heard anything. I didn't want to be responsible for anything horrible happening to him, too. I'd better take this straight to Rivera, I thought. Though he'd probably have some reason to discount the connection to the other murders. Which he didn't think were even murders.

But first, I called Susan on my cell and explained why I'd be late to work and that I'd make it up later. Thank the gods for an understanding boss. I knew what kind of verbal abuse I would have gotten if Donna, Her Royal Bitchiness, were still in charge of my department.

I headed for the police station, sloshing along sidewalks where the dirty snow had become dirty brown slush. Trying to avoid the cold splatter from the other pedestrians' sloshing, and failing. Now I was chilled to the bone from my sodden boots and pantyhose. Aarrgh. Showing up at Rivera's office, not to mention my own office, covered in disgusting guck wasn't my favorite way to start the day. The weather in New York was…well, as somebody, I think it was Jerry Orbach, on *Law & Order*, once said: "If you don't like the weather…or was it the neighborhood? Or both?…wait ten minutes." But ten minutes later, the streets were still swimming in the brown stuff.

Luckily, I found Rivera in, ignoring the fact that he obviously wasn't glad to see me.

He greeted me with a grunt and a yawn and motioned to a chair across from him at his desk. Today he was decked out in a godawful mismatch of brown pants, gray shirt, and blue jacket. Why they didn't teach wardrobe skills in the police academy, I'd never know. More important, I could see that he was in a foul mood.

He opened a desk drawer, took out a bottle of aspirin, washed it down with the ever-present caffeine-free soda on his desk, and glared at me. "Just what I needed to add to an already rotten morning," he said. "To what do I owe the pleasure of this visit? Not another so-called 'murder,' I hope?"

Trying to start off right, I said, "Sorry to trouble you, Lieutenant, but I thought you'd better hear this. That is, if you haven't already. Heard it, I mean." Why did he always make me so nervous that I ended up sounded like a gibbering idiot? Or a ditzy female, which I had no doubt was what he thought of me?

"Oh, right," he said, dripping sarcasm, grabbing a pen and notepad. "Okay, from the top."

"Sorry to disappoint you, but there's been another murder. Lucy, a homeless woman who's been a regular at my corner for years, was found stabbed to death this morning."

He put down his pen. "Already knew about that. We figure it for a robbery/homicide. The neighbors told us she had a baseball cap she kept her money in and it, and whatever cash she collected, was gone. Beats me how people can kill somebody for a few dollars, but it happens. Probably a junkie." He shook his head.

Trying not to be too argumentative, I said, "Lieutenant, I don't think it was robbery."

He yawned. "And why not?"

I took a deep breath and tried to compose myself. Bad enough that Lucy was dead, but having to go through my usual rigmarole with Rivera was getting to me. "Toot sweet," as Donna used to say. "Look, I know this is going to sound strange—"

"What else is new, coming from you?" He snorted.

Deep breaths, Marabella, try to relax. Remember, you've got a job to do, no matter how irritating he is. I'd have to change the part of the story involving my mother. "Okay. I, um, snuck into my neighbor, Sam's, apartment before they cleaned it out."

"Breaking and entering, huh? Looking for clues, I imagine?"

"I didn't break in, the apartment was still open," I said.

"If it was open, it wasn't open for you to snoop around in."

Ignoring him, I said, "And I found a pad of paper with the imprint of Sam's changing his will, that he never got to finish writing. The next day, Lucy, the homeless woman, told me she saw somebody sneak into the building. And that the person looked familiar. And that she'd probably remember who it was and tell me when she did. Now she's dead."

He looked up from his notepad. "So far, you haven't given me anything that would lead me to believe, number one: this was connected to your other two so-called murders, and number two: that this was anything but a robbery/homicide."

Fighting for self-control and losing, I said, "Look, there's now been three dead people, all centered around my building. Don't tell me you think it's a coincidence?"

He yawned again. "I do. Not only that, you're always thinking everything's a conspiracy, somebody running around killing people. For what purpose?"

By now, I was on fire. "Lieutenant Rivera, how about the purpose of someone wanting to get their hands on their share of three million dollars, in a timely fashion?"

He shook his head. "Boy, speaking of conspiracies. You're telling me that somebody did away with an old man with a heart condition for his money, which they'd most likely get pretty soon anyway? And that another old person, walking downstairs, trying to balance her cane and her laundry in a dark basement, was killed because of the same money? And that a homeless street person, whose own money went missing, was killed for the same reason?"

"Lieutenant! You are either too stubborn to admit you could be wrong or you just won't take me seriously! There's a serial killer out there, preying on old and helpless people!"

He gulped his soda. "Well, you're finally making sense. I agree with you."

Ah. "That's great! I've convinced you, right?"

"No. You're right that I won't take you seriously." He smirked and got up from his chair.

Grrrr. I got up, too, glaring at him. "You'll see. I'm right. And you'll be sorry."

He glared back at me. "Believe me, I already am. For wasting my time, listening to your cockamamie conspiracies. Good morning, Ms. Vinegar."

Chapter 14

At least everyone at work was sympathetic, which helped my mood, if not my conscience. Even though Carmen, after hearing the story, said, "Hey, Bella, no way was this your fault. She was just in the wrong place at the wrong time."

I thanked her and tried to put all of it on hold and concentrate on my work, which was a heavy load today. I had to come up with a press release and media alerts about the guest lecturer in the biology department, which involved research about the guy. And another release about the free rabies clinic John's department was sponsoring. And the pages for the annual report needed to be proofread. Hopefully, there were no terrible problems, so it wouldn't have to be sent back to the printer. Oh, and I needed to schedule a couple of photo shoots of students receiving special awards. The actual picture-taking was done by Carmen and not me, thank the gods, or the students would be unrecognizable blurs. A non-visually oriented person didn't usually make for a good photographer.

When I finally was able to get out of the office, I caught the subway home, not eager to deal with any more slush. After my thoughts turned to what I'd like to do to

Rivera, they turned to Lucy again. What a good soul she was. What a kind person she was. Always cheerful. Never complaining about her lot in life. How she never worried, because she had such faith in the Lord.

Well, the Lord couldn't save poor, harmless Lucy from a vicious killer, who never would have hurt her if it weren't for me. My meddling, my sleuthing, my nosiness.

From the time I was a little girl, I'd been obsessed with finding out what was going on around me. I even started a spying club—shades of *Harriet the Spy*—in sixth grade, with a couple of my friends. The only problem was that nothing interesting ever seemed to happen in my neighborhood. So after a while, the other kids got bored. Too bad, because a few weeks later, I woke up one night to flashing police lights. Turned out one of our lowlife neighbors had been running high-stakes poker games and got raided. The man and his buddies were hauled away in a police car. I was very disappointed that I wasn't able to find out what happened after that, because he disappeared.

When I reached my building, I tried not to look at where Lucy's body had been. Or where she used to stand, day after day, with her wide, toothless smile and her Yankees cap at her feet. Thinking about Lucy made me feel sad and guilty. Then it made me furious. Lucy was the latest of the good, kind people who were victims of this ruthless killer.

Lucy, I thought, wherever you are, surely with the Lord, I'm going to find out who did this to you and make them pay, big time. I know that doesn't make me any less responsible for what happened to you. But it's all I can do for you now. I brushed away tears on my sleeve, wishing I had a clean handkerchief like the one Lucy always carried, as I went up to my apartment.

Chapter 15

Walking to the subway for Rose's *shiva*, I was grateful that the snowy, cold weather seemed to have left us, hopefully till next winter. There was even a hint of spring to come in the air, and an intermittent glimpse of the sun when it peeked out of the clouds.

I realized that I'd literally been in mourning for days. Having to cope with the deaths of three people I cared about was too much to bear. I went to bed sad and woke up sad, barely able to keep from bursting into tears.

When I changed to the Brooklyn-bound train, I told myself that Rose's sister didn't need my depressing mood to add to her grief. *Better buck up before you get there.* I closed my eyes and took a couple of cleansing breaths. Aah. It really did help. I had to be grateful to my late therapist, Dr. Ditstein, for that. Before our relationship, I never knew how to help myself relax.

Miriam Kravitz was definitely not what I had expected. Far from being a frail elderly person, she sailed into the lobby of the Greenspan Building, a senior citizens' apartment complex, like a battleship: black-suited bosom preceding her, full steam ahead, no nonsense. Steel-gray hair permed in rigid waves, firm arms and legs, penetrating eyes. Very much a personality. And formidable. Total opposite of her sister. Where Rose was soft and shy and unassuming, Miriam was a determined, obviously sharp woman with the energy of someone half her age. I later learned that she'd spent many years as assistant principal of a Brooklyn high school.

She smiled, gripped my hand with plenty of strength. "You must be Marabella. Thank you so much for coming. Please, come upstairs, we're almost ready to begin."

No elevator for her. She charged up two flights of stairs. I followed in her wake, puffing as we reached the door of her apartment. *Damn*, I thought. *I'd better make a date with Toniann and get back to aerobics.* Or without Toniann, who was otherwise occupied these days.

The apartment was crammed with thick drapes and rugs, dark furniture and heavy mirrors, which Miriam must have moved from a previous home. The place was full of people, all speaking loudly, I assumed because of hearing problems. Probably mostly senior citizens who lived in the building. Miriam, I gathered, was quite the social director. She ran the exercise program, the Bingo nights, was a reader at the weekly Friday night Shabbat services, arranged the birthday parties and the trips. And was president of the Greenspan's tenants' committee. I got the impression that some of the residents were a little afraid of her.

As she marched in and out of the kitchen, I heard someone mutter, "There goes the admiral."

Someone else said, "Shoosh, she just lost her sister, have a little respect, she's in mourning."

Everyone quieted down during the brief service. And started up again as soon as it was over, between eating and drinking. There was an enormous amount of food and diet soda. I filled a paper plate with goodies and a paper cup with soda and took myself to a chair in the corner of the living room.

After a few minutes, Miriam grabbed a nearby chair and fixed her eyes on me. "Okay, it's all arranged."

"What?" I said, scarfing down a mini-brownie, the chocolaty taste thick on my tongue. Pure melt-in-your-mouth sweetness. Ahh. Unfortunately for my hips, I had no self-control when it came to brownies. Even having been almost killed by a box of poisoned ones, a gift from a killer. And, though it was hard to believe, John liked my hips. Scrumptious, he called them. Amazing man.

Miriam spoke *sotto voce*, pointing to a short, stocky man with a receding hairline, talking to someone across the room. "My son, Ronnie, the ADA. By the way, he happens to be single." Divorced, five years now, no children." She gave me a penetrating gaze. "I think you two would be perfect for each other."

What was it with that generation, that they had this compulsion to match make? "Um, sorry. I have a boyfriend. But thanks, anyway." I smiled at her.

She sighed. "Too bad. Anyway, Ronnie already fixed it with your lieutenant. So, how soon can we go there?"

No flies on the admiral. Trying to swallow without choking on chunks of chocolate and nuts, I said, "Um, it would have to be after work. Or on my lunch hour."

"Where is your office? I'll come pick you up."

I took a sip of soda. "Isn't that a lot of trouble for you? We could just meet at the police station."

"No trouble at all. Besides, I was thinking of signing up for a couple of courses, maybe at your college."

The fact that she'd have to take two subways to get to Chelsea College didn't seem to faze her. "Actually, you could take classes at the community college right in your neighborhood, much easier."

"It would be an adventure. New buildings. New people. New things to learn." She folded her arms across her chest.

I wondered why on earth she'd be interested in CC. Just nosiness about where I worked? Checking me out? Who knew? But I'd bet a dozen brownies that taking classes there wasn't all that was on her agenda.

I wrote the address, phone number, and directions to the college on a slip of paper and handed it to her. "Okay. I don't have any idea of Rivera's schedule. We'd better make an appointment. And I think the phone call should come from you. I'm not exactly on his A-list."

"Why not?"

"I'll fill you in on the way over to the police station. Just let me know day and time," I said, getting up from my chair.

"Take a couple brownies with you," she said, grabbing a half-dozen, and throwing in a few chocolate chip cookies and two pieces of pound cake, for good measure, into a paper bag—plus some cans of diet soda. "To wash it all down. Thank you so much for coming and for all your detecting help," she whispered.

Call me a chocoholic. Call me a person without willpower. I didn't care. I took the bag, thanked her, and went out the door.

Chapter 16

I mulled things over on the trip back from Brooklyn. The subway was a good place to mull, since no New Yorker wanted to make eye contact when out and about.

Priorities, priorities. What to do first? Well, besides getting Rivera to do an investigation of three deaths, which I was sure were related, the question was: Who was the killer? The almost certain answer was a member of Sam's family, because of the will.

The next thing on the list: Have my mother check out the beneficiaries' financial status. And their lifestyles. Who knew what kind of stuff was going on in their personal lives? Gambling, infidelity, embezzling, blackmail, porn, fraud, debt, bigamy, the possibilities were legion.

But a little voice in my head warned: *What if the killer figures out that you're the one who took the pad? And thought Lucy told me who came back to Sam's apartment?*

But, I told the voice, *the killer could also think someone threw the pad out, right?*

Remember what happened last time you played detective? You promised to leave crime-fighting to the cops.

But this was Sam and Rose and Lucy, I told the voice. *I can't just forget about them. Or make believe I thought it was natural causes. There's nothing natural about murder.*

When I got off the last subway, I remembered I was running out of cat food and ducked into Pet Smart. God forbid that my cat didn't have his choice of Fancy Feast dinners. I picked up some cans and a bag of kitty litter.

By the time I got home, I'd scarfed down half of Miriam Kravitz's brownies. *Today on the lip, tomorrow on the hip.* When I opened the door to my apartment, my mother and Zilla both woke up from naps. At least my mother wasn't cranky and grouchy. I wished I could say the same for Zilla, who woke up like a bear in spring. In other words, grouchy and ravenous. Hopefully, food would calm the savage beast. I went into the kitchen and opened one of the cans, dumped half in his dish and filled his water dish. And put the new litter in the pan.

After I got him settled, my mother and I sat down to our dinner. Spaghetti with ketchup sauce. The sauce came straight from a bottle of ketchup. *Who makes spaghetti sauce with ketchup? No point saying anything.* At least it wasn't leftovers. Yet.

After we went back to the living room and were sitting on the sofa, I asked my mother if she'd seen or heard anything more in Sam's apartment. I'd decided not to say anything about Lucy yet. I didn't want to make my mother even more nervous about me, if I could help it.

"No. But come to think of it, maybe what I heard were the cleaning people."

"Cleaning people? Then you would have heard a lot more noise, things being lifted, carted out of the apartment."

She shrugged. "Maybe I was dreaming, or hallucinating."

"Ma, you're trying to keep me from worrying, right?"

She nodded.

"And you're trying to keep me from finding out who did this, right?"

"And from getting killed."

"Okay. I understand. But you should understand that I can't leave this alone. They were my friends."

She sighed then nodded her head slowly.

"So, let's get to work."

"I'm ready when you are, sweetheart." She fished out her bifocals and the pad and marker.

"First, we need to make a list of anyone who could be a possible suspect," I said.

"Which means members of Sam's family," she said. "Let's have it."

"Two brothers and wives, one sister and husband. Their children wouldn't count, since it was the parent who'd inherit. Plus Jennifer, his niece. Wait, don't we still have the list from Sam's address book?" I asked.

"Right here," she said, retrieving the sheet of paper from her bosom. What else did she keep in there? God only knew.

"Whatever I might need in the future," said the mind-reader. "Okay, I'll take them in order. Jeremy and Tamar in Riverdale, in The Bronx, first. I'll scope out their house, look for bank statements, check out his office."

"How are you going to do that?"

She smiled. Sphinx-like. "Follow him to work, of course. By the way, does his wife work?"

"Don't know. But I'm sure you'll find out."

"Of course."

She licked the marker, thinking. "Next stop, Glen Cove, David and Cheryl. Then Abby and Larry in Tarrytown. And Jennifer, in Park Slope, in Brooklyn. I'll start on it tomorrow."

"Hey, please, don't overdo it, okay? Take your time, please. I don't think there's any big rush."

"Ten-four."

She was back to trucker mode again. Maybe she drove a semi in a previous incarnation?

"No, sweetheart. I just like the lingo. By the way, as long as I'll be out and about, I'll pay a visit to the doctor, get a look at Sam's medical records. And the pharmacy." She stretched out on the sofa and closed her eyes.

I went into the bedroom and got out my sorry attempts at knitting. Being a non-visual person didn't help my efforts. Luckily, the women in my knitting group, the Yarn Marms, were patient and happy to help beginners. Though the most experienced one, Bunny, aka The Yarn Guru, shook her head and said, "I've never seen anything like it," every time I made yet another mistake.

At least each mistake was different. Mistakes or no, knitting helped me to concentrate on other things. Unraveling helped even more. Shades of Miss Marple. Unraveling her knitting helped her unravel a mystery, usually murder, and usually with more than one body involved.

As I started to unravel the results of my latest mistake, I thought about the components of the three deaths and what I knew so far. Or what I *thought* I knew:

Sam's death: though the verdict was heart attack, he didn't have serious heart disease. Argument with someone—presumably family member—the day he died. Said he was planning to change his will. Overheard by Rose. Killed by: overdose of heart medicine, nitroglycerin? Something else? Maybe succyinylcholine, the one I'd heard about on TV dramas? Need autopsy: toxins, puncture marks, etc. Also: check prescription for heart medicine. Cops said only half a bottle of pills left, when was it renewed?

Rose's death: afraid person coming out of Sam's apartment saw her; fell in laundry room, said she was pushed. Sister said Rose was always careful walking, with cane and supportive shoes. Rose died in hospital after nurse said she was recovering. IVs, monitors, tampered with? Check with nurses, doctors, etc. Need autopsy.

Lucy's death: after pad of paper with indentation of first lines of changing his will found (by Mother) in Sam's apartment, someone—presumably the killer—looked for pad—noises overheard by Mother. Person seen going in and out of the building and vaguely recognized by Lucy.

Thinking about poor Lucy meeting her death just because of where she was standing and for talking to me, trying to be helpful, made me feel sick to my stomach. I didn't know much about Lucy, or even whether she had any family. Maybe there was a way I could find out. I'd heard that she ate at a soup kitchen and stayed at a homeless shelter when the weather got bad. I could ask the people there what they knew about her life. I promised myself to plan to do something in her memory. That was the least I could do.

I looked down at my hands and realized I'd unraveled an entire ball of purple wool. But there was something else, something that I'd tried to push away, that I didn't want to think about.

But there it was, snaking its way into my immediate consciousness. The someone I was looking to find, the someone who'd been looking for the pad of paper, might very well end up looking for me. As Sam's next-door-neighbor and friend, as someone Rose might have confided in as to what she heard and saw, and as the recipient of Lucy's recollection about the person sneaking into the building.

Chapter 17

Soft candlelight, soft music, tables for two covered with linen tablecloths and tucked into corners, heavenly smells coming from the kitchen. The restaurant was living up to its reputation as a romantic place to eat. And John looked good enough to eat, too. He was wearing a brown jacket that matched his eyes, a rust-colored shirt, and a chocolate paisley tie. His dark curly hair was even curlier from the shower. Yum. I'd vowed to banish all thoughts of the murders, and Li Li, from my brain tonight. I wanted this to be a lovely, romantic dinner. And I had high expectations about what would happen after dinner.

After a quick kiss on the mouth, which made me hungry for more, we ordered drinks and dinner. Steak, rare, for John. Ugh. Nothing that was still bleeding for me, thank you. Chicken for me. Why did I always choose this in restaurants? Fear of unknown food? My mother's warnings about undercooked whatever, botulism from things in jars and cans, Legionnaire's disease…no, wasn't that from something in the air conditioning?…and what was that thing you risked from undercooked pork, besides the wrath of God, if you were Jewish?

I had to tell John about Sam. He reached for my hand across the table. "I'm so sorry. I know how fond of him you were. But it can happen, with an older person. Did he have any medical problems, like a heart condition?"

"All he had was angina, a mild case, under control with medication, he told me."

John squeezed my hand. "That's what he told you, Marabella. Maybe he didn't want you to worry about him, so he didn't tell you the whole story."

"And there was a lot of money involved, allocated in his will."

"But you told me he lived so modestly."

"I know. I guess that was just his way. Um, there's more."

He looked alarmed. "More?"

"Tell you later," I said, seeing that our dinners were arriving. I inhaled the aroma of my chicken dish: redolent with lemon and butter sauce and sage. Mmmm. The less said about John's rare beast, the better. I hoped it was really dead. I thought it even smelled like blood. After we finished and were sipping our wine, I told him the rest.

"Rose Adelman is dead, too."

"Rose Adelman?" He looked puzzled.

"Another elderly neighbor. A good friend of Sam's. And she heard an argument in Sam's apartment, before he—"

John patted my hand. "Go on."

"She thought she saw something, somebody, running out of Sam's apartment, who she thought saw her, too. And now she's dead." I gulped a mouthful of my white wine.

"Be careful with that. You know what can happen," he warned.

"Not to worry," I said.

John had unfortunately experienced the results of my drinking. I either threw up or passed out, or both. Neither of which was attractive or conducive to romance.

"How did she die?"

I told him how I'd found her in the laundry room and what she'd said to me. And what her sister said about what happened in the hospital. I figured I'd better not add Lucy's murder to my report.

He sat back in his seat. Then he reached for his wine glass and gulped.

"Be careful with that," I tried to joke. He didn't have my problem with alcohol.

"You went to the police." It was a statement, not a question.

"But the lieutenant, Rivera, didn't take me seriously." I told him about Miriam Kravitz and her plans.

He frowned. "Marabella, this is not good. I have a horrible feeling that you're trying to play detective again. Is that what—"

I shook my head. "Don't be silly. I had enough of that last time."

"Right. Promise me you'll leave it up to the cops?" He was still frowning.

I decided not to let him know about what my mother found in Sam's apartment. Or what she'd heard. It would only make him crazy. I managed to change the subject to something much more delicious. "How about that coffee aanddd…" I gave him my best salacious smile.

He grinned. But he still looked worried. I was counting on the fact that I'd be able to get his mind onto steamier things very soon. Hopefully, without the Marx Brothers vying for my attention.

Chapter 18

Toniann and I met the next day after work for our fittings at Gloria's Bridal Shop, a few blocks from her parents' house in Brooklyn. The place was decked out like a fancy wedding, with ornate white trellises trailing artificial white blossoms, a mock wedding cake on a stand. A large music box played, "Here Comes the Bride," in the window next to the bridal party mannequins.

The fitters had Toniann hoisted up on a small bench in front of a huge mirror, measuring and pinning. The dress was gorgeous, a shimmering white satin that flattered her figure, which didn't need much flattering. Perched on her head was some kind of headband made of what looked like white feathers.

"Are those from actual birds?" I asked, hoping not.

"Not anymore," one of the fitters said, with a raucous laugh.

I turned my head so I wouldn't have to see the remains of what must have been beautiful birds and tried to concentrate on my friend, the soon-to-be blushing bride.

The shorter fitter pointed at me. "Your turn. Your dress is all ready for you to try on. I bet you're so excited."

I could hardly wait. You know how kids used to put a buttercup under their friends' chins, to see if their faces would look yellow? Well, whenever I was anyway near that fateful color, my face grew yellower and yellower. Why Toniann would subject her best friend, her maid-of-honor-to-be, to becoming a yellow ball with legs, was beyond me. I followed the fitter, who was displaying the wretched bunch of yellow fabric on a satin hanger. She directed me to the dressing room, holding the dress while I undressed. We went over to another bench in front of another large mirror. I climbed up, faced the glass, and groaned.

It was worse than my worst clothing nightmare. My medium-pale white face had become a butterball. Aarggh. I wondered aloud if I could put some kind of green, blue, purple, whatever, around my neck to offset all that yellow.

"Such a sense of humor." The fitter guffawed. Then she started measuring and pinning. And warning me not to move or I'd get stuck with one of her pins. But I couldn't help it, since everything in me was screaming to get out of that yellow thing.

"Ouch!" I looked down at a pin stabling my skin, oozing a few drops of blood.

"You can't get blood on your dress!" After yanking out the pin in my right thigh, she yelled to a salesperson, "Kleenex!"

At least the blood would have added some color. But having my skin pinned was painful, so I made a supreme effort to stand still.

She resumed her pinning without comment. Until she got to the top part of the dress.

"Whoa! We'll just have to find a way to make the bust more generous," she said.

My chest was pretty generous, though miniscule

compared with my mother's endowment. But huge compared with Toniann's.

Then she hollered to another fitter. "We're gonna need some extra fabric for the bust."

Many thanks for that announcement, I thought. At least there didn't seem to be any men in the shop at the moment. But I didn't appreciate my measurements being broadcast in public.

Toniann giggled. "Some people have all the luck."

Trying to stay still and not gesticulate while I was talking, to avoid more stabbing, I said, "Never mind luck. How about food? As in dinner? I'm starving."

"Just a few more inches and we'll be done for today," the fitter said.

"Today? We have to do this *again*?" I yelped

"Unless you want to go topless," she said, with a cackle.

Chapter 19

The next day, Miriam Kravitz called me at the office to tell me we had an appointment with Rivera that afternoon at five-thirty. Great, the perfect end to an already horrible day.

I'd had to spend quality time with my old nemesis, Professor Myra Newsome—aka Nasty Nuisance. Besides being a royal pain, Newsome was a card-carrying bigot.

The good professor's complaint of the day was that I'd only publicized her daughter's engagement in our internal newsletter. She expected the announcement to be in *The New York Times*, at least. She planted herself across from me in my office, hands on hips, scowl on face. A powerful perfume odor wafted toward me, making me sneeze.

I blew my nose and gritted my teeth, imagining them taking a bite out of her. "I'm sorry, but we don't send out press releases about faculty members' personal or family news, Professor."

Myra Newsome was a thoroughly narcissistic woman, pushing fifty or so, who acted as if she were still a twenty-something. She wore clothes that were years too young and too short for her age. Today she had on a ruffled pink blouse and short maroon skirt, ending in high leather boots. She also spoke in a girlish tone, giggling, when she encountered a man. Being deluded about her age and appearance might have accounted for her misconceptions about other things. Namely, her own importance.

Newsome glared at me and drew herself up to her full height, which, without the boots, was about the same as mine. "And just why not? Isn't that what we pay you people for?"

I bit my tongue then took a couple of deep breaths, not caring if she thought I was weird. I needed all the ammunition I could get. I smiled and said, "Professor, I can see that you're upset."

Upset was the understatement of the year, since the woman practically had smoke coming out of her ears. And as for what was coming out of her mouth…

"How dare you patronize me, you little twit? Who the hell do you think you are? You're here to serve the faculty members, meaning people like me, in the academy, you ignoramus." Her face was bright red and she was snorting like an angry rhino.

I was afraid she'd have a stroke. Not that I cared. But knowing her, she'd find a way to blame me for it. I'd better try to calm her down. "I'm really sorry, Professor Newsome. I wish I could do something about it. I know it's a stupid rule. However, someone in *my* position hardly has the power to do anything about it, you see." Grovel, grovel. "But maybe you can send the announcement to our alumni magazine. I'm sure they'd be happy to publish it. You could include a photo, too. Of the engaged couple," I tossed in, for extra points. *Oh, what havoc have I wrought?*

The last thing in the world I, and our department, needed was to have to publicize every cockamamie event in the faculty's personal lives. I could see it now: bar and bat mitzvahs, high school graduations, heck, middle school graduations.

She did not look overjoyed. But her face was beginning to regain its original color and her breathing seemed more normal. "Hmmph," she said and turned around to leave.

I sat back in my chair and took care of my own breathing for a few minutes. Then I got up and went into Susan's office. "Aarrrgghh!" I pretended to tear my hair out.

Looking up from the pages she and Carmen were going over, Susan gave me a sympathetic look. "Newsome, right?"

Carmen volunteered, "She's a real—"

Susan gave her a forbidding look.

Carmen shrugged. "Rhymes with witch."

"And itch," I said, imagining Newsome full of itching powder. Which gave me a bit—okay, a whole lot—of satisfaction. I heard my phone ring back in my office. It was Miriam Kravitz, telling me she was around the corner. I grabbed my jacket and pocketbook, waved goodbye to my colleagues, and went downstairs to meet Miriam at the front entrance, girding myself for my session with Rivera. I couldn't wait to see which one of them came out on top. I was betting on Miriam.

Chapter 20

Dressed in a business-looking gray suit, Miriam led our way into the police station, determination in every bone of her body. The desk officer took our names, buzzed Rivera, and directed us right to his office. Amazing. Miriam's son-the-ADA must have some clout. Or maybe Rivera wanted to get our meeting over with as fast as possible.

Miriam strode into Rivera's office, reaching out to grab his hand in what looked like a firm grip. He smiled at her, actually stood up—a picture of wardrobe-dysfunction in a brown striped shirt, green jacket, and gray pants—and asked her to sit down. As for me, I got a cursory nod and a point to a chair. Also amazing was that he'd found two relatively comfortable chairs to put in the room.

"Nice," I said to him, patting the chair before I sat.

A scowl. Then a change to Lieutenant Pleasant. "Mrs., uh…"

"Kravitz," Miriam said.

A benevolent smile. "Mrs. Kravitz, first, let me say that I'm very sorry for your loss."

"Thank you," she said.

"And I understand that you have some information about your sister that could be helpful." Out came the notepad and pen.

Miriam leaned forward in her seat. "I certainly do."

"Okay. From the top…uh, please." Another smile.

Would wonders never cease?

She went through the whole thing, not leaving out any of the pertinent details, listing everything in chronological order. "So here is my case: First, Rose heard the argument and Sam's threat to change his will and got a glimpse of someone running out of his apartment. Then she told Marabella that she was afraid that the person thought she got a good look at him or her. Next, Marabella found her on the floor in the basement, and she said she'd been pushed. The next morning, the hospital nurse told me Rose was improving. And then, all of a sudden, she was dead."

Rivera nodded, scribbling away on his notepad.

She leaned forward in her chair. "So, what are you going to do?"

He looked at her. Ignoring me, of course. "I'd say you made a good case."

"For?"

"An investigation. Which we were about to launch anyway." He glared at me.

Miriam sat back and let out her breath. "Thank you. But please, tell me exactly what you're going to do, and how soon?"

"I really can't share details like that. But I need to ask your permission about something, just in case."

"About what?" she asked, leaning forward again.

"Just in case our investigation warrants it, we'd need your permission to conduct an autopsy. Which would mean exhuming your sister's body."

Miriam stared at him for a few minutes and finally said, "There's no other way?"

I patted her arm. "Miriam, the lieutenant said, 'Just in case.' It might not even have to happen.'" I shot Rivera a look and he nodded.

Rivera pressed on. "But if we have reason to believe there was foul play, it might be necessary for our case."

"Just do what you have to do to find my sister's killer," Miriam said.

I folded my arms across my chest. "Not only was there foul play in Rose's death, but also with Sam's, Lieutenant. And Lucy's."

Another glare. Then he turned to Miriam, and stood up. "Mrs. Kravitz, I assure you that we will get on this right away. I'm going to take charge of this case, *personally*."

I assumed this was our signal to leave and got up, as did Miriam. She walked over to Rivera and gripped his hand again. I hoped she gave him a good sprain. I was itching to stick my tongue out at him, but managed to control myself. I should be used to our unpleasant relationship by now, right? Anyway, I was eager to get home and see what my-mother-the-ghost-detective had discovered.

Chapter 21

After feeding the voracious feline and consuming last night's leftovers, my mother and I settled down on the sofa to go over our day's events. I gave her the upshot of the interview with Rivera, including the possibility of an exhumation and autopsy of Rose Adelman. Like Miriam Kravitz, my mother was appalled.

She shook her head. "I've never even heard of a Jewish autopsy, never mind digging up the body. Isn't it against our religion? Maybe you should consult with a rabbi. How about the one who officiated at my funeral…what's-his-name? Not that he was anything to talk about. No charisma."

Besides this suggestion being in questionable taste, I was flabbergasted about her sudden interest in religious observance, she being someone who'd hardly ever graced the inside of a synagogue, even on the High Holidays. My parents had referred to themselves as "cardiac Jews," meaning Jewish-in-food-only. The food that seduced the taste buds, restaurant meals thick with butter and fatty meats that sank to the bottom of your intestines like a pile of bricks: brisket smothered with onion gravy, potato pudding, chicken livers sautéed in chicken fat. My mother's cooking had had similar ingredients, minus the heavenly taste. This way of eating may well have contributed to my father's early demise from a stroke when I was twelve.

"Ma, Miriam Kravitz is an intelligent woman. I'm sure she'll consider this with a great deal of thought." Miriam was also a determined person. Even if she felt the idea of an exhumation and autopsy of her sister was an anathema, religious or otherwise, she wouldn't let anything stand in the way of finding out how Rose died.

Besides being intimidated by Miriam, I felt a growing admiration of her. I'd spent years being a weak sister, years of dependence first on my mother for my decisions in life and then on my late therapist, Dr. Ditstein. I'd added Xanax to that state of dependency. Basically, I'd been stagnating: staying in a job with a lousy boss—my previous boss—lousy salary, lousy atmosphere. Enduring a non-existent love life, partly because I kept finding Mr. Wrong.

But my whole, horrible, scary experience finding Ditstein's dead body, a second body, being thrown in prison, and enduring three attempts on my life had made me a stronger, more independent, more decisive person. Not to mention finally—hopefully—finding Dr. Right, in the form of a handsome, sexy, loving veterinarian. If he didn't end up with Li Li, that was. How I could feel so jealous and so, okay, hot, about John at the same time, was illogical. Logic, shmogic, the guy lit up my heart, as well as other parts of my body. Then my thoughts went to parts of *his* body. *Better stop that, Marabella, and get back to the here and now.*

My mother was giving me peculiar looks. "You're not having a hot flash, are you, sweetheart? You're much too young for that. In fact, I was almost—"

I cut her off, not eager to hear her 1001 tales of menopausal misery again. "No. Let's go over what you found out in your travels."

"Just a minute," she said, digging for her bifocals in her bosom, which rested comfortably in a turquoise top I'd bought her at Macy's. On sale, of course, since she wouldn't hear of me paying full price. One of the worst insults you could hurl at another kid in my neighborhood was: "Your mother pays retail."

She settled the glasses on her nose and picked up her notepad and marker. "Jeremy Lipson." She made a face. "There's something wrong with the name Lipschitz? Sam's brother Jeremy is a doctor, a pediatrician. It's a lucrative practice and his finances appear to be in order. But you never know, do you? Remember how your Uncle Max was making so much money, we all thought his practice was doing very well? Until he got caught for Medicare fraud. Well, that was your father's side of the family, anyway. And lucky for him, he got off with only having his medical license revoked and paying the money back."

"Ma," I said.

"But—"She paused for dramatic effect."—Dr. Jeremy is supporting not one, but two mistresses!"

"Wow. That has to cost plenty."

She nodded. "He's shelling out tons for furs and jewelry, not to mention fine dining at the ritziest establishments in town."

"But how does he…"

She grinned at me. "Aha. He's been getting advances on his life insurance and is rapidly going broke."

"Does his wife, um, Tamar, know?"

"Tch, tch." She shook her head. "The wife's always the last to know. Not only that…"

"There's more? Another mistress?" I was feeling dizzy.

"There's no flies on his wife, either. She works in advertising. She patronizes the top-of-the-line for her outfits and hairdos and is also partial to only the best in furs and jewelry. Plus, their kids went to pricey colleges, which they're still paying off."

"Geez. With all that money going out, he's probably worth more dead than alive." Then I remembered. "Except that he's been raiding his life insurance."

My mother peered at her notes. "David Lipschitz, Sam's other brother, *seems* to be on the up-and-up. He's an administrator in a medium-sized software company, and it looks like his finances are more or less in order."

"What about David's wife?"

She nibbled on the marker. "Cheryl. She's been in and out of rehab for the past five years."

"For?"

"Drugs. Prescription pain killers. She got hooked after she was in a bad car accident, poor thing. And that exclusive rehab place costs a pretty penny, let me tell you."

"Nothing but the best for Cheryl. So there's money problems there, too. What else?"

She peered at her notes again. "The sister."

"Abby Goldfarb," I said.

"She's doing okay. She's an associate professor of English at NYU. But her husband—"

"Is an alcoholic," I said.

She nodded. "Right. And that's the problem."

"Well, duh."

She frowned. "No need for sarcasm, sweetheart."

"Sorry."

She waved her marker in my direction. "I'm talking about the problem with his employment."

"Which is?"

"He can't keep a job. He was a senior manager at a marketing company, making good money, till they fired him for drinking on the job. Then he headed up a social service organization, till he was fired."

"He must have been faking his resume."

"Then he worked as a sales director for a car company."

"Until he was fired," I said, thinking, *Didn't the guy ever hear of AA? Or rehab?*

My mother went back to her notes. "Evidently not," said the mind-reader. "Jennifer, the niece."

As far as I was concerned, Jennifer was better than any of them, hands down. I bit a cuticle, hoping there was nothing wrong there. "What *about* Jennifer?"

"Don't do that, sweetheart. It'll make you bleed. And bitten cuticles are not attractive."

Not to mention what gnawing on a marker did. I stopped biting. "Jennifer?"

My mother looked at her notes. "She works for a health care company and is doing quite well in her firm. Everybody likes her, and she just got a promotion."

"Good!" I said.

"But you never know, do you? She lives in a nice apartment in Park Slope." She closed her eyes. "I remember when Park Slope wasn't such a pretty place. Before we moved to Forest Hills when you were little, your father and I lived in that section of Brooklyn. It was a fourth-floor walkup and our neighbors were—"

"Ma, please."

She gave me a huffy look. "All right, all right. But what have I got these days except my memories?"

"Ma!" The mother-martyr routine was the worst.

"Anyway, Jennifer is a success at her job and has a boyfriend, Mark Hirschfield."

"What about him?" I asked.

"He's also in health care. In fact, he works in the same company. To sum up: Jennifer's and Mark's finances seem to be in order."

I breathed a sigh of relief. "Okay," I said, as Zilla came strolling in from the kitchen, jumping up to perch on the chair. After a few minutes, he turned his furry hindquarters to us and settled in for a snooze.

My mother shook her head. "Why is that cat so unfriendly?"

"Maybe he was raised in a dysfunctional litter. Actually, it's just his basic personality. Plus the fact that you've taken over his territory by displacing him on the sofa." I couldn't help thinking this might have a permanent impact on him. And not for the better. Maybe I should ask John about that. Wait a minute, what could I say: *My cat is upset because my ghost-mother is occupying the sofa? Any suggestions?* I doubted if John's veterinary expertise included how to teach your pet to get along with your ghost.

Contemplating Zilla, my mother said, "You know, we *could* share, if you think it would make a difference."

"Forget it. He'll just have to learn that he's a cat and you're a…were a…" I'd better get back to business. "Did you have time to get to the doctor's office and the pharmacy?"

She looked at her notes again. "About the doctor, Dr. Bornstein. You were absolutely right, sweetheart, about Sam's condition. He had a mild case of angina, which was being controlled with medication."

"Aha," I said.

"And Sam had just refilled his prescription."

"Then the bottle should have been almost full. But the cops only found it half full," I said slowly.

"Aha," we both said.

Chapter 22

I met Toniann at aerobics after work. I was amazed that she'd managed to find the time, with her wedding coming up so soon.

"Are you kidding? If I didn't get a break between Otis and Peter's mother…"she said, between leg lifts.

"Understood." I turned over to work my other leg and the other side of my backside. As usual, the Healthy Woman Fitness Center had the music turned up so loud, we had to shout at each other. I looked around as we stood up for our cool down. Toniann and I were the only ones over thirty, including the instructors, and probably the only ones who still had most of our hearing. The twenty-somethings considered the volume level not only normal, but constantly asked for it to be turned up.

"Do you think we'd be better off at a regular, coed gym?" I asked Toniann, as we walked to our lockers.

"Nah. We'd be smelling stinky-man sweat and listening to grunts *and* loud music."

After showers, we made for the whirlpool. Other than a very large woman who looked half-asleep, we were the only ones there. "Ahhh," I said, leaning back against the wall.

"Ditto." Toniann closed her eyes.

"You're looking a little thin. Are you eating?"

She sighed. "Too nervous. Peter's mother is driving me nuts. She doesn't like the church, she doesn't like the caterer, she doesn't like the menu, she doesn't like the invites…"

I'd never met the woman, but I knew Peter was his widowed mother's older son. Poor Toniann. Hopefully, they'd be able to move far enough away so they'd have some peace. Peter had just graduated law school and already had a few bites from law firms. "Hey, are any of Peter's possible jobs out of the city? Maybe even out of the state? Not that I wouldn't miss you lots, but…"

"I'm hoping for one in LA. Or one in Chicago. Or DC. Or even," she said, making a face, "Albany. At least, she'd have a long drive. But even though it would mean being closer to her, I'd love to be able to stay in the New York area."

As we got out of the whirlpool, I said, "I'll keep my fingers crossed for you. But now I need to talk to you about what's been going on with—"

"The murders," Toniann said.

We went to an ice cream place near the gym. We ordered an everything-sundae for her and fat-free, sugar-free vanilla frozen yogurt for me. Which I knew would have all the flavor of a kitchen sponge. Yum. I gave her a recap of recent events: Lucy's murder, Miriam Kravitz's suspicions, the dirt on Sam's relatives, his state of health, the bottle of pills. Luckily, my friend was pretty incurious, so I could finesse the circumstances as to how I found all this stuff out. Plus she already knew I was an incurable snoop.

After I told her everything, I got a lecture instead of questions about my methods.

"Marabella! Geez Louise! You're at it again, aren't you? D'you *wanna* get yourself killed? D'you have a death wish or something? Here you are, sticking your nose into a dangerous business, again. There's already three dead bodies, forgodsakes. Do you wanna be number four?" She pointed a nicely manicured finger at me.

She had a point. Did I really want to get down and dirty with a killer, again? Did I really have a death wish? I didn't think so, but—

I flashed on a teenaged me, riding no-hands on the back of a motorcycle on an icy road in New Hampshire. The bike belonged to my no-good boyfriend, whom my mother had warned me against. That made it all the more exciting to be with him and engage in all sorts of self-destructive, fun activities, such as combining alcohol and various kinds of pills, prescription and otherwise. And when we weren't on his bike, we were in his car, which we shared with the gun he kept in the back seat. Thank the gods my mother never knew half of what was going on back then. But I was a rebellious teenager in those days. I was older and wiser now. Wasn't I?

"Toniann, I understand what you're saying and I know you're looking out for me. But—"

"But nothing. At least last time, you had an excuse: the cops thought you did it. So, what's your excuse this time?"

I looked down at my plate. "I have three dead friends. That's my excuse."

She patted my hand. "I know. It's a terrible thing. But don't you think that maybe some of it could have been accidental? I mean, you *are* talking about old people and a homeless woman who lived on the streets." She looked at me hopefully.

"Not with all the circumstantial evidence. Number one, Rose heard the argument and Sam was talking about changing his will. And she saw someone run out of Sam's apartment the day he died. Number two, someone attacked Rose in the laundry room. Her sister said Rose was getting better in the hospital. Then Rose died. All of a sudden. Then Lucy saw somebody sneaking in and out of the building who looked familiar. She promised to tell me who it was when she remembered. And she's killed," I added, for good measure, "Put all that together with the fact that almost every member of the immediate family, the heirs to Sam's estate, has some kind of financial problem: mistresses, rehab, alcohol."

Toniann sighed. "You might be right. But I'm scared for you. If this killer has already killed three people, what's to stop him or her from killing a fourth person, namely you?"

Though I wasn't announcing it to her or the world, I was plenty scared for myself, too.

Chapter 23

When I got outside, I could hardly get my breath, the wind was so strong. Papers were flying all over the sidewalk and shop awnings were swinging. I tried to walk as fast as I could to the subway and still breathe.

On the ride home, I figured out my next steps. I could probably get a better sense of Sam's family by checking them out in their own milieu, where they'd be in their comfort zone and not on guard. I remembered that as I was leaving Sam's funeral, I heard one of them mention a grandchild's upcoming bar mitzvah. I'd ask my mother to check out the details. Knowing the high lifestyle of most of Sam's family, such an occasion would certainly involve a posh caterer. And a posh caterer needed lots of waitpersons, right?

Okay, I could do that. After all, I'd had experience. Once. As broke college students, my girlfriend Sarah and I signed up as extra waitpersons at a faculty dinner. I did pretty well, all things considered, meaning that I'd been generally oblivious as to which direction I was going, and only dropped a couple of plates.

I'd have to lie about my experience. And I'd have to wear a disguise, one that didn't look too fake. A wig or maybe dyed hair, maybe heels, so I'd look taller than the family remembered. Fake long fingernails, since mine were always bitten down to the cuticles, and then some.

When I walked in the door, Zilla began his ritual of circling my ankles. My mother informed me that dinner was ready. First things first, I told her, and went to the kitchen to feed Zilla, trying not to trip over my own feet or his. Then I sat down at the table for whatever my mother had cooked up tonight. I had no idea what I'd just eaten, till she informed me that it was a medley she'd created of leftovers. It didn't even have an aroma, probably because of all the medley-ing. I had to start bringing home Chinese takeout, pizza, whatever. My excuse would be that I didn't want her to exert herself. And I needed all her energy to catch this killer. I sat down at the end of the sofa and related my plans. Needless to say, she was upset. In fact, she sounded a lot like Toniann.

"Do you want to get yourself killed? Can't you leave this to the police? Not that this detective…lieutenant, person…was in a big hurry to do anything."

Yadda, yadda, yadda. I knew she meant well and was only looking out for me, but, hey, I was an adult, fairly intelligent, and fully capable of taking care of myself. Another thing: if I didn't try to figure out who did in my friends, who would? I doubted if this case was top of Rivera's list. Or if it was even *on* his list. Just because Miriam Kravitz's son-the-ADA had intimidated him into yessing Miriam, didn't mean he had any intention of following through with an investigation.

"Yes, I know, sweetheart," said my mother-the-mind-reader. "But you have a strange way of getting yourself in real trouble. I get worried about you. And—" She tossed in the mother guilt pill, "—you know my heart isn't very strong."

Oh, God. She had been very ill for a long time before she'd died of congestive heart failure. After she came back the first time, she'd seemed pretty frail, though when the occasion, such as saving my life, called for it, she was able to draw on her reserves. But I was concerned about her strength and didn't want to push it.

Not only that, I started thinking about the killer. And wondering why he or she hadn't come after *me*. Was he just practicing on the old and the helpless? Honing his skills before he came after me? Working up to dealing with me? Did this make me a sitting duck, waiting for the hunter?

Well, even though I might be panicked, I could try not to panic my mother and drive her into a health crisis.

Hoping her mind-reading abilities were taking a break, I said, "Ma, I promise you I'll be very careful. I don't want you to worry about me. It's not good for you. And *I* don't want to have to worry about me. It's not good for me, either."

Chapter 24

When I wasn't thinking about the murders, I was thinking about Li Li. That problem was keeping me up nights. When I told Toniann at lunch, she said, "She sounds like a complete phony baloney. You'll see, he'll catch on, don't worry."

"Well, I'm not about to sit around and wait for him to wake up and smell the perfume," I said.

"Oh, c'mon. Why would he want that skinny teeny bopper instead of you?" she said.

Why? I could think of at least three reasons. "Number one, she's a manipulative little witch. Number two, she's petite, slim, and graceful. Number three…or maybe should this be number one…she's a master at stroking the egos of poor, unsuspecting males. Number four—"

Toniann interrupted, "But, Marabella, remember, you said that John likes women with a little flesh on them, right?"

"But—"

"And don't you think he's got enough sense to appreciate someone with no BS, like you?"

I stirred a couple of Splendas into my tea. Splenda was my diet substitute for the five food groups I dearly loved and could have lived on happily ever after: pizza, pancakes, donuts, bagels, and chocolate. Which would have provided me with a couple hundred pounds ever after.

"Maybe. But most men can't resist that type of woman. Besides, I'm not the only one who wishes Li Li would disappear. I could name at least a half dozen women on campus who hate her guts."

"Well, then, whaddya wanna do about it?" Toniann said, between sips of coffee and bites of whatever luscious, super-high-calorie sandwich she was devouring and I was lusting after. I looked down at my hips and sighed. I still felt twinges when I remembered my unfortunate pre-teenage years. Whenever I'd walk to my seat in class, a loathsome boy named Tommy McGowan used to point to my hips and lead a chorus of his loathsome pals in: "Saddlebags, what you got in those saddlebags?"

"Marabella."

"Sorry, I zoned out," I said, picking at my Dieter's Special (Translation: a lovely cottage cheese salad.)

"Well, whaddya wanna do about the little home-wrecker?"

I drew my finger across my throat.

"Seriously, you could write her a poison pen letter. Signed in fake blood. With a skull and crossbones—"

"Don't be silly, we're not in junior high. Maybe I should try to make John jealous, what d'you think?" I bit a cuticle.

She looked skeptical. "Nah. Besides, who could you make him jealous with? That new dean you told me about, the one who looks like a bad imitation of Danny DeVito? Or the guy in administration who weighs about three hundred pounds? Didn't you say they were the only unattached, straight males under sixty there?"

I felt offended. "I'm sure I could find somebody, if I tried. After all, John isn't the only guy around." Even if he *was* the best-looking, kindest, most loving, and most marvelous in bed.

She chewed her pastry and thought for a minute. "Well, you could *really* go after her."

"Like how?" I sipped my Splenda tea.

"Spreading rumors about her, that she's making it with everybody in sight, that she's planning to blackmail the married ones. Stuff like that."

The idea of doing that made me feel sick. I would not like myself if I became the kind of person who could do that. Not to mention what John would think of me if he found out.

"Look, some of my colleagues have already done nasty stuff to Li Li." I related the ladies' room mirror writing incident.

Toniann shrugged. "Sounds like she's pissed off lots of people. So maybe you won't even have to do anything, somebody'll do it for you."

And then people might think I did it, anyway. Great. I decided to forget about Li Li right now and change the subject to the wedding. Which was in barely two weeks. "So, is everything going okay? Other than your future mother-in-law?"

She sighed. "If only she lived in someplace far away, like Alaska. But Peter is being a darling. And my family isn't driving me too nuts, for a change."

"Hey, how about we do a bachelorette party, just the two of us, at a bar?"

She giggled. "Sounds like fun. But you can't really drink, can you? Don't you throw up or something?"

"Only if I don't pass out first. Don't worry, I'll take it slow and be okay. And it'll be fun. Besides, it'll calm your pre-wedding jitters."

"Right. And help me forget about Peter's mother."

"Soon to be your beloved mother-in-law," I said, with a grin.

She swatted my arm as we got up to leave.

Chapter 25

My mother's nosing around about the Family Lipschitz had paid off. They'd be gathering for Abby and Larry Goldfarb's grandson's bar mitzvah at Sheldon's of Sleepy Hollow. Sleepy Hollow was in upstate New York, a nice train ride from the city, along the Hudson. I'd heard from somebody at the office that Sheldon's was the premier location in that area for a Jewish child to be displayed to his relatives. The caterer was also a favorite for local Jewish extravaganzas: Sidiris, in Tarrytown—named for Sidney and Iris Finkelstein. But rumor had it they were the Leona Helmsleys of Jewish caterers: so mean to the help, they couldn't keep their wait staff from one event to the next. Perfect for this eager, klutzy wannabe.

At Grand Central, I took the Metro North train up to Tarrytown for my wait person interview. Thankfully, I got the job just in time for the Goldfarb bar mitzvah. The woman I met with was the Sidiris wait staff recruiter, poor thing. Her hair badly needed styling, and her face needed propping up. She looked as if all the life had been drained out of her. And she was probably not much older than me.

She gave me printed instructions, directions to Sheldon's, and, after asking my dress size, a navy blue uniform. Smiling wanly at me, she said, "I'm sure you'll do just fine. And there'll be lots more events coming up. Wedding season is starting, you know. So there's a lot to look forward to."

"Sounds great!" I grabbed the papers and uniform and left. If I ever decided to branch out into my own PR business, a company like Sidiris could sure use my services. Hard to believe that such smart businesspeople didn't know how to keep their help. Oh, well, not my problem.

Back in the city, my next stop was for a wig and false fingernails. Plus shoes with a little lift. They wouldn't be ideal for being on my feet all night. My feet would just have to grin and bear it till I got them into a good soak at home.

The beauty supply shop was a Barbie-look-alike dream come true. A person could instantly change into any one of hundreds of other people at the drop of a wig I decided to become a platinum blonde, about the farthest thing from my natural hair, which was chestnut brown.

Besides, I'd always wanted to be a blonde and so did most of my childhood girlfriends. Except the few lucky ones who were born that way, and with golden ringlets, yet. I used to stare at them in class and at recess, hoping that if I was very good, somehow my hair would be transformed into golden ringlets. So much for trying to be good.

The other reason I wanted a platinum wig because of its star quality: Lady Gaga, Madonna, Dolly Parton, and, let's not forget Marilyn Monroe. I also thought it would go along with my new persona as a wait person: glamorous but humble. Neither of which came naturally to me and would serve me well as part of the disguise.

I tried on half a dozen platinum wigs, gazing into one of the mirrors. I coveted them all and finally settled on the most outrageous, most Gaga-like. For my new false fingernails, I picked out platinum with silver sparkles. Might as well go with hair and nail coordination.

My next stop was a nail salon. Trying not to choke from the chemical smells, I asked the manicurist to glue the things on, enduring her disdainful looks at my bitten-down nails and ragged cuticles. I figured if I tried doing it myself, I'd probably end up gluing them all together. Like the pants' legs I sewed together in seventh grade sewing class.

In a discount shoe store, I found the perfect height-enhancers: soft-soled canvas with a wedge heel. These would not only give me an inch or so, but would be relatively kind to my feet, I hoped.

I couldn't wait to get home and parade my new self to my mother and Zilla, the only ones I could trust with the preparations for my scheme. I opened the door of my apartment quietly, hoping they were both asleep, which they were, so I could surprise them. I ducked into the bedroom and dressed myself in the uniform, which was a bit too tight in the bust. All to the good, I thought, since it should at least keep the men's eyes focused on my chest instead of my face. I pinned up my hair and arranged the wig over it, slipped on the shoes and marched into the living room for inspection.

"Ahem," I said to the sleeping beauties.

Zilla jumped off the chair, wound himself around my elevated feet, and emitted loud "Mmrowws," which meant, "Dinner, now."

My mother also had her mouth open and was staring at me in what seemed to be shock. "I never thought you'd look good as a blonde."

I grinned and struck a pose. "Glad you like it."

"And I was right, you don't." Then she looked down at my fingers in horror. "What are those things, tattoos? They're impossible to get off. And you can't be buried in a Jewish cemetery with those things. I heard a story once, from my neighbor, that her husband, who got them in the navy, couldn't be buried in the family plot. So she had to follow him to some strange burial ground where they didn't know a soul."

I tried not to laugh, since I didn't want to hurt her feelings. "First of all, Ma, those 'things' aren't tattoos, they're fake fingernails. They're just glued on. And they do come off, trust me. Second, it's not true about tattoos being forbidden in a Jewish cemetery. Anyway, I have to feed the feline now. We'll go over our strategy later, okay?" I made my way into the kitchen.

The Goldfarb bar mitzvah's catered affair was scheduled for the next day, Saturday, following the service at the local synagogue. After my mother and I got to Sheldon's, we'd scope out Sam's family. While I tried to concentrate on not breaking too much china or spilling too much soup.

"See if you can get a sense of anything that doesn't smell right. Especially after they've had a few drinks. Hopefully, you'll see or hear something that can help us."

"Roger."

My mother was back to her wannabe-trucker self.

Chapter 26

Sheldon's of Sleepy Hollow was done up in two themes that could destroy the sensibilities of anyone with any taste: glitzy and Headless Horseman. Personally, I preferred the headless one. As a stand-alone, the pumpkin-head images, black horses, and poor Ichabod weren't too awful. But as a companion to the overdone, phony elegance, the whole thing was not a pretty sight.

At least a dozen gaudy chandeliers lit up the banquet room. The chairs were a sickly shade of purple—muted grape, someone commented with actual admiration—with wall-to-wall carpeting in the same color, with the added attraction of huge embellishments of woven grapes. On the hors d'oeuvres table, a large horse carved from ice stood in its AstroTurf corral. I wondered what would happen when it melted. Would it drip down onto the table and soak the grape-embellished muted grape carpet? Chopped liver pumpkins decorated the other tables. At least, they didn't color the liver orange. But I bet they tried. Aarrggh. Just thinking about that possibility made my stomach roil.

My mother looked around the room. "Very elegant affair. I haven't been to a bar mitzvah since…it was

Cousin Irwin's son, Jason, out on Long Island, do you remember? They had it at a hotel, and the waiters were terrible, and so was the food. And worst of all…"

I frowned at her, hoping that would do it. I couldn't tell her to be quiet when all these people were wandering around. Though nobody could hear her, it was distracting, and they could notice that. But they were all too busy talking, probably about people who weren't there.

I hurried into the kitchen, which was enormous. As was the chef. Everyone had to inch by her white-jacketed bulk to get at the serving dishes. But I had to admit that the food smelled wonderful. I inhaled the woodsy aroma of oven-roasted rosemary chicken, the bittersweet smell of caramelized vegetables, the syrupy odor of maple glazed sweet potatoes. A major treat for a nose like mine. Hopefully, the help got to eat leftovers after the party. Hopefully, not from the guests' plates.

I grabbed bowls of salads, stashed them on a tray, and headed out to the banquet room, willing myself not to drop anything. It worked, until I caught sight of a couple of hors d'oeuvres floating off the large side table against a wall. I barely managed to save my load of china by doing a quick balancing act. Luckily, the crowd was so busy shoving each other to get to the table that a few dainties disappearing into thin air didn't even register. I tried to signal my mother surreptitiously, but it didn't work. Oh, well, I guess she was hungry. Or just wanted to remember the taste.

A voice in my ear said, "Right, sweetheart. Now I just need something to wash it down."

"But…" What was the use? I prayed that she'd try to use a little discretion, even though I knew the concept didn't exist in her universe. I trudged into the kitchen for my next load, bowls of soup, and carefully made my way back out to the tables. I seemed to have gotten the hang of it and everything went smoothly after that. Until the guests, having had several drinks already, became surly.

That made the head wait person, a skinny redheaded woman, whip us into a frenzy, yelling, "Let's get moving, people! They're hungry out there!"

We became whirling dervishes, racing in and out of the kitchen, grabbing plates and cups. I charged into the banquet room with my tray and headed for my assigned tables. Lucky for me, one of them, the second-best table, was occupied by Lipschitzes, dressed to the nines: Jeremy and Tamar and their offspring; David and Cheryl; Jennifer and a young man who, I assumed, was her boyfriend. Tamar and Cheryl were jeweled up to their eyebrows, with necklines that plunged as far as was barely decent, on either real designer outfits or really great knock-offs.

But their couture and jewels didn't come close to matching the bar mitzvah grandmas at the head table. Abby was queen of the overdressed—sequins glittering on her barely covered plump bosom, and enough jewelry, if it was real, to feed a third-world country for a year. Another woman, who must have been the bar mitzvah boy's other grandma, about Abby's age and with as much bad taste in jewelry, was yakking away in a voice you could hear in Brooklyn.

As I reached the second-best tableful of Lipschitzes, I tripped over an ice cube that had dropped from somebody's drink and ended up on the floor on my behind. I could hear loud snorts of laughter from the Lipschitzes. That wasn't the worst of it. Most of the plates were broken, lying in pieces on the muted grape carpet. I could feel my wig twisted half off my head. I must look like a fright, I thought. I was thankful that I hadn't stabbed myself with shards of china and other than my dignity, and the plates, everything seemed okay.

Except for my mother. She rushed over to me, whispering in my ear, "Are you all right? Here, let me fix your hair."

"Stop. You can't do that. Don't worry about it," I whispered behind my hand, hoping they all weren't still watching me on the floor.

She backed off, looking hurt. I'd deal with that later. I picked myself off the floor, adjusted the wig as best I could without a mirror, and went into the kitchen, looking for something to sweep up the pieces of china. Needless to say, the head wait person was not happy. I knew she'd fire me right then and there if she weren't so short of help. Instead, she just gave me the evil eye. "Sorry," I mumbled, "tripped on an ice cube—"

She barked, "Go clean up the mess and get back out there with more plates. And better not break any more, or I'll dock your pay."

My mother tch tch-ed and whispered, "No wonder they can't keep their help."

I was feeling sorry for the rest of the wait staff, since they had to deal with these conditions on an ongoing basis, that was if any of them ever came back, and scurried out to clean up. Thankfully, I had no more mishaps during the rest of the evening, before I collected my pay and returned the uniform. We all got to take doggie bags home of the worst parts of the roast chicken and already-dried-out stuffing, along with broken bits of pastry. Whoopie. At any rate, it would be a lot better than whatever would be waiting for me at home.

"That's not being nice, complaining about your mother's cooking," said my mother, on the way home. "After I've been slaving away in that tiny, so-called kitchen of yours."

"Sorry," I mumbled, dying to get the wig, now unbearably hot and itching like mad, off my head. But trying to unpin a wig on a moving train wasn't easy to do without sticking myself in the eye with a bobby pin.

Dealing with the wig made me think of a horrible possibility. When it slipped partway off in my fall, one of the Lipschitzes could have recognized me. And figured out that I must have been spying on him or her.

"Let me help you, sweetheart." My mother was poised to start unpinning.

I grabbed her arm before my fellow travelers who weren't sleeping or drunk would notice the wig lifting itself off my head. After some peculiar stares, possibly due to my clutching an invisible arm, I quickly pretended to be doing arm exercises. That resulted in even more stares. At least I didn't have to worry about anybody on the train bothering me, since they must have thought I was a nutcase. My problem now was trying to keep the seat next to me empty, so that no one would sit down on my mother. And to try not to think about what could happen if the killer thought I was after him or her.

Chapter 27

When I checked Zilla's food dish, it was still full. I'd forgotten he didn't like liver. I washed out his bowl, unearthed a can of Fancy Feast Whitefish and Cheese in Gravy and spooned in half of it. "Finicky, finicky," I muttered.

I made my mother and me tea and we settled on the sofa. "Okay, give."

She took a sip. "Ahh, just the way I like it, not too strong. Thank you, sweetheart." Reaching into her bosom, she drew out the pad and marker. She was decked out in the blue-green top and matching pants I'd bought her. She reached in again and dug out her bifocals. "Now, let me see…mmhm, mmhm. Okay, here we go."

I sipped and waited. My mother always had a flair for the dramatic, so I tried to be patient. But it wasn't easy. "All right, already. What did you see or hear?"

"Don't rush me. I'm an old woman. And patience, my dear, works a lot better than rushing around like a chicken without a head."

Grrrr. "Sorry."

She read from her notes. "One of the brothers, David, was huddling with the other one, Jeremy, about the terrible state of his finances. He, David, was begging his brother for a loan. Jeremy threw up his hands and said he was done lending his brother money that he'd never get back. And that it was only going to be thrown away on David's wife, Cheryl's, rehab stints. And that Jeremy needed his money for his own family's expenses. Then Abby said her husband, Larry, the one who drinks, lost his most recent job. She was nagging him about how they were going to help pay for their grandson's bar mitzvah. Right in front of the boy, too. Can you imagine? Anyway, the husband said he'd take out a big life insurance policy on Abby and bump her off to pay the bills." She shuddered. "What kind of people?"

"I'm sure he was trying to make a joke, or just get her to shut up. Anything else?" I was trying to digest what my mother had said.

"Yup. Tamar, Jeremy's wife, was complaining to David's wife, Cheryl, that she hadn't had a new fur coat in a couple of years."

"Poor thing," I murmured.

"And every time she asked Jeremy, he said there were money problems. She couldn't imagine what he was doing with all their money. Why is the wife always the last to know, I'll never understand. She'd have to be blind, deaf, and dumb."

"Ma."

"Okay. The other wife, Cheryl, looked very out of it. I heard Jeremy say to Tamar later that he wouldn't be surprised if Cheryl had to go back to rehab. And that the rehab place was eating up David's money."

I thought about all this. "Sounds like they're all getting pretty desperate for cash." I yawned. "Guess I'm more tired than I thought. Going to bed, now. Goodnight, Ma." I kissed her forehead; tucked one of her ugly, handmade afghans around her; and went to my bedroom.

I clicked onto the internet to do a quick check of my messages, hoping for a nice little email from John. What I saw instead was: "This is a warning! Mind your own business if you know what's good for you!"

This made me furious. How dare someone, who'd already killed three of the kindest, most decent people I knew, threaten me! Before I could think straight, I emailed back: "Who do you think you are? You can't scare me! You murdered my friends, and you won't get away with this!"

I printed out the threatening email and my response, figuring I'd better show them to Rivera, though I wasn't hopeful about how he'd react. Then I turned off my computer and picked up my knitting, to calm myself down. Zilla wandered into the room, jumped onto the bed, and started undoing my stitches. He was enjoying himself so much, I didn't have the heart to get mad at him. So I handed him the yarn and got ready for bed.

I couldn't sleep. I lay awake, thinking about the message I'd just sent. Brave, maybe. But maybe resulting in harm to my well-being.

I'd worry about that later. Right now, I'd think about being a strong, fierce woman warrior. I fell asleep dreaming that I was Boudica, the warrior queen, on a magnificent horse, armed to the teeth, leading an army of ancient Britons against mighty Rome…

Chapter 28

My idea woke me bolt upright the next morning. I was ready to rock and roll.

Attention, you coward who emailed me that threat: I am a Vinegar woman, and Vinegar women don't quit. Even when things get scary.

Time for me and my-mother-the-ghost-Vinegar-woman to go into action. And I had just the plan. I'd meet with each sibling and spouse and tell them there was additional money from bearer bonds Sam collected that weren't accounted for in the will. That Sam had once mentioned years ago he'd made these investments. And must have forgotten about them.

And when Sam's lawyer cashed out the bonds, it amounted to another million dollars. As executor of the will, I was to decide how to disburse the money. I could decide that the money should go to a charity. Or several charities. Or set up a scholarship or foundation in Sam's name. Or divide the money among the relatives.

It was all a humongous lie. There wasn't any more money, or any unaccounted-for bearer bonds, or anything. This was really going to test my ability to lie. I'd have to do a lot of practicing. Maybe it would help to keep reminding myself that I was lying for a good cause. Even better, I could think of it as acting.

This brought back memories of my acting debut in eighth grade. I played the part of Gertie Goodnick in the end-of-year play, *Small Town, USA.* Gertie was the town gossip, constantly making up and spreading rumors on the phone. Actually, I was pretty good, if I did say so myself. The only downside was being called "Dirty Gertie," by one of the boys in the cast for months afterward.

By conjuring up my thespian abilities, I could make Sam's relatives nervous about how to give the money away, asking each one which charity would be best to give to in Sam's name: a hospital, a college, a research foundation. Telling them that I was in charge of this extra money, that I was the only one who could decide what to do with it, decide what or who would most benefit. I was banking on the pure, unadulterated greed of most of the family members.

This, hopefully, could smoke out the killer. And incidentally, set me up as the next dead body.

Wasn't there any other way? Unfortunately for my well-being, I didn't think so. I'd just have to be super careful. And practice the whole story with my mother. Though she'd have a fit about my putting myself in danger again. But, I could argue, with my-mother-the-ghost-detective to protect me, what did I have to be afraid of?

I paid a visit to Rivera after work. I thought he'd have apoplexy after I showed him the email and my reply.

"You did *what*? Are you really that dumb or just really nuts? You're just begging for trouble, aren't you? We have more important things to do than keep getting you out of trouble, Ms. Vinegar." His face was bright red.

I looked down at my lap. "I guess I just didn't think this through."

"Understatement of the year." He opened his desk drawer, pulled out a bottle of something…probably aspirin, maybe something even stronger?…and swallowed a couple with gulps of a decaf soda.

I hoped I wasn't giving him a heart attack.

"You're going to drive me to an early grave. And right now, you're giving me a gigantic headache."

"Sorry," I said.

He picked up his pen and notepad and sighed. "Okay. From the top. Why do you suppose someone would want to do this to you?"

I bit a cuticle, reluctant to confess my sleuthing, "Well, I've been, um, trying to find out who killed Sam and Rose and Lucy."

This got him boiling mad again. "Didn't I tell you that we would take care of any investigation? That you should keep your nose out of it?"

I was just as mad as he was. "First, I'd like to know how your investigation has been going. I bet you haven't even started yet, right?"

"It's none of your business. It's a police matter, as you very well know. Now, let's hear it. What kind of trouble did you stir up this time?"

I took a couple of slow, deep breaths, the way my therapist had taught her patients. "I got a job as a wait person at the Goldfarbs' grandson's bar mitzvah, that's Sam Lipschitz's grand-nephew."

"What does this have to do with anything?"

I took another breath. "If you let me explain." A glare from the lieutenant. "I wanted to check out Sam's family, who, you may or may not know, benefit from Sam's will, to see—"

"And just what did you expect to find? Some clues in the hors d'oeuvres, maybe? A hot tip under the table?" He snickered.

"No need to be sarcastic, Lieutenant," I said.

"Well?"

"They're all very hard up for money. One half-brother is supporting his family and two mistresses."

Rivera raised his eyebrows. "That doesn't make him a murderer, just a philanderer. Just wait a minute, exactly how did you find all this out?"

Think fast, Marabella. "Um. I followed him."

"Are you aware that stalking is a criminal offense? I should cite you for that. And for breaking and entering your neighbor's apartment." He smirked.

"I didn't break and enter. The door was unlocked," I reminded him.

"Go on."

"Another relative, a brother-in-law, is definitely an alcoholic, who can't keep a job."

"Did you stalk him, too?"

"No. I heard his drunken voice on the phone when I called to tell his wife that Sam was dead. Also, he never stopped drinking at the bar mitzvah, from the beginning to dessert."

"Anything else?"

I figured I'd better not mention the dope, you should excuse the expression, on Cheryl and her prescription drug addiction. "I heard the bar mitzvah boy's grandparents arguing with each other about how they were going to help pay for the cost of the dinner, the band, all of it. That's the couple with the alcoholic husband," I said, helpfully.

He'd been scribbling notes. "I got that. Okay, is that it? Besides mixing yourself up in police business, you've been playing a very dangerous game. For instance, did it ever occur to you that maybe the guy you followed to his girlfriends' places saw you?" He glared again.

I had the grace to look embarrassed. "Guess I didn't think about that," I mumbled.

"No kidding. You just run with that nose of yours first, don't you?" He tapped his pen on his desk.

I looked down at my lap. "Um, there's one more thing. My wig almost fell off when I tripped on an ice cube."

Rivera blew out his breath. "Your *what*?"

Better get it over with in a hurry, I thought. "I wore a wig and false nails for a disguise."

Rivera held his head in his hands. "I don't believe all this. I don't *want* to believe it."

I barreled on. "I slipped on an ice cube and my wig started to fall off. I was on the floor next to the Lipschitzes' table and maybe somebody recognized me and got nervous."

He groaned and stood up, ushering me out of his office. "We'll look into this. I don't suppose it would do any good to warn you about dealing with dangerous people, would it?"

Actually, I was a little frazzled about the whole thing. "I'll try to be careful," I said. No point telling him about my plan to use myself as bait to smoke out the murderer. Sometimes, I was even more afraid of Rivera than the killer. Rivera would look for any excuse to lock me up, so I wouldn't cause him any more problems.

Now it was time to go home and do some strategizing with my mother. Another person I was afraid of. I was not looking forward to her reaction when I told her about my—our—plans. But once she saw how determined I was, and that there really wasn't any other way, how could she refuse?

Chapter 29

My mother and Zilla were actually sharing the sofa. Well, not exactly sharing. My mother was curled up at one end, wearing her new maroon tee and navy sweatpants. Zilla was at the other end. An uneasy truce if I ever saw one.

"Ha! Are you Hatfields and McCoys getting along?"

Zilla's response was to bound off the sofa and wind himself around my ankles, emitting vociferous "I'm hungry" sounds.

My mother's was a "Hmmff."

"Well, at least you're both…"*Alive* had almost left my mouth."…um, well and not injured."

My mother gave Zilla a forbidding gaze. "He wouldn't dare."

She didn't realize that when he was fixated on his dinner, nothing anyone said or did mattered. After I fed him and we humans fed on spaghetti with ketchup sauce, I sat down on the sofa next to my mother. "I have a plan," I said.

"Not if it puts you in any more danger, you don't," she retorted.

I hoped my powers of persuasion were up to the task. "Ma, I'm already in danger." I told her about the threatening email.

She fell back against the sofa pillows, clutching her chest.

Oh, God. "Can you breathe? Are you in pain? What should I do?"

"I'm all right, sweetheart. But I'm very frightened. What should you do? What you should do, my darling daughter, is to stop with the plans, stop playing detective. That would make me breathe a whole lot easier, I'm sure."

Great. Pile on the guilt, why don't you? Not that everything wasn't hard enough these days, I had to deal with my mother's fears. I had enough of my own, thank you. Even though most of the time I sailed on, acting as if nothing got to me. That was the way I protected myself from crashing, losing control. The thing I feared most. At college parties, that made my reputation as the pot smoker who never got high. Nobody knew it was because I only pretended to inhale. I was afraid if I did, God knew what could happen, what I'd do. But wasn't pot kind of like hypnosis? That you wouldn't do anything under the influence that you wouldn't do anyway?

"Sorry if I made you worry about me, but I'm worried about *you*."

"I know," I said, feeling even more guilty, if possible.

"All right. What's your plan? I know you'll do it, even if I think it's a terrible idea. And I'll end up helping you anyway." She sighed loudly. "Do I have a choice?"

The mother-martyr again. Aarrggh.

She wagged her finger at me. "That's not a nice way to think about your mother."

I really hated her mind-reading ability, which had definitely gotten sharper since she—

"Sorry. But you realize that I don't really have a choice, since whoever has been killing off my friends already threatened me."

She sat up and folded her arms across her chest. "You shouldn't have answered that email. That's just asking for trouble."

"Well, I brought them both to Rivera."

"A lot of good that will do, I'm sure," she said.

Zilla strolled into the room and jumped up on the chair. Ignoring us, he went to work on his after-dinner toilette.

My mother said, in a stage whisper, "Do you think he knows I don't like cats? Do you remember the terrible cat Aunt Evelyn had? Not only did he scratch everybody who came into the house, she swore he jumped into Howard's crib and tried to snuff the life out of him—"

"Ma, cats don't do that. They don't smother babies. That's an old wives' tale."

She sniffed, obviously not believing me. "Hmmff. Though, considering what Howard became later on, maybe it wouldn't have been such a bad thing."

She had a point. My cousin Howard was, as far as I knew, the only genuine sociopath in our family. He started his career at the age of eight, trying to set neighborhood dogs on fire (too traumatized from his early experience to pick on cats?) progressing to burning down garages, and graduating to setting an office building ablaze. When he was cut loose after serving years in an institution for the criminally insane, he was back to torturing animals. He met his end in a fire he set at a zoo.

"Tch, tch. Such a terrible thing for our family's reputation," my mother said.

I told her my plan. She leaned back against the pillows and closed her eyes. Was she sleeping? Was she all right?

"Ma, are you—"

"Shh, I'm thinking."

That's good, I thought. At least she didn't outright condemn it.

She opened her eyes, ready for business. "Here's what we know: they're greedy and they have money problems of one kind or another."

"Right."

"So we, you, I mean, make an appointment with each one, to discuss what to do about this so-called extra money."

"Right."

She fixed me with a look. "And you'll meet each one in a very public place, preferably in broad daylight. Or else I'm not in."

"Why?"

"Because I'm your mother and I said so."

"Hmm. I guess that lets out caves or dungeons."

She shook her head. "Where did that smart mouth of yours come from?"

"Sorry, I was just trying to lighten the atmosphere." I stood up and went to the bedroom for my cell, for the family's names and phone numbers.

"Another thing, set the meetings at a place convenient for you. That puts you in a better position to deal with them," she called.

"Brilliant, but how can I do that if I don't know what's in their area?" I yelled from the bedroom.

Silence. Then, "Sweetheart, there's always a local diner or a park, isn't there? Just Google it."

Before she became really ill, my mother had taken an internet course for seniors and loved it. "Thank you, Miss

Marple," I said, walking back into the living room.

She tried to look modest, and failed.

I decided to call Abby Goldfarb first, figuring she'd be easier to deal with than the men. I didn't think she was the overly suspicious type, seeming to be more concerned with her appearance than whatever was going on around her. I remembered that at her grandson's bar mitzvah party, she was practically hysterical about losing one of her (real or fake) jeweled bracelets, making people look under their seats and causing a minor commotion, interrupting the boy's thank-yous, until someone located it.

When I got the doting grandma on the phone, I went into my role as a benign, altruistic dispenser of largesse. "Of course, being the charitable person I know you are…"

She made appropriate noises into the phone.

"I know you'll want to have a voice in the decision as to what to do with *all this money*."

Was that the sound of heavy breathing? "Oh, yes, of course."

We arranged to meet at a tea shop near the Tarrytown train station next Saturday around noon and said goodbye.

"Broad daylight is good." My mother yawned and stretched out on the sofa.

As soon as I heard her snores, I grabbed my jacket and pocketbook and quietly left the apartment. I headed over to the nearby soup kitchen, to see if I could find out anything about Lucy. Did she have a family? Had she left them because of some terrible thing in her past? Were they nice people? Was she just a helpless, lonely old woman, who ended up on the streets because of poverty or disability?

I walked the few blocks to the kitchen and went inside. Volunteers were dishing out soup, preparing sandwiches and making coffee. Whatever the soup was, it smelled a lot better than my mother's cooking, and probably tasted better, too. Looking around the room, I caught sight of a large, white-aproned woman who appeared to be in charge, and went over to her.

She turned and gave me a broad smile. "Hi, hon, I'm Mary. You can just sit right down here." She led me over to a chair at a long table.

"Um, thanks, but…"

"Don't be shy, hon, you're looking pretty hungry." She attempted to deposit me into the chair, still beaming at me.

She had a point, what with a steady diet of my mother's cooking. Trying to stay upright, I said, "I'm here about Lucy. I need to know if she had any family."

Mary stopped smiling, took out a tissue from her apron pocket, and blew her nose loudly.

I patted her dimpled arm. "She was such a good person. I've known her for years. I used to see her down the street, outside my building."

Sniffling, Mary said, "Lucy was a treasure. When she came here, she'd try to make the other clients feel as if they were dining at an elegant restaurant. And that they weren't taking charity, they had a benefactor happy to provide for them. So for a little while, they felt like they had some of their dignity back." She broke into a teary smile.

I choked up. Lucy was an even better person than I'd thought. "I didn't know that about her. Actually, I really didn't know anything about her. Do you know if she had any family?"

She shook her head. "I never knew. She never talked about her past life."

This made me even sadder. The idea that Lucy was going to be buried in an unmarked grave after her body was released from the morgue, with nobody to mourn her, was awful. But wait, Mary and some of the people here who knew her, could be there, right? And so could I.

"Look, I'll let you know when her…um…body, is released for burial. Then those of us who cared about her can be there."

Mary's broad smile was back. "To show her how much we cared, the way she showed our people here. Thank you, Miss…"

"Marabella. I'll be in touch."

Chapter 30

All hell broke out on campus the next morning.

Someone, maybe more than one someone, had trashed Li Li's office, pulling things out of her desk drawers, tossing papers all over the place, emptying her wastebasket onto the floor. The dean of the science department called everyone into his office, one person at a time, to meet with him and a couple of campus security officers. Asking what did we know and when did we know it. I was dreading the questions. I was a lousy liar. My face usually gave me away, which was why nobody ever wanted me as a card partner. Or wanted my real opinion as to whether what they were wearing looked good on them, or if I thought they'd gained weight, or if they were looking older. Though maybe I was getting better these days. I'd managed to fake my way through the Goldfarbs' bar mitzvah party and was hoping to do the same with Sam's relatives.

I didn't want to make enemies by being a ratfink snitch. I especially didn't want to make an enemy of Carmen. I was a little scared of her reaction if I didn't produce the PC answers to the questions.

I hadn't realized so many women at the college had reasons to dislike, if not really hate, Li Li. During huddled discussions before the interrogations, I found out that, besides Margaret Wilson, at least half the staff on our floor had confronted Li Li and/or their boyfriends, fiancés, or significant others about tete-a-tetes: coffee dates in the cafeteria, laughing conversations in the halls, little "favors" she'd begged from the "big, strong, wise men," such as problems starting her car, worrying about walking to the parking garage alone after dark.

Even Susan, my normally down-to-earth, common-sensical boss, had had an unpleasant encounter with Li Li that I didn't know about.

Susan's good-looking, sexy boyfriend, Theo, was supposed to pick Susan up from work one afternoon for dinner out. Well, instead of five o'clock, Theo didn't show up till almost six. Susan must have had smoke coming out of her ears. Li Li, spotting a new "big, strong, wise man," had waylaid him on his way to our office. She claimed she had a printer malfunction and prevailed upon him ("pretty please") to help out a poor little female. Li Li had provided a reason for Susan and Theo to temporarily break up again. Since they both were pretty stubborn, it happened a couple times a year.

So of course Susan had a sour taste in her mouth about Li Li. Not that she would ever say or do anything. That wasn't her style. Theo got the worst of it. It took two weeks of huge bouquets of flowers, notes of apology, and begging, before they were back together that time.

Word must have gotten around about the Susan, Theo, and Li Li incident. No such thing as secrets on Chelsea College's campus. Word had also gotten around about other women who had a hate-on for Li Li, present company included.

All this news had reached the ears of the more-than-eager Professor Newsome in the English Department. We found out that she was the one who'd relayed it to the dean. Newsome had been after Susan's job ever since Susan came on board. Anything bad she could attach to Susan or her department was pure gravy to Nasty Nuisance. The result was that the dean was taking a special interest (Were we persons of interest?) in Susan, me, and a bunch of others—namely Carmen and friends. John had already been questioned, as to whether he knew if anyone had been threatening Li Li. Luckily, he hadn't taken my rants about her seriously, so I was off the hook, at least with him, so far.

When it came my turn for the inquisition, which probably wasn't a fair thing to say, since the dean was usually a reasonable man, I'd already done some deep breathing (*thank you, Dr. Ditstein*) to calm myself down, as much as I could. I sat down across from the dean and the security guys, smoothed my skirt, and waited.

He was silent for a few moments, maybe trying to unnerve me, get me to confess? It was definitely working, except that I had nothing to confess about the trashing of Li Li's office. But maybe I was being a bit paranoid. Anyway, the wait gave me time for a few more deep breaths.

"Ms. Vinegar, do you know anything about anyone threatening Dr. Chang?

Oh, God. "Um, no, nothing." I hoped my face wasn't on fire. For some crazy reason, that made me think of: "Liar, liar, pants on fire." I had to get a lot better at lying before I dealt with Sam's relatives, that was for sure.

He gave me a penetrating look. "Have you seen or heard anything that could provide us with any information?"

Deep breaths, Marabella. "No, nothing."

He sighed. "All right, Ms. Vinegar. You may leave. But if you recollect anything, anything at all, that has to do with this incident, you have a moral, not to mention legal, obligation to report it."

"Legal?" I asked, before I could stop the word escaping from my mouth. *Marabella, someday your curiosity is going to kill you.* This thought did not do anything to calm my nerves.

He stared at me. "This incident is considered workplace harassment. And whoever is responsible will be charged. So, it behooves—" *Behooves?*"—anyone with any knowledge of this to disclose the information. Otherwise, the person who holds back information could be considered a party to all this."

I could smell the fear dripping down the inside of my blouse. Getting up, I said goodbye and found my way out. I was sure he could see right through me. Through my lies. I resisted the temptation to look down and see if my pants were on fire, underpants actually, since I was wearing my usual skirt, blouse, and blazer ensemble.

Marabella, what have you gotten yourself into this time? Maybe I should have been more assertive with Carmen and company, scrubbed the mirror, and gotten them to lay off. Ha! Something told me they wouldn't have taken kindly to my efforts. And that I probably would've ended up with a few choice bruises and a warning. *A warning.* Thinking of the dean's warning made me shiver.

Maybe I'd better tell Carmen what the dean said, whether or not she wanted to hear it. After all, I didn't know who'd trashed Li Li's office, even though Carmen and her buds came to mind. But supposing somebody else had done it? There was plenty of hatred of Li Li to go around. I hoped that nothing else, something even worse, would happen. Even though I hated Li Li for all her manipulations too, deep down, I didn't want to see her get hurt. Or worse. Who knew what damage an angry girl-friend or fiancée could inflict?

Then I flashed on what could happen if John thought that I did it. Just when things seemed to be going along swimmingly…well, except for Li Li and the fact that my apartment was now off-limits to romance—okay, sex. And having to hide my sleuthing efforts from him. I preferred not to think about his reaction to my interviewing murder suspects, using myself as bait. It was hard not to share things with him, but some things, like murder, were better not shared. And I planned on trying not to think about anything involving death, Sam's horrible relatives, or threatening emails during our next weekend together.

Yippee! This would be our first weekend together in a while. That was the good news. The bad news had to do with other members of John's and my families. The four-legged ones.

In order to spend a weekend away, I'd be forced to tote along my curmudgeonly cat. Either that or risk John's horror at leaving my pet alone for two days. I couldn't very well tell him that my mother would take care of Zilla, could I? Or, for that matter, even ask my mother to fill in. Or leave them alone together for that long, though they seemed to have worked out an armed truce. Too bad I'd gotten off Xanax. I could have used it on one, or both, of them.

Besides dealing with Zilla, there were Harpo, Chico, and Groucho, the St. Bernard littermates at John's house. Even though I was now relaxed enough around them to be only mildly intimidated, there was Harpo's infatuation with me to cope with. Being showered with affectionate drools and growls if John tried to make a move on me wasn't my idea of a good time. For some ungodly reason, John thought it was hilarious. For any privacy, John had to lock Harpo and company out of the bedroom, while they serenaded us with howls and scrabbles at the door.

I reminded myself to pick up a cat carrier and cat treats at Pet Smart on the way home. I shuddered to think about trying to coax Zilla into it. Since I'd brought him home as a tiny, adorable sprite—a perfect example of unforeseen circumstances—he'd never been out of my apartment. Let alone shut up like luggage, and in a terrible snit. My mind conjured up an image of a raging, pacing tiger in a cage.

Chapter 31

At the fancy tea shop bar near the Tarrytown Train Station, I ordered an overpriced cup of tea from the spike-haired wait person, declining her offer of a ninety-nine-cent piece of pastry that smelled like a sugar cookie and made my mouth water. When my stomach tried to say yes, my hips said no. I was cursed with the short, wide-hipped woman's dilemma. Wide hips and large breasts ran in my family the way long legs and flat chests ran in Toniann's.

Though my bosom had never reached the…heights? The mass?…of my mother's. This had caused her to constantly complain about wearing my clothes, until I'd finally bought her new clothes. She could've wafted in and out of Macy's with her own selections, but I didn't want to encourage her in this. Bad enough that I'd see something on the table, like ketchup for her spaghetti sauce, that I could swear I never bought. Hopefully, whatever items she pilfered were small enough not to cause a problem. Maybe she went on shoplifting forays after hours. I didn't want to know.

After being only a half hour late, Abby Goldfarb breezed in. Loaded with jewelry and makeup, a fur—though it was almost seventy degrees outside—and, would you believe, a hefty amount of cleavage showing at noon? She was a grandmother, for God's sakes. But, hey, everyone to her own taste—lessness, right? She'd put on a few pounds since the bar mitzvah, too, which added to the effect. Evidently the results from the fat farm hadn't lasted long. She was on the pudgy side and being short didn't help. Her hair was a brassy blonde, resembling no natural color on this earth. She was wearing colored contact lenses, bright blue, that looked as if they belonged on a mannequin. But I couldn't help noticing the dark, puffy bags under her eyes. Couldn't be easy, living with an alcoholic loser.

I gave her what I hoped was a welcoming smile and waited for her apology for being so late. None came. After helloing me and tossing her dead animal on a chair, she excused herself to get her tea and the ninety-nine-cent pastry. The only occasions when I'd been up close and personal with a fur anything involved Zilla's hairballs. I fervently believed that fur looked a whole lot better on the live animal than dead on a human being. But I was here on business, not to judge Abby's lousy taste and ethics.

She was back in her seat. "Okay, let's get to work, though I don't see why Sam appointed you as his executor. When he had family, that is," she said, between sips of tea and bites of pastry.

Inhaling the seductive sugary essence while I sipped my tea, I tried to sound like a rational, disinterested party. "You have a point. But Sam didn't want to play favorites. You know how much trouble that can cause in a family." I gave her a sympathetic smile.

"Hm."

I pulled out a file from a briefcase I'd brought along. After I put the file on the table between us, I made as if I were studying the pretend information on the pages. "It turns out that years ago, Sam began collecting bearer bonds. I guess he must have forgotten about them when he made out his will."

Abby stopped sipping and chewing. "How much? Exactly?"

So much for not beating around the bush. I could sense the *eau de greed* dripping from every pore in her body. "Well, let me think." I ruffled through the pages in the folder and tapped my pen on the table, to whet her appetite even more and wrack her nerves.

She was practically bouncing out of her seat. If she were a dog, she'd be drooling all over the table. "How much?"

My, my, weren't we getting anxious. "Hmmm," I said, watching her squirm in the chair.

"How *much?*" She was leaning so far forward, her cleavage was on the verge of popping out of its confines.

"It looks like around another two hundred fifty thousand each."

Abby and her bosom sat back in her seat and finished off the tea and pastry. She gave me a 1000-watt smile. "This is a nice surprise."

I smiled back.

Then she frowned. "Uh, you did say two hundred fifty thousand more?"

I smiled again and patted her hand, hoping to catch her off-guard. "That's right. I guess you and Larry could make good use of the extra money."

She leaned forward and said in a low voice, "You bet. He just lost another job, the schmuck. And who knows how long I'll have *my* job, in this economy. We've already committed a lot of the money from the will to pay off some of our debts. We took out a second mortgage on the house. And we promised to help our son pay for our grandson's bar mitzvah. I don't think we can." She groaned.

I patted her hand again. "*Mazel tov* to your grandson. But it must all be very hard on you." Sympathetic tones.

She let out her breath. "Damn straight. But this will definitely help. Uh, do you know when I might expect the money?" She reached for the dead animal.

I told her about my possible plans for the money to go to charity. "Being a charitable person, I'm sure you'll approve of whichever one I pick."

Her eyes blazed. "What? You're kidding, right? You're going to give the money *away*? You can't do that!"

I patted her arm. "Hold on, Abby. I haven't decided anything yet." Then I thought of something. "But why don't you get together with the others to discuss where you all think the money should go?"

She shook off my hand, glaring at me. "That's a thought. But you damn well better make the right choice."

If looks could kill. I smiled. "I'll let you know as soon as everything is decided."

She stood up to leave. "Fine," she spat.

"Glad I could help." I watched as she walked to the exit.

She was barely out the door when she started to light up a cigarette. Even from where I was sitting, I could that see her hands were shaking so hard, she finally gave up. Abby Goldfarb was one desperate woman. Desperate enough to kill three people?

Chapter 32

The next morning, I got a call from Miriam Kravitz. She was upset and excited at the same time. Rivera had finally been persuaded, probably by her son-the-ADA, to exhume her sister's body and order an autopsy, once Miriam, the next of kin, agreed. Which was the reason for her being upset and excited.

"I understand that this is upsetting, Miriam. But it really is good news, if we want to find out what happened to Rose," I said.

She cleared her throat. "The idea of digging up my sister's body is…"

"I know. But think of this: Rivera is finally taking this seriously, at least seriously enough to find out exactly how she died."

She snorted. "Hmmph. You mean my *son* convinced him to take it seriously. I haven't seen that lieutenant make any moves on an investigation so far, have you?"

"It doesn't matter. At least it's going to happen. Did you give permission for the, um, procedure?"

"Yes, of course. It's the only way we'll be able to find out what happened."

"Good. Did Rivera tell you when it'll be done?"

"They're going to do the…exhumation…this week. After that, the medical examiner takes over."

I thought for a moment. "Miriam, once we know what killed Rose, if it's what we think, some kind of poison somebody put into her IV or something else, then maybe we, or your son, can convince Rivera to find out what killed Sam, too."

"But, Marabella, don't you need a relative to agree to the whole procedure?"

Hmm. That could be a major problem. Oh, wait. "Maybe not. If Rivera has reason to believe that Rose was murdered, maybe he doesn't need the family's permission for an exhumation and autopsy for Sam. It would be part of an official homicide investigation."

I heard Miriam sigh. "Okay. Let's hope we get to the bottom of this soon. Meanwhile, I hope you're being careful. After all, you're dealing with a double murderer."

"Triple," I said, without thinking. Oh, God. Now I had to tell her about Lucy. Needless to say, she was horrified.

"Marabella," she said. The voice of the admiral was loud and clear. "You need to be careful. Do not take chances. I'm beginning to be quite fond of you, my dear."

"Me, too," I told her. I gave the phone a brisk salute and said goodbye.

Progress, I thought. Rivera's people were sure to find something fishy about poor Rose Adelman's death. When Miriam visited Rose in the hospital, a nurse said she'd been on the road to recovery from the vicious assault in the laundry room. Something had to have gone wrong after Miriam's visit. Recovering one minute, dead the next? Not in any way a natural death, I bet. But what could've happened? I started to think. Okay, in a hospital, in the ICU, on various IV medications and monitors, who could get to Rose without being noticed?

Someone who looked like they belonged there, that's who. Someone in a uniform, dressed as a doctor, a nurse, an IV tech. Even someone pretending to clean the room. But the staff would be careful who went into an ICU, wouldn't they?

And that someone would have done…what? Put something in one of Rose's tubes. Or pinch off whatever tube was vital to Rose's breathing or heart rate. Those terrible images were making me feel sick.

But I had to think. *Deep breaths, Marabella.* Okay. A person would need some kind of medical know-how to do a medically related murder, right? At the very least, they'd have to know how to put something lethal in a tube or even how to shut it off and quickly restart it, so the death looked natural.

So which member of Sam's family had any medical training, besides Jeremy, the pediatrician? A nurse, tech, EMT, medical assistant, anything dealing with human or even animal healthcare. Maybe I could ask John what kind of training a person would need to give an IV to an animal.

And what made me think he wouldn't be upset about what I've been doing? Well, I wouldn't have to tell him, would I? Sure. I'm just asking about who gives IVs in a vet's office out of idle curiosity, right? Right. Better off asking my mother to do a deeper check into the family's background. That ought to do it. That and doing the rest of the pretend-there's-more-of-Sam's-money interviews with greedy Lipschitzes. And using myself as bait.

Deep breaths, Marabella.

Chapter 33

When I got to work, I found Susan at her desk, tapping furiously with a pen. A habit she had when she was nervous or worried. Or both.

"What?" I asked, sitting down across from her, hoping something terrible didn't happen to Theo or her family.

She stopped tapping and groaned. "You won't believe this."

If she knew what'd been going on in my life, she'd know I could believe just about anything. "What?"

"Carmen."

I had an awful feeling in the pit of my stomach. I bit a cuticle, held my breath, and waited for her to give me the bad news.

It was bad all right. Carmen had been charged with harassing Li Li, trashing Li Li's office, and even more stuff. Stuff I hadn't known about.

Groaning again, Susan said, "Over the weekend, Li Li's car windows were smashed, her tires were punctured, and *BITCH* was scrawled on the hood—"

In red lipstick, I bet. Like half the female staffers on campus didn't use red lipstick? Susan and I were among the few who wore the paler shades of rose or mauve. The time I'd tried using a bright red, I looked like a female version of Bozo. (Bozarella?)

"—in red lipstick. So they added destruction of personal property to the charges."

I blew out a breath. "What did Carmen say about all this?"

Susan drummed on her desk with the pen. With this news, I was surprised she wasn't drumming with a pen in each hand. Or something heavier. "They asked her if she and her friends did these things and she said that she wasn't going to rat out her friends. And that she wasn't one bit sorry it happened. You aren't one of the friends she wasn't going to rat out, by any chance, are you?" She fixed me with a look. My face must have shown the hurt I felt and she quickly apologized. "I'm sorry, Marabella. I should've known you wouldn't be involved with something like this. Please accept my apologies. I'm just so upset." She started tapping and groaning again.

"Not to worry. Look, we know that Li Li doesn't exactly have a lot of friends on campus."

A snort from Susan.

"But for Carmen to get herself in this kind of trouble, when she really needs her job—"

Susan's head shot up and she drummed furiously. "Right. What are we going to do? Not only does she need the job, we really need her help. And right in the middle of student recruitment, too."

I leaned over and patted her arm. "Well, first of all, we don't know that she's even guilty."

"But look what she said."

I thought for a moment. Carmen prided herself on her big mouth. When she was growing up in that rough neighborhood, she said, she was known as "The Mouth."

"You know Carmen. She always has to act tough. And I sometimes think she really enjoys acting like an overgrown juvenile delinquent." Just remembering some of her past antics made me smile.

Susan actually smiled, too. "Thanks. I never thought about that possibility."

I sat back in the chair. "I think we need to talk to her as soon as possible and get the real story out of her. What do you think?"

Susan nodded.

"Where is she?" I was afraid I'd find out she'd been locked up in jail.

"Home, I guess. She's been suspended without pay until the authorities decide what to do. The dean and the police are discussing it as we speak. I'm worried about how she's going to feed those kids. And her mother, who isn't well." Susan shook her head.

I stood up. "I think we should go see her. Can we get away right now?"

She checked the to-do list on her desk calendar. "I just need fifteen minutes to return a couple of phone calls. We better call her first. Do you want to do it?"

And warn her off? Well, I didn't think we had much choice. Taking two subways from the West Side all the way to Astoria, Queens, and finding nobody home wouldn't be my idea of a good time.

I agreed to make the call, figuring Carmen might be less nervous if she spoke to a colleague first rather than her boss, and went to my office to check her home number and address. We also needed directions, since I could just see Susan and me lost in the wilds of the Queens subway system forever. Like that old song about Charlie and the MTA, the Boston subway system.

Carmen's mother answered the phone. I told her who I was and asked for Carmen. She sounded very nervous. "Why you want to talk to Carmen? She have enough troubles. She don't need no more."

"Please, Mrs. Rodriguez, I work with Carmen. I think it's terrible what happened to her."

"*Si, si.*"

"I'd just like to come over and talk to her. To see how we could help."

"We? Somebody else?"

"Just me and our boss, Susan," I added quickly, before she could object, "Susan cares about Carmen and wants to help her."

A deep sigh. "Okay. I go ask if she want to talk."

I heard labored breathing going away from the phone. Carmen's mother suffered from COPD after years of a two-pack-a-day smoking habit. There was what sounded like banging on a door.

After a few minutes, I heard Mrs. Rodriguez's difficult breathing again.

"She don't want to talk to you," she said.

I gritted my teeth. *Damn you, Carmen. We're trying to reach out to you, you ungrateful woman.* "Mrs. Rodriguez, you want to help your daughter out of this mess, don't you?"

"Oh, *si, si*. Very much."

"Okay, then. She needs to let us come and talk to her and strategize."

"*Que?*"

"Um, make a plan, how we're going to help get her out of this."

"*Bueno,* okay."

"So please tell Carmen that we're coming to help her. Okay?"

"Okay."

She sounded a little less nervous. I nearly forgot about directions but asked her to get them from Carmen. She did, and it was a good thing we asked. I hoped we could find our way there without any problem. And that

Carmen would be cooperative and willing to work with us.

Chapter 34

Cooperative? Carmen? Not when it came to her tough-girl persona. I must have been delusional. Having to fight with the person we were trying to help was the last straw—after taking two trains and getting off at the wrong stop on the last train.

Carmen's mother had graciously invited us into the living room, motioning to a sofa that was covered by a beautiful, multicolored afghan. When I complimented her on it, she beamed. "My daughter made it."

Carmen was her usual charming, belligerent self. Even more so on her home turf. She stomped into the room, planted her feet in front of us, crossed her arms over her chest, and bellowed, "Whaddya want?"

Susan and I, by unspoken agreement, started off gently. "Carmen, we never knew about your design talent. It's gorgeous!" I said, as she glared at us.

"Enough with the flattery. Whaddya want?" She looked terrible. She was wearing a too-tight ratty tee shirt and too-big scruffy pants, her hair was unwashed and hanging over her face, and the part of her face I could see looked haggard. She looked as though she'd aged ten years. The sparkle was gone from her eyes, and no wonder.

Susan leaned forward. "We want to help you. What can we do?"

Carmen planted her feet even wider apart. "Ha! Why do you care, anyways? Besides, you guys probably think I'm guilty. Guilty before being proved innocent, right? Isn't that the way it works with people like me? Blame the 'Rican, right?"

Susan groaned. "Carmen, please."

Hoping to sound like the tough killer-chaser Carmen was in awe of, I said, "Okay, enough. First, we need you to tell us exactly what happened, everything you know, about these incidents."

She sighed. "Bella—"

Now I had her.

"—you know I can't rat on my friends."

"Bull. Your so-called *friends* are sitting pretty, letting you take the rap for them. Putting your job in jeopardy because of them."

Her shoulders drooped. "I…"

"Carmen, remember what happened to me, when I was framed for murder?"

She nodded.

"Well, I fought back. And you need to do the same thing." Of course, a few minor things had happened along my way, like my almost getting killed and being thrown in jail. I prayed that Carmen wouldn't focus on those details right now.

She pushed her hair out of her face and looked hopeful. "Do you really think I can do it?"

"Sure," Susan and I said together.

"Sit," I commanded, patting a seat between us on the sofa. I figured I should keep up the tough Bella routine since it seemed to be working.

She sat and, when Susan and I gave her a joint hug, started to cry. "I was so scared that I'd lose my job. But I was even more scared of being a ratfink." She sniffled.

"Carmen, if I have anything to say about it, you're not going to lose your job," Susan said. "We need you in the department."

Carmen sniffled again and grinned. "Even with my bad language?"

Susan smiled at her. "Nobody's perfect, not even you."

"Okay, guys, we've got work to do. Carmen, give. The whole thing."

She blew out her breath. "Remember the lipstick message on the ladies' room mirror?"

I nodded.

"What?" from Susan. "Nobody told me."

"Sorry, I should've," I mumbled. "But I didn't want to…"

"Get me in trouble." Carmen had a worried look on her face.

Susan frowned at me. "You and I will talk about this later. Go ahead, Carmen."

Carmen stared at us. "I didn't want to get you in trouble, either, Marabella."

"Never mind that now, let's just get on with it."

Still looking worried, she said, "Okay. It was Margaret Wilson and two of her friends, from accounting."

Susan gaped. "Margaret? She's so quiet and such a…"

Carmen sneered. "Lady? Well, not where her boyfriend was concerned. Actually, almost her fiancé. That was before Arnie met Li Li."

"Oh, no. That little…" Susan said.

Carmen's eyes had their old sparkle back. "Rhymes with witch. Yup. And guess what? That…Li Li didn't even really want him. She just wanted to prove she could get him, especially since he was already taken. That seems to be her specialty."

Oh, God. If she ever really got anywhere with John—too bad Margaret and her buddies didn't finish her off for good.

Susan obviously had been thinking the same thing. "If she tries that on Theo…"She made a slashing motion across her neck.

I took a couple of deep breaths and tried to get my mind back on the task at hand. "Listen, first we've got to get Carmen out of this."

"Right," from Carmen.

"So you've got to tell the dean and the cops about Margaret and company," I said.

Carmen stood up. "She'll kill me! And why would anyone believe me?"

"We'll go with you. And we'll make sure she doesn't hurt you," Susan said.

"Don't worry," I said, with more confidence than I felt.

We said goodbye to Carmen and her mother and headed for the subway. On the way back to the office, Susan gave me a mild scolding. "No more secrets that could affect our department, okay?"

"Okay, I should have thought," I said.

"Thinking is always a good idea. Except during…" She grinned.

"Sex," I said, glad we were on good terms again. Once again, I mentally counted my blessings in having Susan for my boss.

Chapter 35

Trying to keep my balance standing on a crowded cross-town bus, I was on the way for my interview with Jeremy Lipson—he of the wife and two mistresses. Did that make him a slime bag or an idiot? Probably both. How much did his wife know and if she did, did she pretend not to? Did she wonder where all his money—granted, he made a good living in his medical practice—was going? Maybe she didn't care. Or think about anything except filling her closet with designer clothes, furs, and jewelry. Not to mention what she paid for hair styling, mani-pedis, bikini waxing, and whatever else she could lavish on her scrawny body. *Well, we all have our priorities, right?* I wondered if the mistresses were curvy.

Jeremy and I were meeting at a bar-and-grill near his office on Manhattan's Upper East Side, around eleven Saturday morning. I'd dressed carefully, in my one dark suit and white blouse, wanting to give the impression of a no-nonsense, down-to-business professional. I'd have to try not to eat anything that could land on my outfit. And be careful not to spill my tea. I wished, not for the first time, that I had Toniann's knack for looking pure as the driven after scarfing down a meal.

Toniann. The wedding was next weekend. And I hadn't gotten her a wedding present yet. I had to think. What did she need? Okay, if not need, what would she like? And Peter. It had to be something he liked, too. This was hard. I didn't know him very well. I thought about what Toniann told me: they both really liked music, mainly show tunes and jazz. What else, I had no idea. But since he'd just graduated from law school, I knew they didn't have money for extras.

I'd go to Crate and Barrel and pick out something useful and decorative, a little luxury for their table that they wouldn't think of buying themselves. Something not too above my salary level. I calculated what I had in the bank and sighed. *Maybe something fake faux?* Hopefully this year, Susan's request for real department raises would go through.

I elbowed my way off the bus, ignoring the swearing from the other passengers, and headed outside. It had just started raining. Luckily, the bar-and-grill was around the corner. Jeremy was already there, even though I was fifteen minutes early. Guess keeping a wife and two mistresses would make a person conscious of time, if nothing else. I wondered if he ever got their names or their anything else confused—tastes in jewelry? Flowers? Sizes of underwear? I went inside, waved to him, and joined him at his table.

Jeremy smoothed back his expensive haircut and gave me a whiff of pricey cologne. He was wearing a dark gray blazer of a beautiful, soft material and a white shirt, open at the neck. He looked fit and obviously took good care of himself. Well, anyone making it with three women had to keep in shape physically. If not financially.

We greeted each other and ordered drinks, a beer and mixed grill for him, tea and a salad for me. After our food arrived, he picked up a handsome leather briefcase and pulled out a Cross pen and a leather record book that matched the briefcase. "Ms…uh…" He gave me a smarmy smile that threatened to become a leer.

Didn't he have enough on his plate, so to speak? "Call me Marabella," I said, giving him a nice, not-too-flirty smile. I wanted to make him comfortable, but not too comfortable. And I didn't want to distract things by having him snicker at my last name. I picked up my own briefcase, serviceable but definitely not a thing of beauty. When I bent over to fish out my folder of fake papers, I felt his eyes devouring my breasts. *Oh, nice. Go back to the meat on your plate, lech.*

Giving him a cooler smile, I pretended to pore over the pages then looked up. "Jeremy, as you know, Sam entrusted the dispersing of his assets to me. That was because he didn't want to have to choose one brother or sister over the others."

He nodded and reached across the table to put his hand over mine. I pretended to sneeze, apologized, and grabbed a tissue from my purse. I got out a Bic pen and a spiral notepad to make sure both hands were occupied. If that didn't work, I'd just have to keep sneezing or coughing. *Allergies?*

Then I realized my feet were being manhandled (foot handled?)under the table. This was giving me the creepy-crawlies. Could I pretend to have itchy ankles? A contagious rash? Too obvious. I'd just have to act like my upper body didn't know what my lower body was being done to. I wondered how many mothers of his little patients he'd harassed. Probably everyone under fifty.

I continued as if my ankles weren't being unwillingly massaged by his feet, which had become shoeless. *The better to feel you with, my dear?* "So, in the will, the assets were simply divided into fourths, a quarter of the whole for each sibling, with Jennifer entitled to her mother's share."

"Mmhmm," from Jeremy, his now-sockless feet slowly sneaking up on my legs.

I'd better hurry this along before he started on other parts of my anatomy with other parts of his. "But we've discovered there's another million dollars from bearer bonds Sam invested in. It was in a separate account and not included in the will. Maybe because it was years ago, and Sam forgot about it when he made out his will. But there it was, and cashed out, as I said, there's about a million. And I'm responsible for its designation."

A lascivious grin, as his toes crept toward my undefended thighs.

Quick, finish, before he hits the target ."So, I'm talking to each of you, asking for your input as to where this money should go, even though it's ultimately my decision. I had several charities in mind, such as cancer research, AIDS, heart disease, domestic violence—"

He stopped in mid-climb, again reaching for my hand across the table. "Don't you think charity begins at home, Marabella?"

"Well, I—"

"Why not divvy it up among the lawful heirs?" He gave me a dazzling smile, displaying an impressive mouthful of caps.

I pretended to think it over. "Jeremy, I'll have to think about it. But why don't you and the others get together to discuss what you think should be done with the money?" I stood up.

"Good idea. Wait!" He grabbed my arm. "Why are you in such a rush? Stay and keep me company for a while. I'd like to get to know you a little better." The leer again.

I just bet you would, Jeremy-the…was there such a thing as a male nymphomaniac? Packing my papers into my briefcase, I said, "I'm so sorry, but I have to get back. No rest for the working woman." Waving goodbye, I went out the door.

I looked back at the window from the street, where he couldn't see me. Shades of Dr. Lecher and Mr. Hyde. His face had purpled with anger, and his caps were bared in a snarl. He looked as if he wanted to bite someone. Me.

Amazing how a man who'd been ferociously hitting on me could turn on a dime. Well, a lot more than a dime. Enough to kill for?

Chapter 36

When I got home, the first thing I did after feeding Zilla was take a long, hot shower, to scrub away the invasion of Jeremy Lipson's feet. Ugh. Then, wrapping my wet hair in a towel, I sat down at the end of the sofa.

"I have a plan," I said.

My mother sat up. "Shoot."

"Not a good way to put it, Ma, but here it is. I told Abby and Jeremy I think it's a good idea for them all to get together to discuss what should be done with the make-believe extra money. So…"

"Aha. So you want me to find out when and where and go be a fly—or a ghost on the wall, so to speak."

"Exactly." Funny, we seemed to be thinking alike these days. I wondered why.

"Because I can sometimes read your mind, sweetheart."

"Only sometimes?" Thank the gods.

She frowned. "That's not nice and it depends. That's just the way it works. Or doesn't."

Okay, whatever.

"So, I'm off to the Lipschitzes' residences to be a covert operator for my daughter." She stood up.

A covert operator? "Wait," I said, before she could waft into the ether. I went to the bedroom and grabbed a ball of red yarn, rolling it on the floor from the living room into the bedroom. I needed to get Zilla in the bedroom before my mother took off. Fortunately, it worked. I shut the door just as he pounced on the wool. "Okay, all clear," I said.

After she came back and was settled on the sofa, she told me the family was about to gather tomorrow night in Jeremy's office to discuss the imaginary money. They picked it because of its convenience to their workplaces.

"Great. Will you be able to remember what they said?"

She folded her arms across her chest. "I'm not senile. Yet."

Obviously, I hurt her feelings. "Sorry, Ma. It's just that it's important, okay?"

"I know that."

She still looked hurt.

"I apologize. Let me make you a nice cup of tea."

She lay back against the cushions. "Okay. I'll just rest my eyes a minute."

When I came back with the tea, she was fast asleep. She looked so tired, I felt guilty. After all, she wasn't a youngster. I covered her with the afghan on the arm of the sofa and turned out the light.

Let sleeping mothers lie. She had a busy stint of spying ahead of her tomorrow night. Or, as she put it, a covert operation.

Chapter 37

The next night, she relayed the whole scene to me, play by play. I could picture every nasty one of them, stripped of any social veneer, in their greedy, selfish element. Except Jennifer, who still seemed to be what she appeared to be: a decent, caring person.

They arrived at Jeremy's office at almost the same time and immediately started in on each other.

"God, Abby, I don't know how you can put up with him," Tamar drawled, from one of the blue loveseats in the expansive doctor's waiting room.

My mother said to me, "I never saw a doctor's waiting room that big. You remember, my doctor's waiting room was so small, his patients were on top of each other. Not a good thing if you had to sneeze."

"And it looks like he's already put away a few." Tamar looked almost anorexic these days. Even her hair seemed to be thinning.

"Tamar is married to Sam's brother, Jeremy, of the two mistresses," I reminded my mother.

"No wonder she's so skinny," my mother said.

"Screw you, Tamar. Need the key to the liquor cabinet, Jer," Larry, who was already unsteady on his feet, yelled at Jeremy.

"And Larry-the-boozer is Sam's sister, Abby's, husband," I said.

"That poor Abby, having to live with that. Such a shame." My mother clucked.

Jeremy, busy in the staff kitchen, yelled back, "In here, Larry."

"If that were my husband..." from Tamar.

Larry came back, unlocked the cabinet, fished out a bottle and a glass and sat down in the chair next to Abby.

Abby glared across the room at Tamar. "Sister-in-law, dear, I wouldn't talk if I were you. At least my husband isn't screwing another woman. Or two, come to think of it." She gave a harsh laugh. The buttons at the top of her dress looked about to pop.

"Tch, tch, such language from her mouth," my mother murmured.

Jeremy stuck his head out from the kitchen. "Shut up, Abby, mind your own goddamn business! Don't you have enough to do, babysitting your boozer husband?" He said to Tamar, "Don't believe her, hon, she's just a bitter old woman."

Abby sneered. "Old? I'm a year younger than she is!"

David and Cheryl, sitting on the other loveseat, looked at each other. "Forgodsakes, people, I thought we were here to discuss the extra money from Sam." David rattled the keys in his jacket pocket. Cheryl looked drawn.

"David is Sam's other brother, married to Cheryl, who's been in and out of rehab," I said.

"No wonder she looked so washed out," my mother said.

"Money, ha! That's a good one, Davy. More money down the toilet for your addict wife?" Jeremy yelled.

David jumped up, heading for his brother, waving his fist. "Listen, you SOB, don't you dare talk about Cheryl like that! And you should talk, spending all your assets on your bimbos!"

My mother shook her head. "Terrible that brothers should talk to each other like that."

Jennifer, who'd been sitting quietly on a hard-backed chair, ran over to her uncle, putting her hand on his arm. "Please, Uncle Dave. He didn't mean it. Please, come back and sit down."

Grumbling, he let himself be led back to his seat. Then he turned to Tamar. "Bet you didn't know he's just about wiped out his life insurance, Tamar. He's gonna leave you flat broke. Whatta guy."

Tamar turned pale.

"Don't you believe him. He doesn't know what he's talking about, the moron," Jeremy yelled.

"Please, Uncle Jerry. Let's stop this, okay?" Jennifer said.

Cheryl piped up. "He does know what he's talking about, Tamar. And if I were you, I'd check out everything. I bet he even has a secret bank account."

Jeremy came into the room with a tray with coffee and cake and set it on the coffee table. "Got to hell, Cheryl," he said, sitting down next to Tamar.

"Jennifer's the only nice one," I said.

Still glaring at each other, the brothers and Abby served themselves coffee and slices of cake. Tamar and Cheryl declined, taking artificial sweetener for their drinks.

Jennifer, who looked too upset even for coffee, said, "Okay, let's get started. What we don't want, and I'm sure I speak for all of us, is for this extra money of Uncle Sam's to go to a charity." She gazed around the room and everyone nodded.

"Damn straight," from David, between bites of cof-fee cake.

"It belongs to us." Jeremy leaned forward in his chair.

"Right," Abby said, pouring sugar and cream into her coffee.

Jennifer cleared her throat. "Okay, then what should we do about it? Ideas, anyone?"

Larry was refilling his glass. "I've got a great idea. Why don't we get rid of this…what's her name, Mary? Then we get th' money. Right, Ab?" He gave Abby a fool-ish grin and slurped his drink. She looked disgusted.

Cheryl looked around the room. "This isn't getting us anywhere. C'mon, everybody, think."

"It's really none of your concern, Cheryl. You're just an in-law. You don't inherit," Abby said.

David glared at Abby. "But I do, sister dear. And what's mine is Cheryl's."

A snort from Abby. "Right, considering that all your money goes to her 'cures.' And how were your accom-modations this time, Cheryl, dear?"

"If you weren't my sister…" from a furious David. Abby laughed.

Jennifer said, "Okay, everybody, that's enough. I think that our best option might be to try to convince Marabella that Uncle Sam would have wanted us to have this money. And that it would really be carrying out his wishes." She looked around the room. "What do you think?"

"Fine, except what if it doesn't work? Then what?" Jeremy said.

David chuckled. "Well, then we'll just have to fix it so she changes her mind."

Jennifer said, "Oh, I hope you're not thinking of do-ing something…" she trailed off.

Jeremy laughed. "Why no, Jen. We may just have to use a little persuasion, that's all." He looked at David, and they both grinned.

"When I heard that, I almost stopped breathing," my mother said.

Jennifer looked worried. "Please, guys, Marabella is a good person. Don't do anything you might regret, okay?"

"Don't worry, Jen. Tamar, we've got to go, hon." Jeremy stood, pulling Tamar up, and went into the bedroom for their coats.

The others followed.

"And that's the report from your spy on the wall. What an awful bunch!"

I nodded. "It's a good thing you were there, since it seems that Jeremy and David are about to come after me. To 'persuade me' to see things their way."

My mother sat up and gave me a hug. "Don't worry, sweetheart. Mother's here. Nobody's going to go after my daughter without going through me, first."

Of course. Since she was invisible.

"And remember, I can see *them*, loud and clear," she said.

Chapter 38

Thank the gods that instead of spending the weekend worrying about Lipschitzes, I had two nights and three days at John's house to look forward to. Thinking about John caused my hormones to drive me crazy. Aah. Great sex. Great food. Great sex. Fortunately, one of us was a good cook. That would be John. Unfortunately, I had inherited my mother's terrible cooking genes.

When I got home from work on Friday, first on my agenda was breaking the news of my weekend plans to my mother. I sat down next to her on the sofa and spit it out.

She reacted as if I were a sixteen-year-old about to lose my virginity. Good thing she'd never found out about the real thing, when I was fifteen. That was the same year I'd repeatedly threatened to run away from home whenever I caught her reading my diary and listening to my phone calls.

"Tch, tch. That's what young women are doing now? Spending the weekend alone with a man?"

"Not exactly alone, Ma." On to my next challenge.

She looked hopeful. "You mean a chaperone? Sweetheart, I'm sorry, I assumed…"

Come to think of it, I guess you could consider three St. Bernards and a feisty feline as chaperones. Especially Harpo, who wouldn't let John anywhere near me, if he could help it. Not to mention the fun and games John and I would have overseeing the animal play-date. I pictured it like putting a couple of wolves and a tiger in the same cage. We'd be lucky to be able to escape to the bedroom for a quickie.

"No, it's the animals. John's three dogs and Zilla. I'm planning to bring Zilla with me."

Zilla's furry orange ears perked up at his name. "Mmmwroow?"

"Never mind, boy," I said. *The less you know about coming events, the better,* I thought.

My mother sat up on the sofa. "Well, since I don't know anything about your date, I'd appreciate it if you'd tell me what he does, where he comes from, who his family is, what they do for a living."

I gave her the details. When I got to the family farm in Pennsylvania, she started. "A farm?"

"Ma, some people actually live on farms. That's where most of our meat and dairy comes from. Along with our produce."

"People have to live someplace, I guess." She shrugged. "I thought produce mostly came from China these days."

"That's more dry goods and electronics," I said, going into the kitchen with Zilla. I was not going to tell her how to reach me, since I knew if she really wanted to, she'd be able to transport herself there without much effort. This I did not need.

After I fed Zilla, not a lot, because I was afraid he'd throw up in the cat carrier, my mother and I ate whatever it was she'd dished up. Then I went into the bedroom and started packing. A brand-new black lace nightgown.

Black lace bra, black lace undies, black lace teddy. My thoughts drifted to John slowly removing all of them. *C'mon, Marabella, you've got work to do.* I threw in jeans, turtleneck, tee shirt, sweatshirt, and down vest, to cover all the weather bases. John's house was almost an hour upstate and who knew what the weather would be?

Now for the real challenge. I placed a couple of special kitty treats and a soft blanket in the cat carrier and put it in the kitchen, figuring since that was the place he ate, he wouldn't be overly suspicious. I waited. And waited. Then I tried a new tack. I motioned to my mother to not make any noise, speech or otherwise, and went into the bedroom, hoping to keep him off-guard. As soon as I heard a sound, I made a stealthy trip to the kitchen. Foiled. Zilla had already scarfed down the treats and had a paw poised to wash up.

Resigning myself to my plan of last resort, pitched battle, I picked him up, yelping when he deposited a couple of nasty scratches on my arms, and dumped him into the carrier, making sure it was secure.

"Here I am, trying to take care of you, you ungrateful feline, and what do you do?" I said.

A loud, complaining, "Mmrroww," was the response.

After slathering antibiotic cream on my wounded arms and bandaging them up, I vowed to take Zilla to an animal behaviorist, cat whisperer, hypnotist, psychiatrist, whatever it took, as soon as I got John to recommend someone.

Then I felt guilty. Maybe Zilla's behavior was partly my fault. Poor thing was probably terrified. Poor thing? This poor thing just inflicted horrible pain on me. I could even get a disease, like cat scratch fever. Whatever that was. Maybe it was something like rabies, when you'd start foaming at the mouth and running around in circles. Like the raccoon.

When I was little, we used to go to my Aunt Evelyn's summer place in the country. One day, a raccoon came out of the bushes and started running around in circles, making funny noises at us kids. We decided it was friendly enough to make it a pet. Luckily, Aunt Evelyn took one look and screamed at us to get in the house. She called animal control, and a good thing, too, since the raccoon had been rabid.

Well, John would know if I were in any mortal danger from Zilla's attack. Thinking about John made me realize that I'd better hurry up with my packing, since he'd be outside in the car to pick me up in a few minutes. I grabbed a couple of cans of Fancy Feast, a few treats—even though Zilla didn't deserve them—his food and water bowls, litter box and a bag of litter and packed it all into a giant trash bag. Now that I had everything, including Zilla, packed, I tucked the carrier under one arm and dragged the bag into the living room. I rolled out my travel case from the bedroom, hoisted the rest, and kissed my mother goodbye on the forehead.

"Oh, what happened to your arms?" she said.

"Guess." I nodded at the cat carrier, where its occupant was complaining loudly.

She shook her head. "Tch, tch. What a bad cat!"

"It's okay, Ma. I'll deal with it. Take care of yourself."

Chapter 39

When John saw my wounds, he was horrified. Then he kissed my arms, which went a long way toward making the pain worth it. But I was not ready to forgive Zilla, even with the godawful yowling coming from the cat carrier. When he finally quieted down to piteous meows, I melted. For a moment I thought of taking him out of the carrier, before I came to my senses. Did I want to risk more of my undefended flesh being ripped to shreds? Or John's? An even-worse possibility was that let loose in the car, Zilla could go berserk, he could land on John's head or the windshield, and we'd risk a major accident.

So I settled for soothing words: "I'm sorry, Zilla. Poor kitty. We'll be there, soon. It'll be all right, don't you worry."

The sounds of cat snores soon filled the air. Either my conversation had put my cat to sleep from boredom, or he'd passed out from the trauma. Gone catatonic? Whichever it was, I was thankful for the peace.

When we got to John's house, I picked up the cat carrier gently, hoping Zilla wouldn't wake up till I could deposit him in a safe place. I didn't want to worry about his being eaten by the Marx Brothers. After all, there were three of the huge, terrifying animals, and Zilla was smaller than the sides of beef they usually devoured in a few bites. I tried to erase the images in my mind of the three dogs fighting over a fresh-killed, bloody Zilla. Although I thought of Zilla as strong and tough, he was just an over-muscled housecat. He'd never had to fight another animal except me.

As soon as John opened the front door, the dogs charged, practically knocking me down with their drooling excitement. I clutched the cat carrier, hoping to make a quick getaway to the bedroom with Zilla, thinking he'd be so scared, he probably wouldn't come out from under the bed the whole weekend.

Not a chance. Zilla was in major feline attack mode, fur standing on end, hissing and growling up a storm. The Marx Brothers were in full retreat, whining and backing away from the terrifying monster in the cat carrier. Zilla definitely had the upper paw.

"Well, old boy, I guess I don't have to worry about you," I said, walking into the bedroom and opening the carrier. Before I could shut the door, a puffed-up ball of orange fur streaked past me into the living room.

The three dogs turned tail and shot into the bedroom, trying to hide under the bed. No matter how hard the poor deluded animals tried, St. Bernards could not fit under a bed, not even a king-sized bed. They got stuck halfway under. This led to much whimpering. They tried going forward, which got them even more stuck, and backing up, which did nothing at all, except cause them to howl.

As for Zilla, he was sitting on the bed, washing his face. We tried pushing and pulling the dogs out. No luck. They were wedged in so tight, it must have been like being trapped in a vise.

"Wait a minute, I have an idea," John said, heading into the kitchen. He came back with a large bottle of olive oil and a couple of rags. "Okay, you grease Harpo and I'll do the other two."

Giggling, I grabbed a rag and started the rubdown. After a few minutes, Harpo and his brothers slid out, slick as greased pigs. They tried licking the oil off their fur, without success, sniffing at themselves and each other with distaste. Seemed they weren't crazy about a Mediterranean diet. Hopefully, this would be a learning experience about not trying to fit into places they couldn't fit into.

"Don't you guys know you're very big dogs? And you're afraid of a very small animal?" I scolded. They lay down on the floor and three huge heads lowered themselves onto three sets of paws. There are few sights as pathetic as large dogs looking embarrassed.

"I think they've learned their lesson, at least as far as where not to hide. Okay, boys, let's get cleaned up." He led them outside for a scrub and a hose-down.

I looked at Zilla. He was stretched out, full length, on the bed, eyes half closed, the perfect picture of a contented cat. "You're a bully, Zilla, you know that?" I said, secretly proud of being the owner of such a ferocious animal. *Come to think of it, having a fierce watch-cat around could come in handy in a bad situation.*

That made me think of the bad situations that could arise in the very near future. Such as my being attacked, killed, bloodied, dismembered. I shuddered and tried to clear away the scary thoughts. *Deep breaths, Marabella, deep breaths.* By the time John came back inside, I was calmer.

The rest of the weekend was without incident. We put Zilla in John's den. I paid him a visit every couple of hours, to make sure he was okay, feed him, check the litter box, and try to pet him, which he endured with his usual long-suffering demeanor. He spent most of the time curled up on the sofa, a piece of furniture I'm sure he was happy to have to himself.

We managed to lock the dogs out of the bedroom without experiencing the usual whining and scrabbling at the door, since they were more interested in whining and scrabbling at Zilla's door. Gluttons for punishment, I guess. You'd think dogs that big would have good-sized brains.

Our time in bed was heavenly and so was our time out of bed, talking and snuggling. I mentally congratulated myself on managing not to think of Li Li or the murders more than two or three times.

"I could get very used to this," John said, giving me a hug under the covers.

"Me, too," I said, snuggling closer.

Then he said, "What would you think of us moving in together?"

Um. I was definitely not ready for that, for a number of reasons. "All five of us? I don't think your roommates would fit in my apartment. And I'm sure Zilla would agree."

He leaned on an elbow and gazed at me. "No joking. I'm serious, Marabella. I want to wake up next to you in the mornings."

That idea made me feel panicky, then warm all over. Since I didn't want to get into our living arrangements yet, I decided to be generous and spread that warmth around. It worked. I got a reprieve, at least for now. I'd think about it tomorrow and maybe it wouldn't seem so scary.

Chapter 40

Toniann and I met at her last aerobics before the big day. Even though it took time, she needed to work off her anxieties. When we walked to the showers, she said, "I can't believe Peter's mother."

"What now?"

"I just found out she'd tried to get her own caterer for the wedding. Of all the gall."

At this point, I'd believe almost anything of the woman, after all Toniann had been telling me about her. "What did you do?"

She sounded more firm than I'd ever heard her. "I delegated Peter to tell her to back off, in no uncertain terms, that's what."

"Did he do it?

She grinned. "Whaddya think?"

We showered and toweled dried. Toniann was in a rush to get home to re-check the wedding arrangements. "Talk to you soon," she said, starting to get dressed.

"Who said getting married was easy?" I joked, and headed for the whirlpool, the reward for all that huffing and puffing. Turned out I was the only inhabitant, which was a good thing. I enjoyed chilling out in the whirlpool with Toniann, but not the company of some of the others, like the gum-popping teeny-boppers carrying on inane conversations.

"Aaah," I murmured, sinking into the warm water, starting to relax. Suddenly, something was pushing my face down into the water, making me choke. I started to yell for help and sputtered, trying to come up for air, but the something, the person, was too strong. Was this how I was going to meet my end, in a health club whirlpool? It would be funny if it weren't deadly. I thrashed around, straining to get my face above the water. Then I heard running feet and yelling. Somebody lifted me out of the water. After a lot of gasping and coughing, I was finally able to breathe.

"What happened?" from Toniann, who'd come to my rescue. Fortunately, she'd forgotten her makeup case in her locker. When she came back, she'd heard noises coming from the whirlpool.

"Somebody tried to kill me," I said, still short of breath.

Chapter 41

The good news was that the health club manager called the cops right away. The bad news was that one of the cops seemed to be prejudiced against me.

After I gave him my name, he said, "Oh, it's *you*. I heard all about *you*. What did you get yourself into this time?"

I gritted my teeth, making an effort to keep my temper. And lost it. "This is how you talk to someone who was almost killed? Isn't your motto, 'Protect and Serve'?" My fellow health club members crowded around, cheering me on.

He told the other cop to check out the premises. Then he scowled at me. "If you'd just learn to mind your own business, maybe these things wouldn't keep happening to you, Ms. Vinegar."

My Greek chorus booed. The cop stared them down. He turned to Toniann. "Did you see anything?"

"Sort of," she said.

He looked at me. "Okay, get dressed, and we'll go to the station and go over the whole thing. You, too, you're a witness," he told Toniann, murmuring under his breath, "Wait till Rivera hears about this. It'll make his day, for

sure." He pointed us to the locker room and ordered everyone else to get out of the way. "Show's over, folks. Go
back to whatever you girls do in here."

They didn't go quietly, but they went, some of them
putting an arm around me and murmuring words of sympathy. "Thanks, guys," I said, going to my locker. I apologized to Toniann for putting her through this when she
had so much on her mind.

"Don't be silly. You coulda died. Thank God I was
so absent-minded I had to come back."

Fifteen minutes later, we were at the station. The
scowling cop marched us over to Rivera's office.

"Just what I needed," he groaned when he saw me.
He fished out a bottle of aspirin from his desk and swallowed a couple with gulps of his ever-present decaf soda.
"Wish I had something stronger," he muttered, directing
us to chairs across from him. He pulled out a notebook
and a pen, sighed, and pointed to Toniann. "Who are you
and what's your relationship to Ms. Vinegar, here?"

"Toniann Di Lorenzo. I'm her best friend."

"She saved my life," I said.

"Okay, from the top," he said, with a yawn.

"Which of us do you want to go first?" I said.

A frown and another yawn. "I don't care. Just start
talking, one of you."

Toniann and I looked at each other. "Okay," I said.
"I was in the health club whirlpool, alone, relaxing."

"Where were you at the time?" He pointed to Toniann.

Toniann said, "I was getting dressed to leave because
I had so much to do, getting ready for the wedding."

He stopped her. "Okay, I don't need to know why
you were leaving. Then what happened?"

"I just started to relax, when all of a sudden, someone pushed me under," I said.

"Where was everyone else? The other people in the health club?"

"There was nobody in the whirlpool except me."

He looked at Toniann. "You didn't see anyone heading that way? Nobody that didn't belong there? Did you hear anything? Smell anything, like perfume, or aftershave?"

She shook her head. "No perfume, but aftershave? It's a woman's health club, so why would I smell aftershave?"

"Maybe somebody was hiding his identity, pretending to be a woman who belonged there," he said.

"That would be kind of hard," I said. Then I remembered that none of the Lipschitzes or their spouses was tall. So it wouldn't be impossible for one of the men to pass themselves off as a woman.

"Not necessarily. Someone in sweats, or something else unisex, could do it." He looked at Toniann again.

She shook her head. "I really wasn't looking or paying attention. Like I said…"

"She had a lot on her mind. She's getting married in—"

"Moving right along. Maybe you fell asleep in the tub? It happens, you know. Were you two drinking before you got in there?"

As usual, he was ticking me off. "Lieutenant, it's obvious you don't believe me—us—about the attack. No, I wasn't asleep. Or drunk. Or even a little high."

He sat back in his chair. "Could someone have been playing a prank? A practical joker?"

Grrrr.

Toniann's eyes were flashing. "Lieutenant, trying to drown someone isn't a *prank*. It's *attempted murder*, as far as I know." She turned to me. "Right?"

I folded my arms across my chest. "Right."

Toniann sniffed. "I can't think what coulda happened if I hadn't forgotten something and had to come back and heard all that thrashing in the water."

Rivera sighed again, fished out a tissue, and passed it to her. "Is there another way out of that place? *If* someone was there, they couldn't just disappear into thin air."

"I don't know about any other exits," she said.

"Me, neither," I said. Thinking about disappearing into thin air made me think about my mother. She'd be worried why I wasn't home yet. Not to mention a certain feline who'd be in a ferocious temper waiting for his dinner.

Rivera pressed some buttons on his intercom and asked for the cop who'd brought us to the station. "Go back to that health club and check if there's another exit, a back way out, an emergency door. Check for footprints and see if any door has been jimmied. And ask if anybody saw somebody who didn't belong there." He clicked off and sat back in his chair, yawning again.

Looking down at my lap, I said, "Um, there's one more thing…"

Toniann giggled. "Just like Columbo."

"What now?"

"What's happening in your investigation of Rose Adelman's death?"

"That information hadn't been released yet."

"But—"

Rivera stood up, our signal to leave. "This meeting is over. Somebody will drive you back to your cars at the health club. We'll be looking into this. Which means that you and your friend, here—" He directed his scowl at Toniann. "—*shouldn't* be."

As Toniann and I left in the police car, an awful thought occurred to me. Whoever tried to kill me might think Toniann got a good look at them. Her life could be in danger, too. The question was: should I warn her? And have her worrying just before her big day? Besides, she probably wouldn't take me seriously, anyway, right? I decided to leave it alone, for now. And hoped to God that was the right decision.

Meanwhile, there was John's reaction if he found out about my near-death whirlpool experience. Speaking of that, it would be a long time before I'd let myself get into another whirlpool. If ever.

I turned to Toniann. "Do me a favor. Not that you didn't just do a really big one already, thank you," I said with a grin.

She frowned. "It's no joke, all right?"

I nodded. "I know. But, please, don't let John find this out, okay?"

Chapter 42

My mother was not a happy camper when I finally got home. In fact, she was, pardon the expression, white as a sheet, pacing up and down the living room.

She put a hand over her heart. "I thought you were dead, or kidnapped, or injured, maybe."

"Not quite. Are you okay?" I tried to get into the room without tripping over Zilla, who was winding himself around my ankles.

"Other than having palpitations before you got home, I'm fine." She flopped onto the sofa.

Oh, God, palpitations. Her heart failure. Now I was really worried about her.

She waved an arm in the air. "Don't worry, sweetheart. But a glass of water would be nice. If it's not too much trouble."

"Of course, right away." I ducked into the kitchen, grabbing a glass and filling it from the tap.

"Let it run, please. Otherwise, it'll be lukewarm."

"Whatever," I muttered, emptying the glass, turning on the tap again, waited a few minutes and tested for cold, refilled the glass, and brought it to her.

She sat up and chugged the water. "Ahh," she said, with a belch. "That's better."

"Good," I said, relieved. "By the way, did you feed Zilla?"

She huffed and sat back against the pillows. "Do you think I'd let an animal, even one that wasn't particularly nice, starve? I even cleaned out that box he uses for a toilet." She made a face.

"Do you have a better suggestion? I hear that toilet training a cat can take years. Would you like to volunteer?"

She shuddered. "No thank you. But what happened? Where were you all this time? And what do you mean, *'not quite?'* Not quite what?"

I was going to have to tell her. This I did not want to do. "Um, how about we wait till after dinner? I'm really hungry. And I guess Zilla has room for more."

"Mmrrow." He started nipping at my ankles.

She folded her arms across her chest. "No, nope, no dinner for you, young lady, until you spill the beans."

Spill the beans? Young lady? "Ma, I am no longer five years old. Or even six. In fact, I'm…" I couldn't bring myself to say "forty."

She fixed her eyes on me. "What happened to you tonight?"

So, I told her. Tried to make it sound less serious and scary. And failed. The good thing was that she was now focused on Rivera's casual attitude. Instead of on me.

She shook her head. "That man should be relieved of his job. What kind of policeman is that, who refuses to investigate when people are killed? And almost killed."

Taking my stinging ankles into the kitchen, I said, "A very skeptical one. Zilla, you've got to learn not to do that, or it's obedience school for you, my pet." I didn't even know if there was such a thing for cats. Maybe I'd have to hire the cat whisperer from the TV show *My Cat From Hell*.

Chapter 43

The sun was shining on Toniann's wedding day. A good omen. The icing on the wedding cake was that Toniann had just found out her future mother-in-law broke her hip and couldn't be there.

"Thank goodness she's not here to rain on your parade," I whispered.

"Not that I was wishing her ill, but…" Toniann whispered back to me as her mother was adjusting the bridal veil.

Her mother shook her head. "Girls, please. I'm sure Peter's mother feels terrible about missing the wedding."

Toniann rolled her eyes. "Because she's missing her chance to complain about everything, all the way through."

"Toniann…" her mother warned.

Trying to change the subject, I cracked, "Hey, is my chin yellow yet?" I was already itching to get out of my cage of stiff yellow fabric.

"I think that's only for buttercups," said Angelina, one of Toniann's younger cousins, who'd been giggling with Carla, another cousin, in a corner of Toniann's old room. Toniann's room, which had been turned into a guest room, had been redone in pale blue wallpaper and painted white furniture. When Toniann was a kid, she told me, everything was yellow. Of course.

When she was growing up, she'd been surrounded by lots of family, maybe to make up for her being an only child. Her parents wanted an armful, but couldn't have any more after Toniann. One more thing we had in common, except that with my mother's compulsive fussing over me when I was growing up, it was hard to imagine her wanting any more children. Toniann's mother, a small, attractive brunette, a little on the plump side, always seemed to be even-tempered and low-key. Low-key was not a word that lived in the same universe with my mother.

After Toniann's tiny, white-haired grandmother had checked and double-checked the children for spitballs, wads of gum and grime, a limousine took Toniann and her father, mother, grandmother, and me to the church. Peter and his brother would ride in another limo. The others would follow in their own or their parents' cars.

We waited for the rest of the bridal party on the stone steps in front of the tall, imposing church. Peter and Danny, his brother and best man, were waiting inside in the priest's robing room. Toniann's mother introduced me to the middle-aged priest, with thinning hair and a sweet smile, who'd known Toniann since she was born. When the woman at the organ started to play "Ave Maria," everyone stood up.

"Time to go," Toniann's mother said, her voice catching, wiping away tears with a lacy handkerchief. She wore a beautifully cut beige silk suit and a frilly beige blouse, and carried a bouquet of red roses.

We lined up and walked into the church and down the aisle. The little flower girls, cute in gauzy pink dresses, strewed pink rose petals. The bridesmaids, dressed in baby blue gowns, carried white roses. Then came the tuxedo-clad ushers—Peter's cousins—and his brother, Danny. And then, me, the maid-of-honor.

I could feel my face getting hot, self-conscious about my outfit and trying not to step on my dress and fall on my behind. I'd never been too steady on my feet, and the high heels, dyed a matching yellow, didn't help. Teetering on my yellow stilts and trying not to drop my bouquet of yellow roses, I kept telling myself it was only a few feet to the candlelit altar, that I could do this, that it was for Toniann and that I was a grownup. Thankfully, it worked.

I teared up when Toniann appeared on her father's arm. She was exquisite, a gorgeous, willowy vision surrounded by clouds of white, with her gauzy veil, feathered head band and a bridal bouquet of yellow and white roses. Her father, tall and distinguished in a tux, was beaming. As were Peter and Danny, looking handsome in their tuxes.

Peter's younger brother was quite a hunk, with big blue eyes and a great tan, the result of his summer job as a lifeguard. If I weren't already attached to John…

The room was overflowing with, I thought, mostly Toniann's relatives. Peter had a small family. Besides his mother and his brother, there were just a few aunts, uncles, and cousins.

Toniann's and Peter's friends were there, some of Peter's law school classmates, and even Otis Pinckney and his sourpuss of a wife. And John, of course, looking yummy in a tan jacket and white shirt. Everyone was quiet during the ceremony, except for Toniann's grandmother's honks, when she blew her nose into a large handkerchief.

After the ceremony, the limousine carried us to Howard Beach, Queens, to a hall that specialized in catering traditional weddings, located, unfortunately, near

JFK. When we got out of the limo, we had to shout to each other over the noise from the planes.

The ballroom's décor was elaborate: a winding staircase with a gold banister from the upper floor for the bride to walk down, huge gilt-and-glass chandeliers, high ceilings surrounded by decorative molding, brass wall sconces and best of all, on the other end of the room from the dark mahogany tables, a large tiled dance floor. The band, which luckily could be heard above the airport noise, was playing '50s music, Toniann and Peter's choice, when we arrived.

The musicians switched to slow, romantic music when Toniann descended the staircase and the newlyweds took the floor. Then it was my turn to dance with the best man. Danny was a great dancer, and swept me along with him. Soon he was pulling me closer and I could see John looking uncomfortable at our table. Ha! Good to keep him on his toes. But I didn't really want to upset him and was happy to hold his hand when the dance was over.

The wine was flowing and the hot and cold hors d'oeuvres were delicious. The best man made a champagne toast and Toniann's father broke down while trying to say something and gave up, giving the couple a bear hug instead. There were food stations with the traditional Italian fish specialties: scungili, calamari, pulpa. The fishy odor made me breathe through my mouth. Eeww. I didn't know which was worse, the looks of these things or their smell.

For a non-fish eater—especially anything squirmy or with tentacles—there was also rare beef roast for those who liked their meat barely dead and roast chicken for the more civilized, like me. Plus tons of various vegetables and fresh, handmade pasta bathed in thick, rich, marinara sauce. I inhaled the cinnamon, caramel, and sugar aromas at the dessert station before resigning my-self to tea and Splenda. John thought I was silly, but I was afraid I'd burst open my gown, especially since I hadn't skimped on the out-of-this-world pasta.

Big as the ballroom was, it was crowded, with all the family and friends. There was just enough space for the long table piled high with gifts, including mine—a pol-ished wood salad bowl and matching salad servers. The rest of the tables were clustered together to make room for all of us. And some of Toniann's relatives, like some of mine, had voices that could be overheard, whether you wanted to hear or not.

I'd pretty much tuned out the conversations at the other tables until something got my attention. At the next table, one of Toniann's aunts, who spent winters in Palm Beach, was talking to a younger woman about a murder in Florida.

"They made it look like natural causes, but it wasn't, it was murder!"

"How did they do that?" the younger woman asked.

"Easy. When you've got medical training, you know how to fool around with somebody's medication, like their IVs. This killer—and would you believe, it was the *victim's own grandson?*—had been a medic in the army. Well, his grandma was in the hospital, recovering from pneumonia, when he killed her."

The younger woman shook her head. "Terrible. Why would somebody do something like that, and to his own grandma?"

Toniann's aunt said, "A *lot* of money. So the grand-ma was hooked up to all kinds of machines but seemed to be getting better, according to her doctor. But the next day, she was dead. It took a while for the police to figure it out, because they thought it was natural causes. And you know how it is when an older person dies, they don't bother about it much." She shrugged.

"So, how did the police finally figure it out?"

"Somebody remembered seeing the grandson sneak into her room in the middle of the night. And right after that, the grandma was dead as a doornail."

I shuddered.

"Hey, where did you go?"

I realized John had been trying to talk to me and I apologized. But it took everything in me to be able to concentrate on him and everything else around me. I was itching to get back home for a strategy session with my mother. We needed to find out if any of Sam's relatives, besides Jeremy, had any kind of medical training, for humans or otherwise. Hey, people who worked in veterinary offices gave the patients medicine and shots and probably hooked up IVs, too. John would know exactly what, of course. But did I really want to get him going about this?

Toniann was getting ready to toss her bouquet and all the single women were jockeying for a good position. She gave me the eye and threw it right at me. I caught it, barely, inhaling the sweet perfume of the roses, my favorite flower smell.

I remembered that she'd been a star pitcher on her high school girls' softball team. Needless to say, I was not a star anything, when it came to sports. Unless you could call reading a sport. One reason was that the girls in my high school were way inches taller than me. My nickname in gym was midget. They kept growing and growing. I didn't. So much for things like basketball and volleyball. I couldn't see over the other girls' heads. My mother, not wanting me to get hurt, got my doctor to write notes about mythical long-lasting periods.

Now that I had the bridal bouquet clasped in my arms, John took it as a sign of another wedding to come, namely ours. He whispered in my ear, "Will you marry me?"

His loving look and the romantic atmosphere made me forget my doubts. Sort of. I whispered back, hoping my resolve didn't waver: "Yes."

I couldn't imagine anyone else I'd ever want to marry. Not to mention that my previous relationships had worked out so badly, it never would have happened. Mainly because of my screw-up mechanism in meaningful relationships. I'd reject them before they could reject me, or I'd get them to reject me, yadda, yadda.

John grabbed me around the waist and gave out a whoop. "Hey, everybody! We have an announcement! We're engaged!"

Toniann ran over and hugged us. "Yay! I'm so happy for you guys!"

As others came up to us with congratulations, I smiled and thanked them. Inside, I was a wreck. Oh, God. Did I really do this? I wished I were still on Xanax. Or still had my shrink. *Please don't let me screw this up, God. Please.*

Chapter 44

I teared up again when Toniann reappeared, now in a powder blue suit, with Peter, in a navy blazer and slacks. One of Toniann's cousins handed out rice to throw and the newlyweds took off in Peter's car, headed for a honeymoon in Toronto. Why Toronto, I'd asked Toniann? Because it was drivable, not too expensive, and a little exotic, she said. Guess that beat out less exotic places like, say, Pittsburgh.

I was still sniffling when John and I kissed goodbye and made a date for next weekend. Hugging me tight, he said, "For a trip to a jewelry store. I can hardly wait to see a diamond on that finger." He kissed my ring finger, wincing at the sight of my bitten-down nails and cuticles.

I tried to cover them up by putting them in the pockets of my gown, before I remembered it didn't have pockets. "I promise I'll try to stop," I said, wringing my hands.

"The ring will look a lot prettier," he said, hugging me again, before we climbed into our separate rides: mine back to Toniann's parents' house, John's at the groom's mother's house, a few blocks away.

With a sigh of relief, I kicked off the heels, climbed out of my dress, and changed back into my normal, comfortable clothes in Toniann's old bedroom. I said good-bye to her parents and grandmother and cousins and caught the subway home.

I fed Zilla, provided my mother with the details, minus my engagement news, and sat down with her on the sofa. Unfortunately, with her sharpened mind-reading skills, at least, when it came to reading *my* mind, I could see she thought I'd left something out of the conversation.

Too bad. I wasn't in the mood for one of her interrogations about every aspect of John's life. I had enough stress to deal with right now, thank you, trying to outwit a murderer and keep myself from biting off every cuticle that was still intact. But I'd promised John to try, didn't I? Maybe I'd have to adopt a new stress-reliever. Like what? Gum chewing was tacky, and besides, it pulled out my fillings. Candy did my teeth in, too, in addition to expanding my hips. I'd given up smoking years ago, after a bad bout of bronchitis. And I'd finally gotten off my long time dependence on Xanax.

Well, I could snap a rubber band on my wrist. Hey, no calories, no loose fillings, no lung cancer, no weight gain, no prescription pill addiction. It could even work. Maybe.

Then there was my knitting, better described as my yarn mistakes. You couldn't bite anything on your fingers when they were involved with knitting needles, especially metal ones. Okay, I guess you could, but it wouldn't be easy. And you could end up stabbing yourself in the face.

My mother broke into my reverie. "Marabella? Eat up, you're going to need your strength. Especially…" She paused. "I know there's something."

She gave me what I could only describe as the equivalent of an elbow nudge, with her eyes.

Forget it, Ma. On to less-personal and more-

detecting matters. I told her about the conversation I'd overheard. "You see? I'm sure that's what happened to Rose Adelman. Remember what her sister said? That her nurse said she was getting better, and then, boom."

"So whoever attacked her in the basement finished her off in the hospital," my mother said. "By the way, there's some nice leftovers for tomorrow night."

I'd have to remember to pick up Chinese food or pizza tomorrow after work. "Maybe by doing something to Rose's IV. Miriam said she was hooked up to all kinds of machines. If that's how Rose was killed, somebody had to have enough medical training to do that. The same with Sam. Somebody gave him something that killed him. So it makes sense to…"

"Find out which member of Sam's family had a medical background, besides Jeremy, the doctor," she said.

"Right."

"I'll get on it right after I finish the dishes."

She always insisted on cleaning up herself, maybe to prove that she was still strong and able to do things?

"No, sweetheart, I just want to be helpful. You work hard every day at that place where they don't appreciate you. They treat you like an indentured servant."

"Please, Ma, not now, okay?" I checked on Zilla. He'd finished his dinner and was washing his face. I picked him up carefully, deposited him and myself in the bedroom, and shut the door. I didn't want to go through another crazed cat episode when my mother did her disappearing and reappearing act.

I settled down with my latest knitting project, a scarf for John. At least, that's what it started out to be, according to the pattern. The problem was that I couldn't make sense of the graph of the pattern in the magazine. No spatial relations ability.

That brought back horrible memories of the spatial

relations test when I was a high school senior. I'd opened the test folder and looked at the pages of various blocks, circles, and other objects. You were supposed to figure out what belonged where and what didn't. After I'd stared at the pages for what seemed to be hours, getting more and more confused, I closed the folder and left the exam room.

Trying to push that scary memory away, I gave up on the pattern and decided to create my own design for the scarf *(seriously?)*, when I heard my mother land in the living room. I opened the door of the bedroom to let Zilla out and joined her on the sofa. She seemed to be having a problem with her breathing, and I hurried into the kitchen to fetch her some water. I handed her the glass. "You shouldn't rush around. It's not good for you. Can you try and slow down a little?"

She sipped the water and let out a small belch. "Aaah, a drink of water always helps. A glass of seltzer would be even better. But thank you, anyway, sweetheart."

Grrrr.

After she finished the rest of the water, she was ready for action, her notes in her lap and bifocals perched on her nose. "At least three of them besides Jeremy have some kind of medical experience."

"That's just great," I said.

My mother peered at me over her glasses. "Don't be so negative, sweetheart. Have a little patience. Okay. Jeremy, of course, is number one, being a pediatrician. David had a part-time job at a vet's office when he was in college."

"What did he do at his job?"

My mother consulted her notes. "Let's see. He helped the vet and his assistant during operations, carrying towels, blankets, things like that."

"So he would have had a chance to see how an IV works," I said.

"Right. Jeremy's wife, Tamar, worked as an aide in a hospital one summer during college."

"Ditto for being around IVs."

My mother nodded. "Cheryl, David's wife, spent a summer during high school as a candy striper."

"Hmmm. Don't know if candy stripers get to see much of anything…"

She gave me a knowing look. "You never can tell. Looks like Jennifer, Abby, and Abby's husband didn't work anyplace where they would've been around IVs. But who knows? You could always get a look at an IV when you're visiting a patient, or have a sick dog or cat."

"Yes, but to fool around with one of those things, I think you'd really have to be a quick study. It can't be that easy to do," I said.

"Or there might be a lot more dead people in hospitals and nursing homes."

Chapter 45

When I got to work on Monday, everything to do with the Li Li incidents had been resolved. Carmen had been cleared and reinstated in our department. (Yay!) Margaret Wilson and two of her work buddies had been fired and were facing charges of harassment and destruction of property.

But Carmen didn't get off that easy. As Margaret and her buddies were packing up their personal things, she screamed curses at Carmen and vowed vengeance. Her partners-in-crime, whom Margaret had bullied into submission, were muttering about Carmen being a ratfink.

All this got Carmen a little unnerved. So, to celebrate Carmen's return to work and to get her mind off Margaret and her minions, Susan and I took her out to a new Ethiopian restaurant not far from campus. I'd heard some of the staff and faculty raving about the food. The place was bright with African masks, sculptures, and woven wall hangings. After we were seated, Susan and I on either side of the honoree, we looked around for our table.

Leave it to Carmen to ask the wait person, "Hey, where's our table?"

The woman pointed to three tall baskets near our

seats. "I assure you there will be no problem with your eating," she said.

"Huh?" from Carmen.

When I glanced around the room, I saw people eating what looked like the tops of the baskets. "That can't be right," I said.

Our wait person came back, bearing three large circles of some kind of flat bread, and put them on top of our baskets. We just stared. The woman said, "These are your tables and tablecloths. Ethiopian-style."

"Oh, I knew that," Carmen said.

Susan and I poked her in her sides. "You're so full of it," I said.

Carmen grinned. Then she called our waitperson over, saying, "I don't see our silverware."

The woman pointed to our hands. "This is how you eat, Ethiopian-style."

"My mother used to kill us for doing that when we were little," Carmen muttered.

Whatever the food was, it smelled delicious, with exotic spices hovering in the air. Cumin? Cardamom? My nose was in scent heaven. The dishes tasted as good as their aroma promised. And part of the fun of the dining experience was getting to eat the tablecloth, together with various foods placed on top.

Unfortunately, it would have been better for Carmen if she'd known what we were eating. Barely a half hour later, she was violently sick all over the sidewalk. Probably because of one of the mysterious spices she must be allergic to. Poor Carmen. So much for her celebration. We promised her our next eating out experience would be someplace where the ingredients were a known quantity.

After we said goodbye and I was on the subway home, I thought about food allergies. I knew that severe allergies to food, like allergies to stinging insects, could make a person go into anaphylactic shock, which could be fatal, if not treated. That made me wonder about what somebody familiar with toxic substances could slip into my food or tea, when I had my next encounter with Sam's relatives. Other than bringing along my personal taster—my mother—I'd have to guard anything I ate or drank as if my life depended on it. Which it very well might.

Chapter 46

I was trying not to show too much joy about the news that Li Li was leaving her job. (Yay!) Especially in John's presence.

"At least she's staying for another couple of weeks." He wasn't looking forward to dealing with the interview process again. "Just when everything was running smoothly in the department. I don't understand why she's leaving. I thought all that mess had been cleared up, since they got rid of those troublemakers." He shook his head.

We were on our way to a jewelry store to pick out my engagement ring. Just saying the words, "engagement ring," in my head, was making me nervous. *Deep breaths, Marabella, deep breaths. Thank you, Dr. Ditstein, for that, at least.*

John parked his car in a garage on the Upper East Side, and we headed down the block to Taylor's Jewelers on Fifth Avenue, supposedly one of the best in the area. I told John I didn't need something extravagant on my finger. I wasn't that kind of woman. My idea of jewelry was my Timex watch on its expandable metal band and, on occasion, a long strand of costume jewelry hanging from my neck.

For my sixteenth birthday, Aunt Evelyn wanted to

give me pearl earrings for pierced ears. I'd already had an unfortunate episode with pierced ears and wasn't about to repeat it.

When my girlfriend Fran and I were fourteen, we went to a shop at a mall where they pierced your ears for cheap, no questions asked about your age. My mother was horrified, but that wasn't the worst of it. Green pus started dribbling out of my ears a few days later. My mother rushed me to the pediatrician—how mortifying is that for a fourteen-almost-fifteen-year-old, sitting in a waiting room with toddlers?—who dosed me with antibiotics and gave me a lecture about infections, sepsis, and death.

So much for my relationship with jewelry. Except. As a lover of all things nineteenth century—I really was born in the wrong era—I swooned over period movies, including the extravagant clothes and jewelry adorning the heroines at the balls. But I couldn't afford to buy real antique jewelry and traipsing around in antique clothing wouldn't have looked professional. Or sane. Though I did own a couple of flea market finds I kept in my closet and occasionally dressed up in when I was alone.

Taylor's Jewelers had a hushed, private atmosphere that spelled expensive right off the bat. The carpeting was a deep blue plush, so thick I felt I could sink into it. Matching velvet-covered wing chairs stood against one wall and a Victorian-era sofa against another. Antique-style mirrors framed the other walls. The lighting was low, emanating from brass wall sconces, except for the lighting on the jewelry cases, which zoomed in like a laser on the glittering pieces. I felt totally out of my league. Any other woman, especially one my age (*Don't think about age, Marabella*), would probably be either blasé about the jewelry exhibit or greedy-excited. I was almost hyperventilating. And trying not to gnaw on a nail or cuticle wasn't helping.

"Marabella?"

I felt an arm go around my waist and made myself smile. After all, the poor man was trying to make me happy, and I didn't need to spoil the moment with my neurotic commitment worries.

John pointed to an old-style gold ring with diamonds that looked like the one the heroine wore in the pre-Civil War movie Toniann and I had seen. The diamonds were in an antique filigree setting, and it had a muted elegance.

"I think this is you," he said.

This time I smiled for real. "How did you know? It's perfect."

Chapter 47

After we left the ring with the jeweler for sizing to fit my finger, John took my hand. "Happy?"

I felt tears threatening. I couldn't speak. I just nodded and smiled as wide as I could without cracking my jaw. "I love you," I said, putting my arms around his waist, even though we were on the sidewalk in such a fancy neighborhood. But I didn't care. I was practically floating down the street.

I was beginning to trust in this relationship. But a voice in my head warned: *Careful, careful, don't let yourself screw this one up. Don't let your guard down on yourself for a minute, or you'll drive him away.* I could feel the muscles in my neck tensing as we got back to John's car.

When we got inside, he gave me a nuzzle and a quick kiss before we started. I began to drift off. But scary thoughts about screwing up plagued me even in my semi-conscious state.

Why can't you just enjoy the moment like a normal woman, forgodsakes? You just got engaged to a wonder- ful man who loves you.

The voice again: *But how do you know that he really does love you? What about his fondness…Is that what you call it?…for Li Li? Maybe he really wants a sweet-talking, manipulative young—C'mon, you're not that old, Marabella—thing who thinks he's a god?*

"Marabella? Earth to Marabella?"

"Huh?"

John laughed. "You were dead asleep, snoring up a storm."

"I don't snore. Anyway, I was just resting my eyes a moment."

"You rested them all the way home. We're back at your apartment." He parked and turned to me with a wonderfully tender leer. "How about if we go upstairs and…"

"I'd love to." *Oh, God. My mother.* "But I have to get up at the crack of dawn. I was supposed to finish a publicity piece yesterday, but…" I raised my palms in a "What can you do?" gesture.

He looked disappointed. "Well, hopefully this weekend?"

I nodded and tried to think fast about someplace that wasn't my apartment. We couldn't go to his house all the time. I still had images of the war between Zilla and the Marx Brothers. "How about that lovely inn in the Hudson Valley?"

"Sounds fine to me. But what about Zilla?"

Aarrggh. If it wasn't one of my roommates causing a problem, it was the other one. "I know, I'll ask Carmen if Zilla can have a sleepover at her house. She loves cats. She already has two." I pushed away the memory of Zilla terrorizing Carmen's cats during the last animal sleepover party. Maybe Zilla would behave this time. Ha! Better hope that her cats have toughened up.

He looked doubtful. "Are you sure it will work out?"

Depends on your definition of "work out." I crossed my fingers and tried not to look him in the eye. "I don't see why not," I said, getting out of the car and blowing him a kiss.

Chapter 48

My next meeting was with Tamar Lipson, Jeremy-the-lech's wife. We arranged to get together at Bloomingdale's luncheon cafe. Tamar was going to be there for one of her high-end shopping trips. She staggered in, toting a hefty Bloomie's bag in each hand, clutching a purse made from what looked like a dead reptile, and wearing an extremely low-cut silver silk top and matching skin-tight pants. She probably thought they made her skinny body look good. She was wrong. I waved her over, wondering how she was going to navigate the seat without ending up bare-assed.

"Shopping is so exhausting these days." She shook her highlighted and low-lighted blonde head, plunked down the bags and inched her way into the seat across from me. "Nobody has any decent help anymore, I swear."

"Whatever happened to the word 'service' in customer service?" I murmured.

"Only another woman could understand." She waved silver false nails in the air.

"Nice manicure," I said.

"It should be, for one hundred dollars a hand," she drawled, arching her eyebrows, plucked within an inch of their life.

"Twenty dollars a finger, not too bad," I said.

We both ordered the salad of the day. Even though she looked as if she lived on a grain of rice a day. She must have thought there was no such thing as too scrawny. And that, hopefully, would give me a good segue into the world of medicine. I ordered my usual tea and picked up a couple of Splendas.

"Wow!" I said, after the wait person brought our drinks back to the table. "How do you manage to keep so slim?" Catch flies with honey, my mother always said.

I swear if Tamar were a peacock, she'd be displaying her feathers. She smirked and preened. "Oh, thanks. Yes, I work at it, every day. With my personal trainer. He's *wonnnderful.*"

Obviously, customer "service" (serviced?) still existed in some quarters. "What's his name? Just in case," I said, pointing to my hips, "I ever get around to really working out."

"Ricarrrdo," she breathed.

Time to get to work. On Tamar. "Well, I really admire your dedication to fitness." I tried to keep a straight face. "You know, staying healthy is so important. My cousin," I lied, "was a real couch potato, ate like a pig, never exercised."

She shook her head. "Bad, bad."

"You're not kidding. She ended up in the hospital with a heart attack, at forty-five."

Tamar clucked.

"And I think being in the hospital was what finished her off."

She stopped sipping her coffee. "Oh, what happened?"

I shook my head. "Nobody knows. Neglect, maybe. You know how some of those nurses are, actually, not even nurses. They're aides. You should see these people. Sometimes, I think they're barely functioning."

She looked indignant. "Hey, that's not necessarily the case. I did that job for a whole summer during college, and, I must say, I was very conscientious, very good to my patients." She added, "Our sorority had a community service component and I picked hospital work."

I tried to look apologetic. "I'm sure you were good to your patients," I soothed. "And you must have learned a lot about medical care there, too."

She perked up. "I sure did."

"What kinds of things did they have you do, anyway?" I added quickly, "My friend's daughter—" Another lie. "—is starting college and needs a summer job. Maybe this kind of job is for her."

"Oh, lots of things. Let's see. Well, of course, the everyday things, like bathing the patients, helping them in and out of bed, things like that."

I frowned. "I don't know how interesting that would be for Claudia. Did you get to see any interesting procedures, operations, stuff like that?"

She finished her drink and sucked on the straw. "Well, not actual operations, we weren't allowed in the OR. But—" She licked the spoon."—I was sometimes in patients' rooms when they were being intubated. That means hooking them up to a tube, usually through an IV. That means intravenous, in case you didn't know." A superior smile.

Well, actually, I did, you twit. "Wow!" I pretended to be impressed. "You sound like you really know your way around a hospital."

She beamed. "My father was chairman of the board of our local hospital and my mother was a hospital volunteer. She took me around with her sometimes, and I could see how she made the patients feel better. When I got older, I even thought about maybe being a doctor. But—" She shrugged. "—I got married to one, and had kids."

"Well, your—and Jeremy's—medical knowledge could certainly come in handy in an emergency, right?"

She narrowed her eyes. "What kind of emergency?"

"You never know. Anyway, we need to talk about the money from Sam's investment in bearer bonds."

She brightened immediately. Amazing what a little mention of money did for this greedy bunch. It almost made me grateful for my own family. Almost. Come to think of it, a will was the cause of big problems in my family, too.

We didn't see much of my family when I was growing up, since at any given time, one group was not talking to any of the rest. What made it even worse was that we all lived in the same neighborhood in Forest Hills, Queens. Imagine your parents dragging you across the street when you ran into your aunt or uncle. The longest feud had been over my grandparents' will. Big surprise. Did any family ever think a will was fair?

Tamar was leaning forward in her seat and asking me a question. "So, how much are we talking about?"

"Um, about a million dollars."

"Divided four ways, that's two hundred fifty thousand each. To the heirs." She blew out a breath.

I dug my notebook and pen out of my briefcase and tapped my teeth with my pen—shades of my mother!—pretending to think. "Well, I was thinking about various charities I know Sam cared about."

Sheer fury filled her face. "You have no right! Who do you think you are, anyway? God?"

I tried to calm her down. "Listen, Tamar, I'm just trying to carry out what I know were Sam's wishes, that's all. I know he didn't want to play favorites here."

She was shaking and, I swear, smoke was coming out of her nose. "Bullshit! Nobody's talking about playing favorites! I'm talking about playing fair with what we're entitled to!"

"Take it easy," I said, which seemed to make her even angrier. I was worried that she'd have a stroke. I hoped she didn't have high blood pressure.

Sure enough, she dug through her purse, which I realized was snakeskin—the very thought was making me ill—and fished out a bottle of pills, swallowing one dry. It took a few moments, but her color seemed a little better. She was still glaring.

I reached for her hand. "Tamar, I haven't made any decision about this yet. The money from the bonds is sitting in a safe deposit box at a bank. It's not going anywhere right now. Why don't you get together with the others and discuss what you think should be done with the money?"

She snatched her hand away, looking at it as if she'd been stabbed, then gathered her shopping bags and stood up. "That's a thought. And you'll let me—us—know what you're going to do."

I nodded. "I'll be in touch."

She marched out, clutching her bags so tightly I could see her knuckles turning white. That was one angry lady. Angry enough to kill?

Chapter 49

After my mother and I finished the moo shu pork and garlic green beans I'd picked up after work, Miriam Kravitz called me about the autopsy results on her sister. Just as we thought: Rose had been murdered.

"The bastard killed my sister!" Miriam said, her voice shaking. "She was smothered to death! They found out because of the blood that collected in her eyes and other places, when my sister was struggling to breathe." She let out a sob.

"Miriam, at least now we know. And we, I mean, the cops, will get him for sure. He, or she, won't get away with it. They probably disguised themselves in a nurse's or another kind of hospital uniform and were able to sneak by the nursing staff."

Miriam was quiet for a moment. "Marabella, there is no 'we' here. You have to leave this to the police, understand?"

"Right." I crossed my fingers behind my back. Did I think she could see through the phone?

"Marabella, I mean it!"

I guess she could. The magic powers of senior citizens. Or admirals. Fingers still crossed, I said, "Yes, yes,

I promise." Eager to get her off the subject of me, I said, "Did Rivera tell you what happens next?"

"He's opening a homicide investigation."

At last. Be careful, don't sound too gung-ho. Or she'll be suspicious and realize I have no intention of leaving the investigation solely in Rivera's ham hands. "Good. It's about time he got on the trail."

"Damn straight. Thanks to my son."

And thanks to the power of the admiral over her ADA son. "Bless your son," I said. Then I thought, why not strike while the admiral was hot? "Miriam, do you think we can get Rivera to investigate Sam's death?"

"Now that we know about—" Her voice caught. "Rose."

"Yes. We know it was the same person. For the same motive. Money."

Her voice had regained its full force. "Of course! The bastard!"

"Okay. I'll go see Rivera tomorrow." I'd be looking forward to it about as much as he'd enjoy it.

"Marabella, if you run into trouble with that lieutenant…"

Ha! When *didn't* I have trouble with him? "Yes?"

"Then I'll call my son."

We promised to keep in touch and said goodbye. As soon as I hung up, my mother was on the alert.

"Okay, from the top."

Was she channeling Rivera? I didn't need two of them, thank you. I joined her on the sofa. "Please find another way to ask me things. As it happens, I'm planning to see 'Mr. From the Top' himself tomorrow."

"Good. I'm glad you're finally leaving things to the professionals. Now tell me what the story is. Please," she said, trying to ingratiate herself to make up for the Rivera impersonation, I guess.

I briefed her on the results of Rose Adelman's autopsy. "I think this proves that Sam was murdered, too, by the same person. Who also killed poor Lucy."

"And who also tried to kill my only daughter," she said, giving me a hug. "Which he would have to do over my dead body."

I was not going to try to process that one. I hugged her back carefully. I could feel her ribs through the pink striped tee-shirt and I didn't want to hurt her. "Ma, you've got to eat more, keep up your strength. You're getting much too thin. This is not good."

She waved her arm dismissively. "I'm fine, sweetheart. Don't you worry about me."

I frowned. Then I tried to joke. "If you're on some kind of crazy diet—what do they feed you up there? Or do they?" I pointed to the ceiling.

She chuckled and changed the subject. "Believe me, you don't want to know. How are you going to talk Rivera into investigating Sam's and Lucy's murders? Somehow, I don't think he'll be taken in by your charms, great as they may be." She smoothed down the pillows she was leaning against.

My charms? Rivera? "Damn straight."

"Please don't swear," my mother said.

"Sorry," I mumbled. I could always count on my mother's wonderful sense of propriety.

"There's nothing wrong with acting like a lady. People will have more respect for you."

"People like Rivera?" I raised my eyebrows. He wouldn't even acknowledge that I might have one teensy, weensy, good idea. About anything.

She nodded. "Even him."

I shrugged. "Fine. Speaking of unpleasant encounters, I have to make an appointment with Sam's brother, David." I thought about what I knew about David as I picked up the list with his phone number. Wife Cheryl, no kids, lived in Glen Cove, Long Island. Executive in a software company. Saddled with bills from Cheryl being in (Was she back in, these days?) and out of rehab for prescription painkiller addiction.

Most of Sam's half-siblings seemed to be victims of problems of their own, or their spouses', making. And these problems all involved a need for money. Big money. Jeremy, with two mistresses—that still blew my mind—and an uber-materialistic wife. Abby, with an alcoholic husband who couldn't keep a job. And David, with an addict wife.

I hoped Jennifer would make a wiser choice in mates than her relatives had. Come to think of it, what did I know about her boyfriend, Mark, was it? Just that he and Jennifer worked in administration in the same health care company, the largest one in New York City. And, as far as I knew, they weren't living together yet. Maybe I'd better ask my mother to check the boyfriend out.

"Be happy to, sweetheart. Let's just see if this young man is on the up-and-up," said the mind-reader.

"And if he's good enough for Jennifer. Such a sweet, caring girl." I'd have to stop thinking of her as a girl, a holdover from when Sam first introduced us years ago. She was a bright young woman, obviously doing very well at her job, since she'd recently had a promotion. Sam was always so proud of her. I could feel my eyes well up. I really missed Sam.

"Me, too." My mother sighed.

"Then please try to stay off my case about tracking down Sam's killer. Okay?"

"I'll try." She lay back against the sofa pillows.

Zilla trotted into the room. I got up off the sofa end, gave him a mock curtsy, and waved my arm toward my place on the sofa. "I even warmed it up for you. It's all yours, buster." I grabbed my cell and went into the bedroom to call David.

When he answered and I told him who I was, there was silence. "Hello?" I said.

"I'm here. What do you want?" An exasperated tone.

Mr. Nice Guy. Maybe that's what drove Cheryl to the pills. "So sorry to bother you, Mr. Lipschitz."

"Get-to-the-point. I haven't got all night."

Grrrr. *Deep breaths, Marabella. You're on a mission, remember? You knew what these people were like, right? So keep your cool and don't let them get to you.* "Sorry. I'd like to meet with you and your wife to discuss the disposal of some extra money Sam had that wasn't in the will."

Silence again. He cleared his throat. "My wife is not available at this time. But that shouldn't be a problem. Just how much are we talking about here?"

"Well…" I said, drawing it out to make him sweat, "it looks like another million. It's from bearer bonds your brother collected years ago and seemed to have forgotten to put in the will."

The voice got warmer. "Hmm. That's an extra two hundred fifty thousand dollars for each of the heirs."

"Um, not necessarily."

The voice turned chilly. "What do you mean by 'not necessarily'?"

"Well, that's why I wanted to meet with you and your—"

"Never mind about Cheryl. She doesn't have a say in this." Irritation again. "What do you mean about 'not necessarily'?"

"It's up to me to decide how to disperse this money, since there were no specific instructions. And the fact that I'm the executor."

"The executor? But you just said this wasn't part of the will. You're just the executor of the will." A note of smug satisfaction.

"That's not the whole story. Sam also specified that I should handle whatever other things needed to be taken care of."

"Forgodsakes! Why is there more and more of this nonsense from you? Why the hell would my brother pick somebody like you to take care of his affairs?" I could hear him huffing, practically snorting, into the phone. I was feeling sorry for Cheryl.

Now I had him going. "Mr. Lipschitz, Sam didn't want to play favorites with his family. And he knew that I would be fair and responsible about his affairs."

Silence again.

"So, I'd like to set up a meeting with you to discuss all this. At your convenience, of course." My voice dripped honey.

An aggravated *hmmmfff.* "I guess I don't have a choice."

Right you are, Mr. Lipschitz.

We set up a time and place. As I started to say, "Goodbye," he slammed the phone down in my ear.

Chapter 50

Rivera was quite a sight in a mustard-colored jacket, blue checked shirt, and gray pants. I wondered if his wife was visually impaired or if he picked out his unique outfits. Or maybe he was color-blind.

"Are you color-blind, by any chance?" I asked, as I sat down on the chair on the other side of his desk.

"Huh?" He yawned and looked at me as if I'd asked him directions to the moon. Obviously, he was totally unaware of his wardrobe disability, for whatever reason. Taking a gulp of his decaf soda and making his usual face, he pulled out his notebook and a pen.

This time, I beat him to it. "Okay, from the top." I grinned.

Rivera was not amused. "You think this is a comedy show? Stop wasting my time. So, fr—let's go," he said, glowering.

"Sorry," I said, not meaning it at all but not wanting to antagonize him further. Or I could kiss any hope of an investigation into Sam's death, correction, *murder,* goodbye.

"Let's have it. *Now.*" Another yawn.

Resisting the urge to salute or say something sarcastic, I said, "I'm glad that you were able to find out what caused Rose Adelman's death. Thank you."

He nodded, pen poised over the notebook. "And? You didn't come here just to thank me for doing my job. So what is it now?"

He leaned forward in his chair, his expression this side of aggravated, bordering on angry.

I was not anxious to beard an angry Rivera in his den, so to speak. "Um," I started, instantly intimidated. Why did he always have this effect on me? I was a tough, strong Vinegar woman, wasn't I? Not easily intimidated, right? I took a couple of deep breaths. In and out. I could see him giving me a strange look.

"Are you summoning up a spirit?" He snorted. "Calling a lifeline?"

I cleared my throat. "Since you've now established that Rose Adelman was murdered, you must realize that she was only murdered because Sam Lipschitz's killer thought she saw something. I mean, why else would somebody kill her? So…"

He interrupted. "So you want to know if we're investigating Mr. Lipschitz's death."

"Right. You know there was a lot of money involved, and Sam's relatives have money problems. In addition to their other problems. And they're not…not nice people." I lifted my chin and looked him in the eye.

"Ms. Vinegar, not being a nice person isn't a crime. If that were the case, you'd be…" He smirked.

I stood up, furious. "Obviously, I've been wasting my time, trying to get any help from you."

He laughed. "Wait. I hate to give you the satisfaction, but we've already begun an investigation into Mr. Lipschitz's death. The body is scheduled for an exhumation this week. We're not exactly dumb, you know."

I could have cried with relief. "Thank you. But why did it take so long?"

He sighed. "I know you think you know how we should be doing things."

"I…"

"The family wouldn't give us permission for an exhumation. And we had no cause to do so until we had the results on Mrs. Adelman. So, now we're able to proceed. So…" Yawn. "…that's it. Now, I've got work to do." He got up from his chair and waved me toward the door.

"Thank you," I said, meaning it, as I walked out of his office.

"Just doing my job," he mumbled, dropping wearily back into his chair.

He always looked so tired, I was beginning to feel sorry for him. But not *too* sorry.

Chapter 51

I hid my brand-new, old-style engagement ring from my mother's prying eyes, though I knew she'd have to know sooner or later. I slipped it on when I got to work, trying not to be self-conscious. After all, I'd always claimed not to want diamonds as my best friend. But this was John and me. And it was truly a lovely, old-fashioned, beautiful piece of jewelry.

I still could hardly believe it. Somehow, I'd managed to be in a relationship without screwing it up. So far. When, I wondered, would I ever be able to trust myself not to self-destruct? Hopefully—

"Woo hoo! Look at the rock!" Carmen said.

"Um, it's not really…"

She dragged me over to Susan to inspect my left hand. "Oh! It's so lovely!" Susan said.

I ducked my head. "Thanks."

Carmen proceeded to haul me around to the other departments on our floor, showing my ring off as if it were the crown jewels, to much oohing and ahhing. And congratulations. And, "When's the wedding?"

All of which I responded to with "Thanks" or "Um."

Carmen gave me a friendly swat on the arm. "Could you believe this girl? She gets engaged to this hunky doctor." She pretended to do some heavy breathing and I felt my face getting warm. "And she doesn't even want to show us the rock, let alone brag about it."

"Carmen, please. I appreciate all the good wishes, but…"

She shook her head and lifted her arms in a, "What can you do?" pose. "Okay, girls, see you all later."

"Thanks," I muttered, and scurried back to my office, Carmen in my wake.

"So. Did you set a date?"

Aarrggh. "Carmen, I haven't even—" Oops. I stuffed the words, "told my mother yet," back into my mouth.

She fixed me with a look. "Haven't even what? By the way, is he great in bed?"

"Carmen!" I felt my face getting hot.

She had the nerve to look abashed. "Okay, okay. I know, you like your privacy," she muttered. "But sometimes, it's a little much. Okay, so what was it that you haven't…whatever?"

So much for distractions. Think, Marabella. "Um," I said, frantically trying to come up with something plausible.

She stared me down, pulling on a thread of her green and white sweater. I wondered how many sweaters she'd unraveled since she quit smoking. Well, losing a couple of sweaters was a lot better than losing your lungs to cigarettes. I had to come up with an answer. Finally, I had it.

"I haven't even met John's parents yet." I went over to my desk, which had a pile of messages. "Got to take care of these. See you later."

The messages were from Professor Newsome, aka Nuisance; the dean of admissions; a guy in the computer services department; one of the counselors from our community substance abuse program; and John, my f— fiancé. My mind stuttered on the word fiancé.

Of course I called John first. He sounded less stressed out than usual. Since the recent—unmourned by practically every female on campus—departure of Li Li, John had had to depend on interns for help in his veterinary assistant program, most of whom turned out to be less than helpful, due to: conflict with class schedules, conflict with part-time jobs, conflict with girlfriends' or boyfriends' schedules, allergies to animals. What someone allergic to animals was doing in a veterinary technician program I couldn't fathom. Maybe he (or she) planned to only deal with the hairless ones.

"I'm glad you're sounding better," I said to John.

"I've finally got a new assistant director." His voice was full of relief.

I, on the other hand, was full of angst. I didn't think I could cope with another version of Li Li. I missed the first part of what he was saying. "I'm sorry, I was distracted. What did you just say?"

He laughed. "You always distract *me*. It's a wonder I get any work done after hearing your voice. Anyway, he'll be here in a few days. I can't wait. I'm swamped."

He? Thank you, God. "I'm so happy for you," I said. And for me.

"So, let's celebrate. How about a close encounter at your place tonight?" He made lascivious sounds.

I bit a cuticle. Here we go again. I was afraid the moment had finally come when I'd have to tell him about my mother. But what to tell him? My mother's ghost has taken up residence on my living room sofa? So not only is the sofa occupied, but I can't make love to you in my bedroom with my ghost-mother in the other room. He'd think I was crazy, hallucinating, or hiding something even worse…even worse than a ghost-mother?…like another man. And what do I tell him about why she'd come back? He'd be livid about my chasing down a killer. Again.

"Marabella? Are you still there?"

I cleared my throat. "Um, John, um, we need to talk."

I heard a sharp intake of breath. Then silence.

"Don't worry, there's nothing to worry about. Nothing's changed between us."

He gave a nervous laugh. "Whew. You scared me there for a minute. I know you've been a little jittery about a commitment, but…"

A little? "Believe me, it's got nothing to do with us. I'll try to explain when I see you this afternoon. But can we make it at that little park a few blocks down from the campus? Please? This isn't easy for me."

His voice was reassuring. "Don't worry. Whatever it is, we can deal with this together. I promise. Okay? See you around five-thirty."

"Thanks." I realized I was already hyperventilating and our encounter was eight hours away. If it got any worse, I'd have to find a paper bag and breathe into it, in the ladies' room. Hoping that no one figured out what the strange noises were coming from one of the stalls.

Chapter 52

I didn't hyperventilate. I threw up instead. Twice. The second time, Carmen followed me into the ladies' room and had the nerve to ask me if I was pregnant. "Not even a little bit," I said.

She snickered. "You know, there's no such thing as a 'little bit' pregnant. You either are or you're not."

"Definitely not," I said, washing my face and rinsing out my mouth.

"Then what's going on? Are you sick? Maybe you should go home. Do you want me to tell Susan?"

I knew her questions were only because she cared, but it was still annoying. "Carmen, it's just nerves."

"Oh, I get it. Pre-wedding jitters, huh?"

I nodded, not a great idea, since my stomach was still queasy.

I figured pre-wedding nerves was about as good an explanation as any. Certainly better than the real story. Anything was better than that .I bit a cuticle as we walked out of the ladies' room and back to the office.

This was a good time to change the subject. "Guess what," I said, in a low voice, so we hopefully wouldn't be overheard by every unattached female on the floor. "Good news for, ahem, single women."

Carmen's eyes got bright and she leaned closer to me. "What? What?"

I hesitated for a moment, thoughts of teasing her, getting even with her interrogation about my intestinal distress, ran through my brain. Just for a moment, though. "John's hired a new assistant. *He'll* be here in a few days." I grinned.

She pretended to lick her chops. "Woo hoo. Let's see, what kind of excuse I can use to sashay down to John's lab after his assistant gets here."

Happy to get her mind off my stomach, I said, "I know. I'll tell John we'd like to meet his new guy to welcome him to the campus. And that we'd like to buy him coffee in the cafeteria."

"Or even better, how about dinner, a nice romantic dinner?"

"Carmen, you—we—don't even know this man. We don't know what he looks like or acts like. He could be a troll, for all we know. Or a total nerd, who only relates to creatures with four feet or no feet. Remember, he's a lab geek." But wait a minute, my fiancé, the farthest thing from a troll or a geek, spent a lot of time in a lab.

Which was exactly what Carmen reminded me. Then she sighed. "Okay, lunch, then. And if he's a troll, it'll be a very quick one for this single woman."

Chapter 53

As I left the office, I was wavering between another bout of nausea and a fit of hyperventilation. *Is this what's called a rock and a hard place? Hold it in or breathe it out? Aarrggh. Okay, try to calm down, Marabella. It's just John. Right. And it's just trying to explain about my mother-the-ghost to him. Right.* I'd be lucky if he didn't cart me off to the loony bin. Call a psychiatrist. At the very least, ask what I've been smoking, drinking, sniffing, shooting up? Treat me like a…what?

I was terrified of losing him. Scared out of my wits, in fact. I couldn't remember being this scared since…since the last time someone tried to kill me. That was another thing. He'd have to know why my mother decided to come back. *No, John, I'm afraid it wasn't just a friendly visit, like, "I really missed my daughter, so I flitted back to see her." Actually, John, she came back because, as she'd put it, "Where else should I be when my only daughter's friends are being murdered? And my daughter herself is in mortal danger?"*

Should I try to convince him she was just a hallucination? That I didn't really believe she was there? Well, that would make me out to be totally bonkers, right? I sighed. This was truly a lose-lose situation if I ever saw one.

Then there was the subject of the conversation: my mother herself. Would she decide to materialize and speak to someone besides me and Zilla? Was she able to do that? Would she even cooperate, if she could? Or would she just be obstinate, deciding not to reveal herself to John?

I was having a hard time making myself get to the park. I was seized with an overwhelming desire to dash home and call John, pleading a stomach virus. Which at this point, was almost true. My stomach hadn't felt this quivery since the night I ate too much of my mother's infamous chopped liver when I was six years old.

But I had to soldier on. I loved John, and I knew I couldn't keep this from him any longer. There was just no other way. Besides, I didn't think it was a good idea to start married life—married life!—with a secret. Especially such an enormous secret. Not that my mother was that big anymore. In fact, she seemed to be getting more frail. But she was a big part of my life now. Well, at least she seemed to be always there when I needed her. So I guess it was: love me, love my mother-ghost?

I dragged myself to the park, where John was already sitting on a bench. Looking apprehensive. But yummy. He was wearing a dark jacket, striped shirt, and dark pants. I could have eaten him up. But he was giving off such nervous vibes, poor guy. *Just wait till you hear what I've got to tell you. Nervous won't begin to describe it.*

I tried to smile at him as I sat down next to him. Then I took his hand.

He looked down at my left hand and took a deep breath. "Well, at least you're still wearing the ring. Marabella, whatever it is, I'm sure it's not as bad as you think."

Ha! That's what you think. "John, first of all, please know that I love you very much."

"Uh-oh."

"No, please. This has nothing to do with us, believe me. Well, maybe just a little." I could swear his ears pricked up. "It's okay, boy," I soothed, patting his hand.

He laughed. "Okay, let's have it."

Fortunately for me, a woman with a baby in a stroller came by and I got a short breather. Then a man with two large dogs, which distracted John, but made me nervous. Unfortunately, they—the man, that was—chose to sit on a bench across from us. The dogs sat on the grass in front of him. When they opened their mouths, I could see they had very large teeth. The better to eat me with.

John regarded the dogs, captivated. "Cute, aren't they?"

I forced myself not to shudder.

Fortunately, they didn't stay long. John turned to me, a worried look on his face. "What did you want to, uh, talk about?"

I began. "Remember our first date?"

A warm smile came over his face and he gave me a hug. "Of course."

"*Wellll*, you asked me about my mother."

He looked puzzled.

"I told you she'd just died of congestive heart failure."

He nodded.

"Um, well, that wasn't exactly the case. About my mother, I mean."

"What do you mean? Is she still living? Was it one of those near-death experiences?"

I shook my head. "No and no. Um, she…she came back."

He stared. "What? What do you mean, she came back? Came back from where?"

I looked down at the grass, now populated by a couple of pigeons and a squirrel, as if it was the most fascinating scene on earth. "She came back from…wherever people go when they die," I whispered, looking up at him.

He just stared.

"I know, I know, you think I'm making this up, or having hallucinations."

He nodded. "Or…"

"Believe me, I'm not making it up, or hallucinating or going crazy. Well, maybe sometimes I act a little funny, but I'm not a full-fledged nutcase or anything." I grabbed his hand again.

He shook his head and smiled. "Okay, I get it. You're just teasing me, right? That's okay. I can deal with it."

I sighed. "I wish I were."

The smile left his face. Now he looked serious. "Marabella, what am I supposed to think?"

I took a couple of deep breaths. In and out. Then I plunged in and got the whole story out, starting with my mother appearing the night of Dr. Ditstein's murder and bringing him almost, but not quite, up-to-date. His face went from disbelief to shock. Then I said, "I bet you were wishing I told you I was a gambler, a compulsive shopper, a drug addict, a klepto."

He just sat there, looking numb. Then he seemed to get his wits together. "I don't care whether your mother is a hallucination or whatever. That can wait. But if she— your mother—appears when you're in trouble, then what kind of trouble have you been getting yourself into now, forgodsakes? "

"You sound like Rivera. I'm not a wayward child," I said. But I could see the wheels turning in his handsome, curly head.

"Oh, no! Don't tell me you're chasing down another killer!"

"Shhh, not so loud." I could see people who were passing by staring at us. "Let's get out of here."

"Right." He got up, pulling me up alongside him. "Okay, now what?"

"Let's just walk and I'll try to explain." I squeezed his arm lovingly.

He shook off my hand, folded his arms, and planted his feet, not moving an inch. "Okay, explain."

Breathe, Marabella, deep breaths. "John, I couldn't just sit by and do nothing while three people I cared about were murdered, could I?"

"*Three?*"

I realized he didn't know about poor Lucy, so I told him.

He looked even more horrified than before. "*Three* people were killed and you want to play *detective*? Are you *crazy*?"

"You sound just like Rivera."

He tightened his arms across his chest. "Good. Rivera knows what he's talking about. Let him handle it." He looked at me. "You *have* talked to him about all this, haven't you, I hope?"

I nodded. "Yes, but..."

"But what?"

"Let's go back and sit down and I'll go through the whole thing."

We walked back to the park. The bench we'd been on was vacant. We sat down and he put his arm around me I figured I better start from the beginning. So I did. About Rose; Miriam and her son, the ADA; Lucy; the exhumation and autopsy on Rose; the investigation into Sam's death.

When I described Miriam, he said, "She sounds like a real pistol," with admiration in his voice.

"Wait till you meet her. They don't call her the admiral for nothing. But why should I do any less than a seventy-something-year-old woman?" I said.

"Because I love you and want to keep you around."

"Good," I said. When I got to my stint as a wait person at the Goldfarbs' grandson's bar mitzvah, he started to laugh. But when I related my meetings with the relatives, using pretend money and myself as bait, he stopped laughing.

John pulled me close. "I'm afraid of losing you. I don't want you putting yourself in danger. Please, for me."

I snuggled up against him. "I promise I'll be very careful."

He turned to me. "And just how are you going to be able to do that when you're risking your life?"

Trying to lighten things up, I said, "Well, maybe my mother could turn me into a cat so I'd have nine."

He shook his head. "Not funny. Hey, wait a minute. Don't tell me your...mother...is a witch, too? Besides being a..."

"That was a joke. She's just a visiting ghost, who comes back when there's trouble. That's all. No biggie." Like this was a simple explanation, for something that bore no relationship to simple. Or logical. Or even sane. And if I was now seeing it as normal or nothing special, what was wrong with me?

John put his head in his hands and muttered, "No biggie. A visiting ghost, no biggie."

I patted his shoulder. "John, dear, I think you should come home with me and meet my mother. She's actually very…" Very what? Interesting? Nice? Smart? Funny?

He picked his head up and stared at me. "Of course. Why not? No biggie, right?"

Chapter 54

My mother was glaring at Zilla, who was batting the pages of her newspaper, when John and I walked into my apartment. Of course, all John could see was Zilla.

"Hey, you two, cut it out. I thought you smoked the pipe," I said, frowning at both of them.

John just stood there, staring at Zilla and the sofa and back to me. "Marabella, there's nobody…"

Oh, boy. Now I had to convince my mother to materialize, or John would think I was even crazier than he already did. But how? Then it came to me: make her feel important. "Ma, this is John. My fiancé. I'm going to marry him. And I need your blessing, your approval. So please, let John see you. And hear you. You'll like him. He's a wonderful man, who loves me, and I love him." I was babbling, so nervous I realized my body was shaking. *This is do or die, Marabella.* I winced. Not a good description.

Then I waited. And looked at John. At my mother. And John.

He looked dazed, as if he couldn't believe the situation he was in. "What kind of weird family am I marrying into?"

That did it. "A very good one, young man," my mother said, sitting up against the pillows.

John's eyes rolled back in his head. I tried to catch him as he fell over.

Chapter 55

After I rubbed John's forehead with a cold, wet washcloth, which reminded me of my first encounter with one of his Marx Brothers, he sat up. "How did I get here? What am I doing on the floor?" He looked dazed.

I bent down and kissed him. "Looks like you fainted, dear. From shock." When I helped him up, his legs were wobbly, so I guided him into a chair.

"Shock." He gazed around the living room. My mother had put on her bifocals and was shaking her head at something in the newspaper, while Zilla kept hitting the pages.

"For shame, what people do to each other. Murder, mayhem. Tch, tch."

He looked terrified. "Oh, God. Now I remember." He turned to me, deliberately avoiding looking in my mother's direction. "It's…"

"My mother." I said. This was not going to be easy.

He whispered, "Is she really…"

"Yes. She came back to help me."

"Of course." My mother folded her arms across her bosom. "Where else should a mother be when her daughter needs her?"

He shivered violently. I wished I had one of those Thunder shirts they advertise on TV, to calm your dog down during thunderstorms or other crises. I put my arms around him instead. "It's okay, boy. She won't hurt you," I said.

She grinned. "I don't bite."

He shivered again, just as violently.

Since I didn't have anything alcoholic to drink, and I didn't think tea or cocoa would do it, I suggested that we go out to the nearest bar for drinks.

"Yes!" He made for the door so fast, I was afraid he'd crash into it. I followed him out and into the elevator.

I couldn't blame him. If he still wanted to marry me after this, he deserved a medal. Two medals. And a really good meal. Not one that I'd cook, of course. I'd treat him to a great dinner after drinks. That was, if he still had an appetite. On second thought, maybe we'd be better off just drinking the night away.

But wait. What was it about getting back on the horse after you fall off? Maybe he needed to be around my mother again, right away, so he'd get used to her?

A voice in my head said: *Marabella, do you want the man to have a heart attack?*

Small doses, okay, tiny doses, of my mother at a time would be much more sensible. And much more healthy for John.

I held his hand tight as we walked to the corner bar, afraid he wasn't too steady on his feet, since his face still wore the same dazed expression. Poor guy. Maybe I've scared him off, maybe he'll run as far as he can, maybe he'll have me committed. Aarrgh.

It was all my mother's fault. Just like when I was a teenager and she scared off my boyfriends. They ended up being afraid to come near me after she gave them dire warnings about what would happen if they ever deflowered her pure-as-the-driven daughter. Of course, she didn't say, "deflowered." I think "took advantage of" was the expression she'd used. And of course, she'd had no idea that I was only 99 44/100 percent pure.

But I couldn't blame her presence now, could I? Only I wished she hadn't been quite so much of a presence around John.

We found a more-or-less quiet spot at the back end of the bar. John ordered a double scotch for himself, and I ordered a regular one, damn the torpedoes. This was a genuine emergency. I waved away the warnings inside my head about throwing up, passing out or other assorted disasters. *Bite the bullet, Marabella.*

John drained his glass before I could venture to take a sip of mine, and ordered another. I knew he was not a real drinker and I hoped *he* wouldn't get sick, pass out or whatever.

After he finished the second drink, he said, "I think I need a couple of those deep breaths of yours. How do you do that, anyway?"

I showed him. Soon we were deep breathing in unison. Then I started giggling. "Sorry, it's just so…" I said, with a snort.

He started laughing, too. "Strange? Weird? You've got to admit," he said, between laughs, "this was something that was…"

I couldn't stop laughing. And snorting. "Out of this world, so to—" Giggle. "—speak?"

He could hardly talk, he was laughing so hard. Then he got serious. "You know," he said, trying hard to stifle a laugh, "I think I need some time to get used to…"

I knew it, I knew it. He was backing out, running for the hills. I stuck out my left hand. "If you want to break it off, I understand, believe me." I gulped, trying not to cry.

He covered my hand with his. "No, no. Just give me a little time to digest all this. I mean, it's not every day that you get to meet your future…uh…ghost-in-law."

Chapter 56

The next morning at work, Carmen grabbed me before I could get into my office.

"He's *here*," she hissed in my ear.

Since my mind was definitely elsewhere, mainly on John and my mother, I didn't tune in right away. "Huh? Who?"

"*Himmm.*" She licked her lips and ran her hands down the sides of her aqua sweater and short black skirt. To further illustrate the point, she made crude slurping sounds.

"Carmen!"

She chortled. "Can't help it, Marabella. I got a peek at John's new assistant. Whew, whatta gorgeous hunk! I sure wouldn't kick *that* one outta bed in a hurry."

"Well, I'm just glad it's not another Li Li," I said, walking into my office and noting the pile of messages littering my desk.

Carmen hummed as she started back to her office. I think it was "The Man I Love." I knew she was lonely, but…"Carmen," I said to her back, "just be careful, okay?"

She turned and flashed me a grin. She had a beautiful smile, inherited, she told me, from her dad's side of the family. "Don't worry, Bella. I'm a big girl. I can take care of myself."

I wasn't so sure. She was so impulsive, especially where men were concerned. She'd married her ex a month after she'd met him on a blind date. And look where that had gotten her. She loved her kids and she was a good mother. But she didn't love the miserable child support she got and that she and the kids had to move in with her mother. Not to mention the emotional scars she still had from his verbal abuse.

I plowed through my messages. Oh, no, another complaint from Professor Nuisance. Now what? I sighed, picked up the phone, and punched in her extension. She was sputtering so loud, I had to hold the phone away from my ear.

"I'm going to the dean about this!" she shouted.

"Professor Newsome, please, try to calm down."

That sent her into a bigger rage. "Don't you tell *me* to calm down, you little twit!"

Deep breaths. I knew that if I didn't address her as "professor" at every turn, it would make her even crazier. "Sorry, Professor. Could you tell me what the problem is?"

Sputter, sputter. "Your *boss* is being sent to the conference on educational psychology instead of *me*. It's outrageous!"

Ah. That was the cause of Nuisance's latest eruption against Susan. "Professor Newsome, I think the reason was that Ms. Davies is writing her doctoral thesis on educational psychology in the community college. So the dean probably figured she could benefit from the seminars at the conference." And I figured I needed to tone it down by acting as if Susan needed the help. But I'd forgotten about Nuisance's jealousy and bigotry about anything Susan achieved, especially a doctorate. "But wouldn't it make more sense for you to be discussing all this with Ms. Davies, rather than with me?"

Nuisance was now in a real rage. "Don't you tell *me* what makes sense! I have *no intention* of discussing *anything* with *her*! I'm just letting your department know that I'm going to the dean. I'm going to the dean, and we'll just *see* about this." She hung up, banging the phone down in my ear.

"Goodbye to you, too, and good riddance," I muttered. I figured I'd better relay Nasty Nuisance's latest rant to Susan, just to alert her, in case Nuisance got anywhere with the dean. Which I doubted, since the dean always struck me as a sensible, rational human being, who only kept Newsome on because she had tenure.

I poked my head in Susan's office. Carmen was still going on nonstop about John's new assistant.

"Marabella, come on in." Susan was dressed impeccably as usual, wearing a maroon suit and white ruffly blouse. She waved me inside, looking as though she'd welcome the hiatus from Carmen's monologue.

I told them about the phone conversation.

Carmen reacted in typical fashion. "That son-of-a…"

Susan shook her head.

"Rhymes with witch." Carmen pulled at some threads on her blue woolly sweater.

I had to give her an A for sticking with her quit-smoking program. Not only that, her breath was a lot nicer. "A lousy, bigoted one. So, what can we do?"

"I know what I'd *like* to do." Carmen drew her finger across her throat. "But I guess that's not an option."

Susan lifted her shoulders in a shrug and looked at me. "I can't think of anything, can you?"

"No. We can only hope that someday, she'll go too far and get herself fired, tenure or no tenure."

"Whaddya mean by 'going too far'? I know she hates

Latinos, too," Carmen said, plucking at another sweater thread.

I shook my head. "I don't know. But somebody like that, all that hate boiling up inside her, it's got to trip her up sometime."

Carmen looked worried. "Do you think she could get violent? Go crazy?"

Susan threw up her hands and stood up. "Carmen, please! And, Marabella, please don't get her started. Nobody's going crazy around here. Guys, we've got plenty of work to do. So let's get to it, okay?"

Carmen walked me out of Susan's office. "Ask John if we can buy his new assistant coffee or lunch this afternoon, okay?" she whispered.

"I can't promise, but I'll try," I said, making my way back to my messages.

There were calls from a local newspaper about new graduates of John's veterinary technician program; from the printer, about the next issue of our external newsletter; and from the director of our criminal justice program, about a student who'd just won an award from the local Boy Scouts.

I was about to refer the reporter to John for information, when I decided to call John myself and have him call her. That way, I got to hear John's sexy voice and hopefully, set up a coffee or lunch meet-and-greet with his new assistant.

It must have been his assistant who answered the phone: "Veterinary."

Wow! Now there were two sexy male voices in that department. "Um, John Adriance, please."

When John picked up the phone, I gave him the newspaper reporter's number and asked him if the phone answerer was his assistant.

"Yup, Rick Borden. He's been an enormous help."

"Well, Carmen and I would like to buy him coffee, lunch, whatever, in the cafeteria. If you guys don't already have plans."

John laughed. "As soon as you mentioned Carmen and lunch in the same sentence, I figured it all out. By the way, I miss you." His voice got deeper and more intimate.

Sigh. "Mmmm. Me too." I cradled the phone under my chin, closed my eyes, and swayed back and forth. I came rudely back to earth when I bumped my hip into a corner of my desk. Stifling a yell, I said, "So, lunch?"

"Okay, fine." Then he whispered, "But I sure wish we were somewhere else right now."

"Me, too."

We said goodbye and I went through the rest of my messages. Most of the people who'd called me weren't at their desks, so it was voice mail phone-tag, as usual. I'd email them, but at least some of them, I knew, would consider it inappropriate for me not to return their calls, no matter how hard it was to reach them. After all, as a PR person, I was there to serve them. How long it took me to get them on the phone was irrelevant. My time and energy didn't matter one bit. Such was the nature of my job, insofar as Chelsea College was concerned. Only the academics, even nasty academics, like Newsome, were respected around here.

Oh, stop griping, Marabella. It pays the bills. And it had a great side benefit, getting to see John at work. Speaking of John, it was time to grab Carmen and head for the cafeteria for our encounter with John's new assistant and Carmen's possible new quarry. Poor guy, I was betting he wouldn't have a chance once she got hold of him. At least, not until things didn't work out. I hated to be so negative, but she'd been having bad luck with relationships after her divorce.

"Hey, let's go!" Carmen was in my doorway. Freshly made up, hair sleek and shiny, loose threads of her sweater snipped off. She looked great.

I told her so and she beamed at me, as we waved goodbye to Susan and headed for the elevator down to the basement. When we got off the elevator, I was grateful there were two of us walking down the dim corridor. I shivered, thinking of the most recent scary story about the basement: a month ago, a secretary in the Biology department encountered a drunken man who seemed to be living in a corner of the passage. He'd tried to grab her. Thankfully, she got away and campus security took him to the police station. Hopefully, nobody else was lurking in the dark, ready to reach out and touch someone. Like me or Carmen.

Carmen tapped me on the shoulder at the cafeteria entrance. "There he is," she breathed, pointing to a table across the room. "Quick, do I look okay?"

"Fine."

John was sitting with a man who, I'd have to admit, was even better looking than he was.

"Wow," I whispered.

"What'd I tell you?" she whispered back, as John waved us over.

Rick Borden looked even better close up. Whiter-than-snow teeth that gleamed, thick, wavy blond hair, and the slimmest blond mustache, full lips, big blue eyes. He was wearing a white shirt with sleeves rolled up that showed off a buff body. Carmen was practically swooning and I had to keep myself from drooling. *Get hold of yourself, Marabella. You're an engaged woman, remember? Engaged to a wonderful guy.*

"Hi, I'm Marabella and this is Carmen," I said, as we sat down. Carmen was absolutely tongue-tied. "We're in the PR department."

"Rick Borden." A million-watt smile and that sexy, sexy voice. "Not really sure what the PR department does."

"We make things up to make the college look good," I said with a grin.

He laughed.

Carmen finally found her voice. "I've never been to the veterinary lab. I'd really love a tour." She sent him an inviting glance.

The million-watt smile again. "Sure, anytime. Just give me a call."

I hoped she wouldn't fall over in a faint. "Let's get some so-called food," I said, leading the way to the buffet. "Oh, and Rick, it's our treat, to welcome you to the campus."

"Thanks, I think," he said, with a grin. "From what John said about the quality of the cuisine, I hope I'll survive. But let me return the favor by inviting you all over to my place for a cocktail party I'm having this weekend."

Carmen's mouth hung open. I poked her with my elbow and she closed it.

"Great!" I said. "What should we bring?"

"Just your wonderful selves, all of you. I'll give John directions. Saturday, around eight. Don't dress."

Carmen stared at him. "You mean not fancy, right?"

"Right." With that, he excused himself and got up from the table. "Be right back with my so-called food," he said, with a laugh.

We had a nice, chatty lunch, the talk being a huge improvement over the food. Rick told us a little about himself: grew up in Cambridge, Mass., went to prep school, father owned a major real estate development corporation, mother a museum docent, three older sisters who were all athletes.

"Wow, did they teach you how to play sports? Or did you have to learn from your dad?" I said.

He smiled. "My dad wouldn't know a baseball from a soccer ball. He's more of a chess guy. But, yes, my sisters were very good about letting me play on their teams. So I learned to appreciate women early on."

Carmen's mouth was wide open. I hoped she wasn't drooling.

Rick finished his lunch and stood up, carrying his tray. "Work is calling," he said, and waved goodbye.

John got up, gave me a quick kiss, and followed.

Carmen just sat there, stunned. "Oh, my God!"

Getting up, I said, "Just be careful, okay? C'mon, let's go."

Chapter 57

Friday night after work I was sitting at a MacDonald's in mid-town Manhattan, sipping my tea. David Lipschitz's idea. Must be a helluva big spender.

Waiting for Mr. Don't-Waste-My-Time to show up. Guess it didn't matter if he wasted *my* time, since he was already twenty minutes late for our meeting. And I hadn't forgotten the veiled, or not so veiled, threat from him and his brother that my mother heard. I'd have to make a big effort to seem poised and self-confident, another test of my acting abilities.

When he finally appeared, he was wearing what looked like a permanent scowl and a tiny cut on his chin that must have been from shaving. Hmm, a bit nervous, Mr. Lipschitz? Short and stocky, he was also wearing what looked like one of those suits advertised on TV: "Buy one, get one free." In other words, cheap. Cheap seemed to describe everything about David Lipschitz. Paying for Cheryl's ongoing stints of rehab must cost plenty. After he ordered coffee, I waved him over to my table.

I figured I might as well start with Cheryl, to throw him off-balance right away. "Thanks for coming, Mr.

Lipschitz. But I thought your wife, um, Cheryl, would be here, too."

He sat down across the table from me, scowling even deeper. "Forget about Cheryl. This is between you and me."

I gave him a concerned look. "Oh, sorry. I just hope there's no problem."

"There's no problem," he muttered, sipping his coffee. "Let's get to it."

Ha! I was betting she was back in rehab again. "Sure," I said, picking up my briefcase and pulling out my fake papers. I went through the whole rigmarole again: the non-existent money from the non-existent bearer bonds that Sam supposedly bought, while David swallowed more coffee.

When I was through, he said, "Okay, that's another two hundred and fifty thousand dollars for each of us. How soon can we get it?"

I pretended to consult my notes. "Um. It's a little more complicated than that."

He leaned forward on his arms. With a shiver, I noticed how strong-looking his hands were. The better to strangle you with, my dear? "What do you mean, *complicated*?" he snarled.

I delivered the rest of my speech, about my decision-making responsibilities.

The man exploded. *Good thing we'd met in a public place. Thank you, Ma.*

"You won't get away with this, miss!" he shouted.

The people at the other tables were staring. So were the counter staff. He must have finally realized where he was and lowered his voice. "I'll take you to court. See if I don't."

With that, he got up and left. Without even a good-bye. I found myself actually shaking. I wondered if I should enroll in a self-defense class, karate, kick-boxing, something. This was one scary dude.

Chapter 58

When I got home, I was still jittery from my encounter with David Lipschitz. I wished I'd thought to pick up a bottle of wine. Even if it had dire consequences. I sank down at the end of the sofa and relayed the highlights of the meeting to my mother and Zilla.

Zilla's response was a large yawn. Obviously, my mother had fed him plenty, or he'd be nipping my ankles to get my attention. My mother's response was to sit up on the sofa and yell at me. That's mother love for you.

"You could've gotten yourself killed!"

I had to stop myself from saying, "No shit." No sense getting her started on my inappropriate language. "You're right."

"Of course I am." She folded her arms across her chest and fixed me with a forbidding look. "Marabella, you've got to stop doing this. These are very terrible people you're associating with."

"Ma, I'm not *associating* with them. I'm *investigating* them. And of course, they're terrible people. Otherwise I wouldn't be investigating them, would I?"

She stood up. "Come, I'll fix you something to eat. You must be starving."

I thought for a minute. "I don't think there's much in the fridge."

"Don't worry, I'll dream up something." She marched into the kitchen.

I shuddered. That was all I needed, one of her made-up concoctions, bits and pieces of leftovers mashed together in a horrible stew. "No, please, don't bother. I'm really not hungry."

"Are you sure, sweetheart? I hope you're not skipping meals. You need to keep up your strength, you know," she called from the kitchen.

"I'll just have a cup of tea. That's all I need." *First*, I thought, *I'll call Rivera. By now, he should have some answers from the ME's office about Sam.*

"I'll make some fresh," from the kitchen.

Is there even a way to make tea that isn't fresh? I wondered, but thanked her, grabbed my cell, and went into the bedroom, followed by Zilla. I scrolled to Rivera's number.

Lucky, or not, for me, he was in. And of course, not happy to hear from me.

"I don't mean to bother you," I began, figuring I'd start with the polite approach. If that didn't work…

"*Suurre*, you don't."

Grrrr. "Lieutenant, can you tell me the results of the autopsy on Sam, um, Mr. Lipschitz?"

"Hmmph."

I heard the rustling of papers, followed by swallowing sounds. Must be the perennial decaf soda. While I was waiting, I glanced around the room and saw something moving on the floor. Several balls of yarn were rapidly propelling toward me. "Zilla, stop that!"

"What? Who are you talking to? Godzilla? Geez." He was back on the line.

"It's my cat."

"Right." I could *hear* the smirk on his face. "I can't give you details. It's a homicide case."

I knew it, I knew it. I bit my tongue down hard to keep from saying, "Told you so." "Ow!" Zilla was using my left leg for a scratching post.

"Godzilla, again?" he sneered.

"Thank you for letting me know." Even though he'd said no details, it couldn't hurt to try, right? I cleared my throat. "How did it happen? Poison? Pills? A lethal injection?"

"Wax in your ears? What did I just say? *No details, capice?*"

"But…"

"Ms. Vinegar," he growled "For your information, I didn't even have to tell you it was a homicide. I was trying to be nice, considering that Mr. Lipschitz was a friend of yours. Now that's it. I'm busy."

"You're investigating? Interviewing the relatives?"

I heard teeth gnashing. "Why, no, we're just sitting here on our butts, of course."

Uh, oh. Better make a quick goodbye. "Thanks for your time."

"My plea—sure," Dripping sarcasm. "Goodbye."

The phone clicked off in my ear. Well, at least I had more information than I'd had before our so-called conversation. I'd call Miriam Kravitz. She'd want to know about it. I debated whether or not to tell her about my own investigation. Better not, I thought. She'd only worry about me. Probably yell at me, too. I already had one mother on my back, thank you.

Speaking of my mother, I needed to find out how Sam was murdered. My mother could zip to the ME's office and check out the notes. Then we'd know if the killer used a lethal injection or another medically related instrument of death. Or something completely different.

That still wouldn't tell us who, of course. Just how.

I left the bedroom, chasing Zilla out ahead of me, and told my mother what I'd learned from Rivera about Sam.

She shook her head. "That a greedy relative should kill a wonderful man like that, for money."

I sat down on the sofa. "So now we know what happened to Sam. But we need to know how it was done. The ME's office would have the autopsy results."

She sat up, ready for action. "I'm on it!"

"Just wait a minute, please," I said, and hurried to deposit Zilla back in my bedroom before she took off. The hell with the yarn. Better tangled yarn than a traumatized cat.

Chapter 59

It took me a while to figure it out. As usual, a doctor's writing is very hard to read," she said, sinking back against the sofa pillows. "Even doctors that treat dead people."

I brought her a glass of water. "Please, Ma, rest a while."

She sat up and sipped the water. "Rest? I'll have plenty of time to rest after I…"

God. One of these days, my brain was going to explode from all this. She was dead. But she wasn't. But would she be again?

"Not exactly, sweetheart." She yawned.

And then there was the mind-reading ability, which she now seemed to have fine-tuned to perfection. "Why don't you nap for a while? We can talk about what you found out later."

She straightened her shoulders. "I'm fine. Okay, here's what I found out. Sam died, was killed, by an overdose of insulin."

Stunned, I said, "But Sam wasn't a diabetic."

My mother nodded. "Right."

I thought about this for a few minutes. "That has to mean, that whoever did this had to have access to insulin."

"And know how to use it," she said.

"So…" I thought some more. "We're talking about somebody who can get hold of insulin easily. If it's not somebody who's a doctor, works in a hospital or a doctor's office or…"

"A relative."

"Of course it's a relative," I said.

"Tch, tch. That's no way to talk to your mother."

"Sorry," I mumbled, "but…"

"I meant somebody who has a *diabetic relative*," she said.

I stared at her. "That opens up a whole new can of worms."

She nodded. "So, now we have to look at the relatives' relatives."

This was too much. My poor brain was just too tired at this point to deal with any more confusion.

"No, sweetheart, it's simple. We have to investigate the relatives' families. To find out who has a relative with diabetes." She smirked. She loved that word, *investigate*. It made her feel like Jessica Fletcher.

But she was right.

The smirk again. "But don't you worry about it. It'll just take a little effort." She closed her eyes.

This scared the hell out of me. "Ma! Are you…" She looked like a, excuse the expression, corpse.

She popped open her eyes and shut them again. "Shhh, I'm thinking."

Planning and plotting. I got up from the sofa, figuring I'd better leave Jessica Fletcher or Miss Marple, whoever she was impersonating today, alone for a while. I started toward my bedroom.

"Jessica Fletcher. When she was hot on the trail of…"

"The man who poisoned his uncle," I murmured, closing my bedroom door. Zilla was stretched out on my bed, fast asleep. Not only had he unrolled every ball of yarn, but he'd tangled them together into one giant clump of wool. I glared at him. Then I remembered how much I liked untangling it. Probably for the same reason I liked doing crosswords. Puzzling something out.

Chapter 60

Carmen was dressed to the nines, even though Rick had told us not to dress. But I didn't want to shake her confidence. And she looked terrific. Figure-hugging red dress, long silver necklace and strappy red sandals. The dress dramatized her dark hair and eyes and full figure. Okay, maybe a little too full. But still. I, on the other hand, wore a charcoal gray A-line skirt and a plum-colored top, more casual. Mainly because a lot of the dressy clothes I had were so old, they practically creaked.

John drove around Rick's street in the Village several times, finally giving up and heading into the only available parking garage in the vicinity. The clouds that had been threatening when John picked Carmen and me up became a thunderstorm when we got out, a couple of blocks from Rick's apartment.

John and I were toting a bottle of nice wine and Carmen had picked up a box of chocolates. My perennial downfall. I promised my hips to limit my intake to two. I could gain weight by inhaling them. Or by eating the box.

We went up the steps soaked to the skin, and the less said about the condition of my hair, the better. Rick buzzed us in and we caught the elevator for the top floor.

Rick had the whole floor in a townhouse. We could hear the blaring rock music before we even got up there. At least, not heavy metal, I said to myself.

Rick threw open the door, a gorgeous sight in a white shirt, open at the neck, with rolled up sleeves—the better to see his biceps. Tight black pants—the better to see the hips and, I imagined, the butt. Carmen looked as if she might faint dead away.

He waved us in. "You poor things, you look like you're drowning! Come in and dry off! So glad you could make it!"

Carmen's cheeks turned the color of her dress, and she gazed at Rick with hungry eyes.

I excused myself, pushing through the crowd to find a bathroom for a quick fix of my out-of-control hair. It was an elegant room: black marble sink, topped by an enormous silver-etched mirror, silver towel bars holding thick black guest towels, black tile floor. Elbowing my way back to John and Carmen, I didn't see how one more person could fit in the apartment. Bodies were jammed up against each other, drinks held precariously, the same with food. Forget conversation. Unless you wanted a shouting match. But some people were actually trying to dance in a few inches of space.

"Wow! You've got a lotta friends!" Carmen yelled to our host, who beamed at her.

I didn't recognize anyone, but why would I? Rick had just started work at the college and evidently we didn't move in the same circles. I remembered that his father was a real estate mogul. Obviously, his friends and acquaintances were of the hard-partying, not-exactly-poor sort. Plenty of bling, designer clothes, plus, from the white powder on one of the tables, designer drugs. John and I looked at each other and shrugged. "Might as well eat, drink, and be merry," I said.

John said in my ear, "But not *too* merry with the booze, okay? You know what happens to you."

I nodded. Right. Throw up and/or pass out. Usually in that order.

The rock music ended and a slower tune came on. "Let's dance," I said to John. As we tried to move in our allotted space, other couples were doing the same. I saw Carmen making her way toward Rick, her face flushed.

But he was already dancing. With another guy. Looking blissful, with his arm around the guy's neck.

"Oh, poor Carmen," I whispered in John's ear. "I'd better go over to her."

She looked as if all the oxygen had left her body. "C'mon, let's get to the bathroom." I dragged her after me, both of us squeezing our way past the crowd. "In," I said.

I marched her over to the sink and handed her one of the guest towels. "Here, wash your face. You'll feel better." As she patted her face dry, I said, "Just think how lucky you are."

"Huh? Lucky? Are you kidding?" She looked as if I weren't taking her feelings seriously.

"Lucky that you found out *now*, before anything…" I trailed off.

She took a deep breath. "Yeah. I guess you're right. Men. Why do I always find the wrong ones? When they don't find me first, that is."

I patted her shoulder. "Hey, you remember how I kept striking out in the relationship department, until I met John."

"Does he have a brother?"

I walked her out of the bathroom. "Yes."

She brightened.

"But he lives on a farm in Pennsylvania. Now, let's say goodbye to Rick."

She made a face.

"Hey, be nice. You can't blame him for your assumptions. And remember, you might run into each other at work. You don't want things to be uncomfortable, right?"

"I guess so." She nodded and we headed out to find John. The loud music was giving me a headache and I wanted to leave.

I knew whereof I spoke about uncomfortable work relationships. The summer after my freshman year in college, I had a job in a department store. It turned out to be a disaster on two fronts: professional and personal. They'd stuck me, the math-o-phobe, in the credit department. By the end of the summer, I'd screwed up everybody's accounts. Even worse was the mistake I made by dating the cute guy in the same department. That ended nastily because I wouldn't give in and it made the rest of my summer at work a living hell.

So, my motto: don't get into any kind of situations with guys you work with. Wait a minute...

I comforted myself with the thought that it was different with John. And that we didn't exactly work together. At any rate, having an unpleasant relationship with people you worked with, male or female, could make your life harder. Which was why I bit my tongue and smiled whenever I encountered Nasty Newsome.

Chapter 61

My mother was still up when I got home. She just couldn't shake the old habit, I guess. When I was sixteen, I got so sick of her hovering that I finally rebelled one night and came home just as she went out to get the newspaper. She dragged me into the house and began the interrogation, which lasted an hour and ended with me being grounded for a week. Thank the gods, all I had to do *now* was put up with her questions. And only answer the ones I wanted to.

"So, where were you so late?" She peered at me over her bifocals, closing the latest *Murder She Wrote* paperback I'd gotten her.

"Ma, I told you, some of us were invited to a party at a colleague's apartment." After I got my coat off, I flopped down on the sofa and kicked off my shoes. Changing the subject, I said, "Did you find out anything about anybody in the relatives' families with diabetes?"

She fished a piece of paper and a marker out of the top of her floral print tee. In between chomps on the marker, she said, "I sure did. Okay, here we go. Abby Goldfarb's husband…"

"Larry."

"…was recently diagnosed with diabetes."

"How recently?"

"Hmmm. About six months ago. And David Lipschitz's mother-in-law has a bad case, even affecting her eyesight. His wife…"

"Cheryl."

"…spends a lot of time caring for her mother." She nodded her approval. "A good daughter, that Cheryl is, no matter what else."

"Anything else?"

"The niece, Jennifer. Her father was diabetic and she helped him with the shots."

"Well, that doesn't mean anything, since her parents aren't around anymore. They died in a plane crash about a year ago."

My mother looked up from her list. "But still. Don't you think you should at least question Jennifer? After all, you interviewed everybody else in the family."

I looked down at my lap. I didn't want to, but, to be fair, it should be done. And who knew, maybe I'd learn something. For instance, about her boyfriend. Should I make it a twofer? He wasn't part of the family. I didn't even know how involved they were. But this was an opportunity to check him out. Not just to see if he was good enough for Jennifer, but whether he could be a killer. Even though I felt bad about treating Jennifer and her boyfriend as suspects, I hated to admit it, my mother was right.

She grinned. "Of course I am."

So I grabbed my phone, went into the bedroom, scrolled to Jennifer's number, and got her voice mail. I left a message, trying to make my request as innocuous and routine as possible: "Jennifer, dear, there are new developments about your uncle's estate, which I need to discuss with each of you. Let me know when would be a good time for us to get together about this. Oh, if your boyfriend is around, would you like him to be there, too? Regards, Marabella."

I felt like a worm for inveigling her in my scheme. But then I thought of Sam. And Rose. And Lucy. And hardened my resolve. Whoever did this was a monster. A dangerous monster. A monster who could be any one of them. Even Sam's sweet, caring niece.

I was tired and got ready for bed. But I didn't think I could sleep right away. With a "Mmmrow," Zilla, who'd been dozing on my bed, opened his eyes. I dug out my newest crossword puzzle book and a freshly sharpened pencil from my nightstand, hoping Zilla wouldn't bat at the book's pages. But he must have been tired, too. He curled himself into a ball next to me, looking at me with half-closed eyes. As if he were keeping watch. I reached over and petted him. For once, he didn't turn away.

Chapter 62

I met Jennifer and Mark at a pizza place in Park Slope. Jennifer was a beautiful young woman, who seemed to grow lovelier every time I saw her. And she knew how to dress to accentuate her light brown hair and fair coloring.

Mark turned out to be what I would call a cute nerd: curly red hair, small gold-framed glasses, button-down blue striped shirt, and khakis. With nervous hands, that he didn't seem to know what to do with. I could imagine him decades earlier with a pocket protector full of pens. Probably I was a bit prejudiced against business types. Jennifer mentioned that Mark was getting his MBA at night from Fordham. Anyway, he was friendly and polite. A welcome change from the others I'd been dealing with. Then again, he wasn't a family member, yet.

After our pizza order came, Jennifer reached for Mark's hand. "We're planning to get married next year. And you'll be invited to the wedding. You've always been so sweet to me." Her heart-shaped face lit up when she looked at Mark.

"I'd be delighted." A nice young couple, I thought. Maybe too nice? Was it all an act? I could feel my sleuthing nose twitching. They could be in on it together. Even though, as far as I, and my mother, could find out, they were both doing very well, salary-wise, at the health care company.

But Mark had let slip about their plans to buy an apartment on the Upper West Side. You had to have a pretty big bundle for that. Even with a good salary. So where did he think the money would come from? Maybe from knocking off Sam and company? After I brought up the fake extra money, I'd question him about it.

I bit into my slice and took a sip of my tea, skipping the fussing with phony papers in my briefcase. B-school students would know if financial papers were real or not, right? I cut to the chase, reciting my spiel about the bearer bonds Sam had invested in years ago and forgotten to put in the will. I had to be hazy about specifics, pleading ignorance of things dealing with money. Ducking my head, I confessed, "I've never been a numbers person." Understatement of the year. "But Sam made me executor, so I need to make some decisions about this money. With your, and the others', input, of course." I smiled.

They looked at each other. Jennifer teared up and Mark handed her a handkerchief. "It's just…thinking about Uncle Sam. He was so good to me," she whispered.

I patted her arm. "I know. I miss him, too." I gave her a moment to wipe her eyes. "Jennifer, I'm sorry, but I do need to know what you think about this. You have a right to an opinion. Of course, I have the final say as to how the money should be dispersed."

Jennifer looked at me. "What would *you* think is the right thing to do? I really value your opinion. You've always been so level-headed."

I felt my heart warm toward her again. *Don't let flattery get to you, even though it feels good*, I told myself. "Well, I thought it would be a good memorial to Sam if it went to a couple of charities." I checked out their expressions and body language, trying to be subtle about it. They didn't look happy. Especially Mark, who was cracking his knuckles.

Jennifer turned to Mark, "Is that definite? I mean, I think it's a wonderful thing to donate in Uncle Sam's memory, but…"

"What, dear?" I egged her on.

"Uh, does it all have to go to charity? I mean, could maybe some of it go to us? I mean, the family?" She looked down at her lap, her face flushed.

I glanced over at Mark. He was scowling. "Jennifer, no decisions have been made yet about this money," I said. "I'm planning to get input from everyone before that happens. So stay tuned," I said, trying to change the mood. I thought this might be a good time to ask Mark how he planned to pay for the apartment, pretending to sound like a concerned (slightly?) older relative. "Mark, buying an apartment sounds like a lovely idea, but…" I pursed my lips, as if I were chastising him.

He made an effort to appear nonchalant. "Oh, don't worry, Marabella. Can I call you Marabella?"

I nodded. "Of course, dear." God, I must sound like a maiden aunt.

"I've just gotten a great promotion, with the salary to go with." He gave a smug smile. "And, I'm lucky enough to be what I guess you'd call a 'trust fund baby.' From my grandfather. It starts to kick in when I'm thirty-five." Knuckle-cracks, again.

Jennifer beamed. "Which is next year."

Hmm. Okay. For now. "That *is* lucky. Guess you'll quit your job then?"

Mark gave a small smile. "Not at all. I'm not sweating this MBA hell for nothing. My inheritance will help pay for the apartment, and maybe a really nice car."

Jennifer interrupted him. "Don't forget about a honeymoon cruise. Around the world. With all the trimmings." Her eyes glittered.

This was interesting. I had no idea she was so materialistic. Maybe Jennifer had always been a little too good to be true. She'd always struck me as a nice, unassuming young woman, who dressed tastefully but not expensively. And her apartment was furnished simply, more utilitarian than showy.

She seemed to collect herself and said, "I've always dreamed of seeing the world, going to exotic places. I've never really been anywhere."

Poor thing. I could really identify with that. I'd once harbored fantasies of being a foreign correspondent. Trekking to dark, dangerous places. Ducking sniper fire and bombs. Escaping from riots. Nearly, but not quite, landing in a foreign prison. Somehow, I'd ended up doing P.R. at a community college. The gods must really have it in for me.

Lucky for Jennifer, she might see her dreams of world travel come true. And it *seemed* to be through legitimate means. *Seemed* to be. That was the question.

For instance, why would a trust-fund baby need, want, even more money? Hmmm. As we all said goodbye, I remembered a line from the *H.M.S. Pinafore*: "Things are seldom what they seem."

Time for a consultation with Jessica Fletcher, aka, my mother.

Chapter 63

The dancers were graceful and the costumes were beautiful. The music, Tchaikovsky, was heavenly. The setting was magical.

My vision blurred. I was eleven years old again, in ballet class at Miss (not Ms., never Ms.) Payton's Dance Academy in Forest Hills. I used to dream of going to a performance of *Swan Lake* in New York City. I brushed back tears and sniffed.

John handed me a handkerchief and whispered in my ear, "What's wrong? Is the story making you sad?"

I shook my head and blew my nose.

"I thought you loved *Swan Lake*."

"Oh, I do. It's wonderful," I whispered back, trying to keep from hiccupping, which sometimes happened when I got teary.

He gave me a puzzled look and turned his attention back to the stage.

After my father died, when I was twelve, my mother sold my father's pharmacy and got fleeced by her shyster lawyer. So we didn't have an extra dime, especially for frivolous things like the City Ballet. With only a high school education, my mother didn't have a lot of options, and she took a job as a truant officer. Not only did it pay *bubkes*, it made me a target of every delinquent in the school district.

After the performance, John and I headed underground to the parking garage for the car. Then we went to a nearby Italian restaurant for a late dinner. We arrived just after it started pouring.

We got a candlelit table in a quiet corner, next to the burning fireplace, where we could dry off. I was hoping John had forgotten about my little episode at the ballet. Not a chance. The man had an amazing memory for details. Especially ones about me. *Better be more careful, Marabella, if you want to keep anything to yourself.* Well, at least he wasn't a mind-reader like my mother. Not yet.

"Okay, what was that all about before?"

No use trying to play coy with this guy. So I told him. "I didn't want to bore you."

He reached across the table for my hand. "You could never bore me. I never know what to expect from you. Speaking of that, I don't want us to have any more secrets. I want us to be able to trust each other. "

I grinned. "Don't worry. What could possibly compare with the big one…" I stopped when I saw the waitperson heading for our table.

We ordered, steak for John, rare (ugh, bloody meat), and roast chicken (very dead) for me. A glass of white wine for me. A beer for John and an appetizer, pulpa, Italian baby octopus(double ugh).Not only did he eat this disgusting mess, he liked to tease me by hanging the tentacles out of his mouth. Aarggh.

"Yuck," I said, making a face.

"Sorry," he said, not looking at all sorry.

Our main course arrived. John's steak was so rare, I could swear it was twitching when the waitperson deposited it on the plate.

"My fiancé, the brutal carnivore," I muttered.

John took a slug of his beer and grinned. "And I suppose a chicken is considered a vegetable?"

"At least it's not still bleeding. Heavily." I tried not to look at the pool of blood on his plate. The blood made me think of Lucy. And Rose. And Sam.

"What?" John looked up from devouring his carrion. "Where did you go?"

Speaking of no more secrets. I guess I'd have to tell him about tracking murder suspects. He'd probably figure it out eventually, anyway .Better he should hear it from me before things got even dicier. Meaning before another attempt on my life.

"John, you know I really love you."

He stopped chewing whatever part of the barely dead beast was in his mouth.

I was afraid he'd choke. "Swallow, please. I don't want to have to do a Heimlich." Which I didn't know how to do anyway.

He swallowed it down with a slug of beer and stared at me. "What now?"

I pushed my food around on the plate, making little piles. "Um. You said no more secrets, right?"

He stared harder. "Okay."

I'd better get it over with, quick. "Um, I've been meeting with the murder suspects, and making them think there's more money from Sam's will, when there isn't. And that I'm in charge about what to do with the money. My plan is to see their reactions to my holding all the cards."

"Are you totally crazy?" He was almost yelling.

I looked around. The elderly couple at the next table were gawking. As were people at the rest of the tables. I could feel my cheeks getting hot and I wanted to crawl under our table. I took his hand. "Shhh, it's not as bad as you think. There's a method to my madness."

His voice got even louder. "Putting yourself out there as bait is a method? How could you do that? Don't you care what happens to you, playing games with a serial killer!"

By now, the overweight maitre d' had been alerted and was waddling his way to our table, scowling. "Let's go, before they throw us out." I stood up, grabbing my still-damp trench coat.

John tossed some bills on the table, got his coat, and followed me out. Glowering at me and mumbling under his breath. Luckily, the rain had slowed down, so we didn't have to race to the car. When we got inside, he drew me close, burying his head on my shoulder. "I can't stand the idea of losing you, Marabella. Please stop."

I kissed him. "I don't want to lose me, either," I said, trying for humor. Needless to say, it didn't work.

He folded his arms across his chest. "Not funny."

"I know." I tried to hug him, but he stiff-armed me. "Just trying to lighten the moment, okay?"

"Not. Okay."

At least, this time, he didn't push me away. "Look, I promise to be very, very careful. I'll try to clue you in on whatever happens. And, worse comes to worst, I'm sure my mother will come through."

He rolled his eyes. "Right. Your mother, the senior ghost Ninja."

"Not exactly. But she does seem to be able to sniff out danger, somehow."

"I don't suppose there's anything I can do or say to stop you from this crazy idea?" He looked miserable.

"Not if you really love me, meaning love me the way I am. For who I am."

He hugged me tight. "You know I do, every beautiful part of your body, including the strange machinations of that brain of yours."

I stuck my tongue out at him. "You know I can't just forget about the fact that three of my friends have been victims of this monster."

He sighed and started the car. "And you could be number four."

Chapter 64

I was emotionally exhausted when I got home and fell into bed .But I would have been better off staying awake, considering the nightmare I had.

Jennifer was chasing me with a baseball bat, followed by her boyfriend with a net, ready to throw over my head. He was grinning evilly, baring fangs dripping with blood.

Aarrggh. I made myself wake up. Sitting up in bed, listening to Zilla's snores, I thought about the dream. Was it a message, confirming my suspicions about Jennifer and Mark? Should I take it seriously?

But what about the rest of that family? Cheryl, the addict, was a sad case. But her husband, David, was desperate for money to pay for her drug problem. Jeremy, of the two mistresses and high-maintenance wife, Tamar, was possibly even more desperate. Abby's husband, Larry, was a lush who couldn't keep a job. That had to be a helluva pressure cooker.

Then I thought, maybe sometimes, a dream is just a dream. I think George Burns said that about a cigar. Or maybe it was Freud. Or Groucho. Thinking about Groucho made me think about the slobbery canine version of the Marx Brothers. And that led to thinking about

John. My fiancé, I thought, gazing at my ring. Speaking of dreams, sometimes I thought this whole thing about being engaged was a lovely hallucination. But sometimes it scared me to death. I still worried about my screw-up mechanism.

At least I seemed to be less scared these days. *And about time, too,* I scolded myself. Meanwhile, I had to get up in the morning for work. I glanced at my clock. Morning was almost here. I inched myself out of bed, to let a sleeping cat lie, and shuffled over to my desk. Pulling out a freshly sharpened pencil and a crossword book to a puzzle I'd already started, I sat down to work. The last thing I remember before nodding off was searching my brain for a seven-letter word for an ancient Asian tribe.

I woke up cramped and grouchy from sleeping at my desk. "It's all your fault," I grumbled at Zilla, who was stretching himself in the middle of my bed. "At least *you* got your beauty sleep, good for you. And now I suppose you want breakfast." With the grace only a cat could pull off, he slipped off the bed and began winding himself around my ankles, accompanied by loud "Mrrowwws."

"I wish I knew if you could understand me or if it's just your morning appetite," I said, trying not to trip over him on the way to the kitchen. After I fed and watered him, I made myself a cup of tea, tiptoed into the living room, so as not to wake my mother, and headed for the chair.

I had to think. What to do next?

"Just ask."

I almost jumped. "Sorry if I woke you, Ma. I tried to be quiet."

Her eyes were only half open. But her mind-reading skills were fully awake. "It's all right, sweetheart. But you were asking yourself…" She had the nerve to grin at me.

Was there absolutely no privacy in this world? Big Mother was not only watching, but could tune in to your every thought?

She sat up with a groan, eyes more or less open. "Don't complain. We've never been a family of complainers."

This was too much. Was I living in an alternate universe? What family was she talking about? Definitely not ours. Our relatives weren't just casual *kvetchers*, they'd elevated it to a high art. I was warned at an early age not to ask my Aunt Evelyn, my mother's sister, how she was. But she told you anyway. The list of her aches and pains, especially those related to her intestines, was legendary. Then there was Uncle Alvin, my father's brother, who gave you updates on the impending doom of his haberdashery store: crooked partners, exorbitant heating bills, undependable workers. And he'd always finish his litany with, "But I can't complain."

"Come, I'll make you breakfast," my mother said, getting off the sofa.

When she didn't want to deal with a subject, she changed it. No point pursuing it. And I was getting hungry. Maybe I could sneak a peek into the refrigerator and see if there was something she hadn't cooked. But she was there ahead of me, just as Zilla trotted out of the kitchen, leaving an empty dish in his wake. Obviously, he'd enjoyed his breakfast. Lucky cat.

I sat down at the table, resigning myself to eating whatever it was, not wanting to hurt her feelings. I could always wash it down with OJ and tea. Which I did.

In between chewing and drinking, I told her about my meeting with Jennifer and Mark. "I'm not feeling good about this. Mark was a little too glib and Jennifer, well, I saw a side of her I'd never seen before."

She put down her cup of tea. "Hmmm. A trust-fund baby, he said."

I nodded, finished the OJ and began sipping my tea. "So?"

She leaned back in her chair and belched. Her new incarnation seemed to have heightened her digestive noises. "Maybe he isn't one."

"One what?" She had also gotten more inscrutable. Or less articulate.

She frowned at me. "Not at all. Maybe he isn't really a trust-fund baby at all. Things aren't always what they seem. Especially people who seem to be trust-fund babies."

We looked at each other. "A case for…"

"Jessica Fletcher," she said, with a grin.

Chapter 65

My mother got the goods on Mark Hirschfield, all right. She announced it when I got home from work. Looking very fashionable in a new ruffled navy top and slacks outfit I'd picked up for her.

"Some trust-fund baby," she sneered, lying back on the sofa pillows. "What a phony!"

She'd found out that Mark's family was just getting by and had always struggled to make ends meet. His father sold insurance. His mother was an elementary school teacher. There was no rich grandfather. Or rich anybody in his family.

"Why do you think he made up that story? Because he's ashamed of his family?"

Perched on the arm of the sofa, I thought for a moment. "I think maybe to impress Jennifer. Or me," I said.

My mother looked at me, a question ready on her lips.

"How does this sound? Mark makes up this story so Jennifer and I don't think he needs any money."

She nodded. "Or maybe Jennifer already knows."

That was hard for me to take. Jennifer being part of a con. In cahoots with her no-good boyfriend. Putting on an act for my benefit. Then I remembered my nightmare. It was possible, I thought.

"I'm afraid it is. Even though I know you don't want to believe it," said the mind-reader. "Sometimes, you're just too trusting, sweetheart."

There were only two possibilities, I thought. Either Mark had fooled Jennifer into thinking there was family money, or Jennifer was in on the scheme to pretend there was.

"Right."

I got up from the sofa and paced. "Well, we don't know yet, do we? And if Jennifer is innocent, should I tell her about him and his lies? Do I have an obligation? She'd be so hurt. But I couldn't just let her go on not knowing what a low-life her boyfriend was. Especially since they're planning to get married and buy an apartment." Since buying an apartment in New York City was out-of-sight expensive, he could be planning to fleece Jennifer out of her inheritance to pay for it. And have her support him in the style in which he wanted to become accustomed.

Which was it? Which was the evil behind the door? This made me think of that story about the lady and the tiger: how to choose? There must be a way to find out what the truth was. Wasn't there?

"I'm thinking, I'm thinking. Give me a few minutes." She closed her eyes, something she sometimes did to help her concentrate. A little while later, she popped them open. "I've got it!"

"What?"

"I'll be a fly on the wall, when they're together." She giggled.

"You'd actually spy on them, in bed?"

She smiled. "Don't worry, I won't look. I'll just listen into their conversation."

She was on to something. "Good idea. So, you can find out if they're putting something over on me, about their plans for the inheritance money, and maybe even…"

"The murders?" my mother said.

Chapter 66

I had to clear my head. I said goodnight to my mother and went to my bedroom, followed by Zilla. I sat up in bed and he jumped up, landing on my feet. Soon snoring noises filled the room.

Good, I thought, *it's like white noise. Should help me concentrate. Try to be objective, Marabella, even though you like Jennifer. It doesn't mean that she and Mark aren't greedy killers. Sure, they seem to be doing very well, financially. Even though Mark was a liar and probably a hustler, too. Probably after Jennifer's inheritance money.*

But would Jennifer kill her Uncle Sam, whom she really seemed to care about? And then kill two more people? And then try to kill me in the whirlpool? I shuddered, remembering how horrible I felt, trying to breathe.

Well, maybe it was Mark. Maybe he did it all. But as far as I knew, he hadn't even met Sam. Had never been in the building. Jennifer had always visited Sam on her own. Maybe because Mark wasn't comfortable with strangers. He hadn't exactly seemed relaxed with me.

But did that make him a killer? A triple murderer? A liar, a nervous Nelly, maybe a hustler. It was hard to imagine either Jennifer or Mark being that cold-blooded.

Another thing: it wouldn't be easy for Jennifer or Mark to get away from their office anytime they wanted to, spur of the moment.

And to kill three people, you had to have ice in your veins. Or a damn good reason. A desperate reason. Neither one of them struck me as desperate.

Desperate. When it came to desperate, Abby Goldfarb came to mind. I remembered our little get-together at the tea bar. She'd bemoaned the fact that her alcoholic husband had just lost another job, putting them in a real financial bind. She was even worried about losing her own job.

Abby. Now there was cold-blooded, for sure. I hadn't seen any feeling from her except about herself and her situation. Even at her grandson's bar mitzvah, she was nagging her husband about their finances, about how they were going to chip in for the event. *In front of the boy, too. Now that's cold.*

So, how could Abby have done it, then? I thought about her job. Associate professor at NYU. This was not a nine-to five job, I knew. Her schedule could be flexible, for sure. Just get somebody to cover a class or two, reschedule a meeting.

Abby could definitely have been in Sam's apartment that day. And could have seen Rose. And Lucy, when she came back to the building. And as a woman, she could have slipped into the health club without too much difficulty. She could've just walked in, while the receptionist was busy doing something. Nobody would've thought anything about it.

Means, motive, and opportunity. I could feel my anger boiling up. This monster killed three wonderful people. Not to mention almost killing me. For money. For greed.

Now I just had to figure out how to prove it.

Chapter 67

When I picked up my mail the next day after work, there was a postcard from Toniann and Peter. By squinting at the picture, I was just able to make it out in the dim lobby—a couple kissing, with dialogue that said, *Glad you're* not *here!* She wrote, *Beautiful weather. Lovely inn. Great food.* She said they'd be back next week. And that Peter had gotten an offer from a law firm in Brooklyn. Yay!

I was so happy, I could have cried. The idea of losing my best friend to out-of-state digs, or even upstate, had been devastating. Smiling, I tucked the postcard in my pocketbook and rang for the elevator.

That's when I heard sounds from the shadows. When I turned around, someone came at me with a heavy object. Abby! I tried to ward off the blows and managed to inflict a few good bruises with my ring before everything went black.

Chapter 68

I didn't want to wake up, but somebody was shaking me awake. I opened my eyes, totally disoriented. Through a fog, I realized I was in a hospital bed and somebody, who must have been a nurse, was leaning over me, asking if I knew who I was. My ears were ringing and my head felt like it had been hit by a truck. I reached up and my fingers touched a thick wad of something wrapped around my head.

"Uhhgggg," I mumbled.

"Don't touch the dressing. And please try to stay still. It's very important."

"But…"

The woman slowly came into focus. She was middle-aged and plump, with short gray hair and glasses with bright red frames. Her name tag said: Elizabeth Carson, RN. "Call me Liz," she said, smiling at me.

I tried to smile back, but the movement made my head hurt worse. "What happened?" I croaked.

Liz gave me ice water and a straw. "Here, sip this slowly. Somebody found you unconscious, in the lobby of an apartment building. My guess is that you fell and hit your head. Anyway, they called nine-one-one, the EMS and the cops brought you here and they fixed you up in the ER.”

“How long? When did I get here?” My lips were cracked and dry and the cool water tasted delicious.

“Since yesterday afternoon. You’ve been out of it almost a whole day. Don’t gulp, drink slowly. Otherwise, the cold from the ice will make your head hurt more.”

No kidding. “Please, can you give me something for the pain?”

She took the empty glass. “I’ll check with the doctor. But I need to know what you remember. Do you know who you are?”

My head was in such agony, I couldn’t possibly think. I started to shake it, no, and stopped myself just in time. “I don’t remember.” I wondered if I had brain damage.

Liz patted my hand. “Don’t worry. It’s very common, after a concussion. You should be back to normal soon. It’ll all come back to you, you’ll see.”

Maybe the problem was that I didn’t want it to come back. Maybe what happened was so horrible, my poor wounded head preferred a state of oblivion. I closed my eyes and was just nodding off, figuring I couldn’t feel any worse after a nap, when Liz came back. She stuck a thermometer in my mouth and wrapped a blood pressure cuff around my arm. She fished a pen from her pocket and wrote on a chart at the end of my bed. Pocketing the pen, she plunked herself down on a chair next to my bed.

“Okay, let’s try to jog that memory of yours,” she said.

Wincing against the pain from moving my lips, I said, “Good idea. But first, can I please…”

She took a small container from her other pocket, got out a pill, and handed it to me, along with the glass of water and straw. "This should do it, but it'll take a little while."

Unfortunately, the pill was very big. I'd always had trouble swallowing large pills. In fact, I still favored Flintstones chewable vitamins. I tried not to gag and finally got it down with the water. "God, that was a real horse pill," I said.

She laughed. "That bad, huh?"

Horse pill. Pills for a horse. Horse doctor. I looked at my left hand and the diamonds twinkled at me. And then I remembered. "I remember!" I shouted, forgetting about my head and immediately suffering the consequences. "Ohhhh."

Liz stood up. "That's great! Tell me who you are and what happened to you."

"I know who I am. Marabella Vinegar."

She didn't bat an eye at my name. Good for her. "Great! Do you know what happened to you?"

I tried to think. "All I remember was that I was in the lobby of my apartment building, waiting for the elevator and the next thing I knew, I woke up in this bed." I gave her my address.

"Well, that's a good start. The rest will come back soon, don't worry. Do you remember if you're employed?"

"I work in the public relations department of Chelsea College. Oh, I'd better call my boss…"

Liz smiled. "You're not ready for that yet. I'll call for you."

I gave her Susan's name and phone number. "Thanks." Then I thought of John. "Oh, and my fiancé. He'll be worried." I gave her John's information. "Could you please let them know where I am? By the way, what hospital am I in?"

She stood up. "Riverview. And don't worry. I'll call

them both for you right away. Is that it? Anyone else? A relative?"

A relative. Oh, God, my mother. She'd be frantic. But how could I… "No, that's it, and thanks," I said. Then I thought of something. "Liz, do you know where my pocketbook is?"

"It's right here in the closet," she said, with a searching look at me.

Realizing I'd better come up with something fast, I said, "Oh, it's my lipstick and mirror. I must look awful, so I want to fix up a little."

"Sure." She got my bag from the metal closet and handed it to me.

I hoped my cell phone was still charged. As soon as Liz left the room, I pulled it out. Thank the gods, it worked. And I still kept one landline in the apartment, in case of a power outage. I whispered into the phone, keeping watch on the doorway in case Liz or somebody else came into the room. "Ma, pick up the phone. I'm in Riverview Hospital. Please get here as fast as you can."

I heard a gasp on the phone. "What happened?"

"Tell you when I see you, Ma. Have to say goodbye now. One of the nurses might come in the room." I clicked off and carefully lay back against the pillows, exhausted, hoping that my head would stop hurting me soon. And that I'd start to remember what happened to me before I ended up in the hospital.

I must have slept for hours. When I woke up, the room was dark. I could hear low voices and the rustling of uniforms as people went down the corridor. My head was still killing me. But I could remember my dream, in living color.

I was standing in the lobby of my building, happy to get a postcard from Toniann and Peter on their honeymoon. I rang for the elevator, and…

Damn! Come on, Marabella, concentrate. You can do it.

Oh, yeah? My aching head said. *I'm on strike. Get back to me after I get a pain pill.*

"Here I am, sweetheart." My mother landed with a groan beside my bed. Luckily, anyone who heard would think it was me. She kissed my forehead and sat down on the chair next to me. "You look terrible. What happened?"

"I'm not sure. I'm trying to remember, but my head…"

She patted my arm. "Don't you worry, sweetheart. It'll come to you. Just be patient."

I pulled the bell. "I'm calling for a pain pill. I don't know if that'll help my memory, but at least it should help my head."

My mother shook her head. "Tch, tch. My poor girl. We've got to get the monster who did this to you."

"Right," I said, nodding my head, causing myself agony.

A nurse with short blonde hair appeared in the doorway. She gazed around the room and looked at me strangely. "I thought I heard voices."

Think fast, Marabella. I smiled at her. "Oh, I must have been talking in my sleep. But I really need a pain pill. Please?"

"I'll just check on your orders. Be back shortly. My name is Bobbie, by the way."

As soon as Bobbie left, my mother said, "Okay, let's get to work."

I groaned. "I can't think."

"Yes, you can. Remember when you were really little and you kept falling down when you were trying to walk?"

"Ma, how could I possibly remember when I was…"

"A year and a half. Anyway, what did I keep telling you?"

Was I supposed to answer that?

"I kept telling you that you could do it. And you did." She folded her arms across her chest.

"Ma, everybody learns to walk, no matter what." I didn't want to hurt her feelings. So what if she thought she saved me from spending my life crawling on the floor?

"But it would have taken you longer. Now, think back to where you were before you landed in the hospital. Come on. You can do it, I know it."

Well, if my mother thought I could do it, who was I to doubt it? Then I heard sounds in the doorway. Bobbie was coming toward me with water and hopefully, a pill. She handed me the water and the pill and gave me another strange look, but didn't say anything. I'd better be more careful or I could end up in the psych ward.

"Thanks," I said, swallowing the pill with water. I handed her back the cup and she left. I figured that saying nothing would be better than trying to explain something that couldn't be explained.

"Okay, let's go. Tell me what happened just before you were attacked."

Besides my aching head, I was amazed at how absolutely exhausted I was. I felt as though the life had been drained out of me.

"Well, of course you do, sweetheart," said the mind-reader. Now, let's get to it."

I took a couple of deep breaths, trying not to move my head. Maybe deep breathing would help recharge my faculties. "I was in the lobby. I checked the mailbox and found a postcard from Toniann and Peter." I smiled, remembering the card: *Glad you're* not *here.*

"Then what?"

"I rang for the elevator and I heard…" I stopped, frustrated.

"You can do it," she said.

"Sounds. I turned around and somebody was coming toward me."

"You're *almost* there. Go, go, go," she chanted.

Was she a cheerleader in a previous life? "It was…" I almost had it. "It was Abby! Abby Goldfarb!" I dropped back against the pillows, forgetting about my head, a big mistake. "Ohhh."

"Hooray!" my mother said. "We did it!"

Chapter 69

John, Susan, and Carmen arrived around the same time, carrying huge bunches of flowers, making a big fuss over me. Which, I must admit, felt very comforting.

I told them what happened and who did it. "By the way, I laid some nice bruises on her face with this." I grinned, pointing to my engagement ring.

John took my hand. "See, it already brought you good luck." Then he got out his cell and called Lieutenant Rivera.

"Don't give him my regards," I said, making a face and instantly regretting it. "Ohhh." I clutched my head.

"I'll call a nurse," Susan said, and went out into the corridor.

Carmen patted my arm. "We were so worried. Thank God you're all right. Sort of."

I smiled at her. "It'll just take a while."

Bobbie came in with water and a straw. She looked relieved, probably because the voices she'd heard were from people other than me. "We just got a call that the police were on the way. When they get here, the rest of you will have to go out. Too many people in the room.

There's a lounge at the end of the corridor and you can wait there."

About ten minutes after they left, Rivera and the cop who'd checked out the health club strode into my room. Rivera looked at me and shook his head. "Well, you almost got yourself killed *again*. What is it with you? A death wish?"

"Thanks for the sympathy, Lieutenant. Nice to know you really care."

He yawned, sat himself down in the chair, and motioned for the other cop, whose badge read *Sgt. Winter*, to get one for himself. "Okay, from the—"

"Top." I grinned at him.

He scowled. "You never stop with the smart mouth, do you? Anyway, we've got work to do here. Tell me what happened to you *this time*." He nodded to the sergeant, who pulled out his notepad and a pen.

I told them the story, starting with my suspicions after Rose was attacked and ending with the murderer, Abby, trying to kill me. "By the way, I managed to inflict some bruises on her face with my engagement ring. So they should still be there, or at least, the signs of the bruises will be there."

Rivera glowered at me. "Ms. Vinegar, I think we know how to check out a suspect." He got up and motioned to Sergeant Winter. "We've collected some DNA evidence from the murders. And we'll want to match that up with your ring. You'll need to hand it over, for now." He stuck out his palm.

"Oh, no!" I said.

"It's just temporary," Sergeant Winter said. "Don't worry, we'll take good care of it." He looked at Rivera, who nodded.

I gave my ring a goodbye kiss, pulled it off my finger, and dropped it into Rivera's palm. "I'm entrusting this to you and it better be in the same condition when I get it back. How soon can I get it back?"

Rivera retrieved a plastic envelope from his plaid jacket pocket and dropped my ring in. "It shouldn't be too long, Ms. Vinegar. By the way, we were able to check out that threatening email you got."

"From Abby, right?"

He nodded. "So it's all probably enough for a charge. You'll need to ID your attacker."

"Of course."

"And testify in court, if there's a trial."

"*If?* With three murders and two attempts?"

Rivera yawned again. "If she takes a plea, there's no trial." He headed for the door, followed by Sergeant Winter. Turning back to me, he muttered, "Sorry this happened to you. Hope you feel better soon."

I couldn't believe it. He actually seemed to care. "Thanks," I said to his retreating back.

My mother agreed. "How about that? Maybe this lieutenant is also a human being."

I smiled at her. "So, now you can go back to…wherever…and rest. And I'm so grateful that you were able to be here. I'll miss you, Ma." I felt a lump in my throat.

She grinned. "Don't worry, I'll be back again. Do you think I'd miss my only daughter's wedding?"

About the Author

Sandra Gardner is a former contributor and columnist for The New York Times. She is the author of four non-fiction books: Six Who Dared (Simon & Schuster), Street Gangs (Franklin Watts), Teenage Suicide (Simon & Schuster), and Street Gangs in America (Franklin Watts). Her coming-of-age novel, *Halley and Me*, won the Grassic Short Novel Prize from Evening Street Press. The first three books in Gardner's Mother-and-Me mystery series are being published are being published by Black Opal Books. *Grave Expectations* is the second book in the series.

www.ingramcontent.com/pod-product-compliance
Lightning Source LLC
Chambersburg PA
CBHW060946120726

47910CB00002B/513